The air had cooled. Shivering, Lisa rearranged her posture, hoping to ease the fatigue in her shoulders or the implacable upward tug on her bound wrists. The rope, extending her arms high above her head clamped them rigidly to her cheeks, restricted her sight to the front. To see anything on either side she had to spin clumsily as only her toes touched a glass plate in the floor. Her bindings raised her rib-cage, emphasising their bars above her in-swept abdomen. Helplessness of this scale indicated a serious intent and Lisa crawled with greater dread of what would happen than prior to her caning. Alone in the empty, windowless room, time had ceased and nothing existed outside the present.

And the longer it takes the worse the suspense.

By the same author:

SURRENDER
JULIA C

EXPOSÉ

Laura Bowen

This book is a work of fiction.
In real life, make sure you practise safe, sane and consensual sex.

First published in 2006 by
Nexus
Thames Wharf Studios
Rainville Road
London W6 9HA

www.nexus-books.co.uk

Typeset by TW Typesetting, Plymouth, Devon

Printed and bound by
Clays Ltd, St Ives PLC

ISBN 0 352 34035 5
ISBN 9 780352 340351

One

Looming shadows concealed every part of the room, though she remembered its stone architraves, ornate mouldings, and the fresco in muted colours on the wall opposite the bed. Muffled hollow sounds faintly drifted. A name – Yvonne von Guilliem – glimmered, woven in gold thread onto her pillow. A smell of beeswax floated from the walnut headboard and mingled with more fragrances from the flower bowl.

The body lying beside her stirred. Lifting cautiously onto one elbow she could just make out the geometry of strong shoulders framing a powerful chest. Vigilant and still, she examined the man's raven hair and coffee skin. His eyelids, closed in sleep, disguised his black pupils and the intense stare that could spear her depths with the instant command of a penetration. Her gaze followed the downward line of his arm lodged on one hip, shading his belly. Below lay his compact thighs, a thick clump of pubic hair, and a flaccid penis domed across his leg. Earlier, brutally erect and breathing fire, its rampant energy had pinned her helplessly onto the bed. The inflexible shaft, constantly grazing her tender clit, made her cry out, expanding the warm ocean wave into vast explosions of delight that swept her, juddering, from top to bottom. Her dear pussy retained the memory of spewing ejaculations deep inside. Each time she moved she could sense the slight telltale squish within her moist channel and a small incipient leak.

Slumped over her hand the glans still had a compelling bulk and weight even in this quiescent condition. As she gently stroked it to and fro, its loose sheath buckled to expose the bulbous cap and she leaned forward to wipe the irresistible plum along her lips. She relished its sleek velvety texture and absorbed a cocktail of scents: a compound of his sweat and creamy sperm, and her own juice.

A drum-roll of thunder rumbled outside and silent arcs of lightning stabbed the sky. On the window's glass beat an urgent flurry of wings and the frantic scratching of claws. A waft of air shook random chimes from the chandelier.

Her nose nestled in strands of springy hair as she sucked the exotic and succulent candy. Provoked, the body grunted but did not wake. She continued slowly, savouring the first stage when, so soft and coiled, so passive and agreeable, she could squeeze the whole length in her wet heat. Its swollen dimensions filled her mind but, before it stiffened again to that demanding state, she could nurture the precious organ with a woman's infinite patience and skill. As she conscientiously served the tube of flesh she loved, it unfurled and hardened until she gagged on the bloated –

'Aah!'

Lisa's piercing scream cut through the air. She lurched back, watching in horror as Thomas Tadpole disappeared in a pool of blue ink which spread to obliterate the distant Luscombe Wood. The flood ran down the sloping board to splash on her knees. 'Stupid! Stupid,' she shrieked, attempting desperately to halt the tide by levelling the paper. Already saturated, it dripped from beneath. She crumpled the sheet to contain the spillage and threw the soggy mess, trajectory-perfect, into the bin. A complete waste of four hours; precious hours that must now be repeated. And with a deadline so near she would have to work into the night to recover the lost time.

Feeling sorry for herself, Lisa sighed miserably. *Deadlines are absolutely the worst thing*. She racked her spine and stretched her arms to wring tiredness out of her muscles. Her slumbering breasts hoisted under the silky scarf, caged in a broad X. As the slithering fabric caressed her nipples she replayed the enjoyment several times, then pattered to the bathroom to wash the blotches of ink from her legs. Her panties had also been drenched and she quickly peeled them off to soak in a basin of cold water. The next essential was to reach the kitchen for another dark brown Colombian and in a few seconds the slug of hot caffeine restored her equilibrium. She wandered back to the studio, ignoring the scene of her latest disaster, and crossed to the window. Beyond her garden boundary the fields rose to a hill where a tangled bundle of trees sprawled to the ridge. One advantage of her location on the edge of the village was that she had maximum privacy. 'But it also increases my isolation,' she announced. *Damn! I'm still doing it.* 'Talking to yourself is a very bad sign!' Portions of her reflection bounced off the panes. The sky's brightness cut off her head but lower down the garden shrubs shaded the window. Its mirror revealed the dim outline of a slim waist swelling outwards to her hips and the top of her legs. Her abdominal curves, neatly punctuated by a sunken navel, narrowed to an unruly accent, roughly triangular. 'Untamed – wild as a meadow.' Privacy allowed her to dress as she wished, or not at all if she preferred adventure. Sipping her coffee, she traced the slope of the hill up to the trees.

'I hope you know that a pervert could be observing from there,' she warned herself. 'He could be focusing binoculars to pin-sharp accuracy.' Nevertheless she held her position, finely balanced between the banal decision to step aside and the urge to remain in sight of the hidden spectator. *Why not? I'm in my prime.* She'd had plenty of offers and rarely refused, but conventional sex had taught her an important lesson: too often it descended to a boring mechanistic exercise ending in routine relief for the man. 'What this woman needs,' Lisa murmured 'is some mystery and drama to bring it alive, and a taste of excitement now and again.' Or even, by some lucky chance, more often

3

than that. Surely the best of all must be pure sex, uncomplicated by sticky emotional relationships? 'I'm sick of rules for natural desires.'

Placing her mug on the floor, she stood upright and began a performance by bunching her globes in her palms, levering the delicate masses in the watcher's direction. *These are for you. How do you want them?* She ran her nails over both areolae and the harsh scrapes projected her teats firmly, eagerly. Giddy and reckless, Lisa turned away from the window and stuck out her haunches to brush the chilly glass in a raunchy display, swivelling her cheeks from left to right and back again. *I'm open for business. Come on in.* What he could now see would steam up his nasty binoculars! Straightening, she faced the window and posed as a model at the end of a catwalk, but from that she imagined a telephoto lens recording her features. In a fluster of panic her boldness, fragile as a twig, snapped. Immediately a deafening knock – retribution for wicked behaviour – battered the door. Stumbling in shock, she grabbed an old coat from a hook, tugged its belt into a knot, and shoved on a pair of gumboots. Outside waited Mr Bennett, secretary of the local art club.

'Good morning, Lisa. Been in the garden? I'm here because it's time to apply for the annual exhibition. I expect you'll be showing this year?'

'I may not have anything ready in time.'

'Is the market buoyant for children's illustrations?'

'Enough for a modest living.'

'Well, just in case, here's your official application. Have you heard the gossip? Our roaming mega-star has returned, at least for a brief visit.'

'Who? Jon Bradley?'

'The very same. But I doubt if he'll be joining us – he's rather advanced for us now. Did you read the critique of his London exhibition? Very good!' Mr Bennett's enthusiasm subsided as he paused at a new thought. 'I distinctly recall his last entry some years ago. A nude female torso, splendidly developed, in a three-quarter view and lit tangentially. An impressionistic blaze of colour, in pastels

4

'... wonderful depth and richness ... gloriously indeterminate, amorphous and radiant. A most sensitive delineation.'

Lisa's eyelids flickered.

'Ah, you remember it too,' Mr Bennett said. 'And the rumours have started.'

'What rumours?'

'About goings-on in that mansion of his. Reports of big limousines and visitors and various lurid tales. Anyway, don't forget the date. We require all the entries we can get.'

Alone once more, Lisa realised she had forgotten her sole experience of modelling. It had been the kind of impetuous choice any girl could make if she felt admired. She balled the application and threw it in the basket. In a similar, less exalted manner than the local mega-star, she had outgrown the art club. 'Jon Bradley ...' On mature contemplation, she decided to hate him. He had inherited a trust fund set up by his parents and shouldn't take work from starving artists. But despite that – and far more serious – he was still in front of her with his first one-man show and its 'very good critique' that she had been too jealous to read. All she had was a ruined Thomas Tadpole.

Lisa dropped the coat, kicked off her boots, and smoothed the scarf luxuriantly over her breasts. The pleasure in these twins! – fluid zones willing to play. Unlike the pointed titties of petite girls these were larger and mobile. Unable to resist their allure, she danced for a while, circling effortlessly, her arms snaking, fluently bending and twisting, pursuing a mental rhythmic beat. Her hips twined and pulsed, her boobs following independently with their own tremors and stately momentum. Her polished thighs and the planes of her belly glowed with light, dispersing their rays in glittering arcs around the room. By the time she entered the studio she was smiling happily.

On the board she laid a pristine sheet of paper on top of her preliminary sketch. In one hour of diligent toil the basic composition could be revived. Then would come a long process of careful painting, ending in the final touches when Thomas Tadpole came to life, sniffing the air for a fresh spot of mischief. Lisa fiddled with the paper and made tiny unnecessary adjustments until, with a listless sigh, she came to a halt. Her respite, the coffee, Mr Bennett, and even the dancing had done nothing to assuage a swirling pit of lust in her crotch. She could not do this now, not yet, not before some crucial release.

Moving the sheets to the plan chest, she replaced them with a slim file retrieved from the bottom drawer. The file's vivacious red had been chosen deliberately for the association with danger and it contained her private pieces. This set of recent drawings would never hang in the art club among the genteel flowers and gory sunsets over the sea. Lisa snorted contemptuously at the committee's horror and its polite tight-lipped refusal. But the harm to her professional reputation might have increased anyway, since the break-in. To be fair, describing it as a break-in might be an exaggeration. 'But I'm certain I shut the kitchen door ... nearly certain.' After mowing the lawn, she had found the door ajar. Of course, it might have been the wind but, fearing an intruder, she had rushed to the studio where her greatest possessions might have been stolen or damaged. The lowest drawer had not been fully closed and she always did that: *Mostly always*. At the idea that a prowler might have examined the file, she still felt sick with anxiety.

Lying on the board, it appeared as anonymous as a million identical files but the contents generated perilous storms of emotion difficult to control. She lifted the cover, gingerly rimming the pulp of her labia.

In the top picture the door of one room opened into a second. Its door, also ajar, led into a third room where another door led to a fourth. The sequence continued, one area into the next, through six rooms. From the rear, a girl came walking forward.

'It keeps on happening.' It puzzled Lisa that peculiarities could emerge in her work that she could not understand; in this case why there were so many doors, or why they were open.

Soon the girl would arrive in the foreground room and inevitably glance to her left, at a woman with the front of her body flattened to the wall and her head to the side. The girl would notice the way she clawed the surface and her strained expression; the panties taut across her ankles; and the man who stood behind the woman, hoisting her dress to expose a pert rump and allow his penetration. The woman, caught helplessly in this dilemma, would meet an innocent stare.

Defenceless against a wave of embarrassment, Lisa flamed, and clumsily raised one foot onto the stool. Her fingers sank into warm succulence. *She's feeling this.*

Keyed-up, Lisa flipped to the next page. In the centre of an empty room a different woman lay supine on a bench, her abundant hair cascading to the floor. She wore a beautifully tailored scarlet coat buttoned from her waist up to the neck, strictly encasing her upper half. In contrast the coat's skirt, like wings, fell to the sides, baring her lower half. Clad in a high-heeled shoe, one of her feet rested on the floor. The other, propped on the bench, revealed, in the gap, a fern of red pubic hair bordering the clearly defined dark furrow. The woman maintained her poise, waiting serenely. 'Doesn't she care about the result?' *No, she's widening her legs.* 'And she's thinking: When will his thick rod slide into my sopping heat?'

Trembling, Lisa switched to a meticulous drawing of a well-proportioned naked man. It had been a simple matter to assemble his perfect physique from her stored recollections, but lewd appetite had introduced a new element. The man peered down at his pointing member which, on its broad helmet – a unique morsel of anatomy precisely designed to attract women – had a smeared layer of creamy solution.

Watching the man regarding himself, Lisa enjoyed the collision between her voyeurism and his self-admiration. Squelching in her own lubrication, she focused on the smudge of fluid. *You know I'm here, don't you?* She pulled out her fingers and sketched the liquid line of a heart that gleamed on the polished top of the plan chest. *There's a present for you.*

In the second scene, reclined on the bench, she had displayed herself to him but now the roles reversed. In a hybrid state, she combined herself and the man; her muscles toughened and bulked and she filled the space he occupied. In a surge of virile power, she saw herself masturbating through his eyes but jumped in shock at a voice, loud in her ear.

'Do you often play with yourself?'

Play with yourself! The phrase scorched her brain as a strong hand pressed onto her own.

'What's your name for this?'

I call it my dear pussy. It's a delicate furry creature.

'And this?' His palms caressed the smooth curves of her buttocks, an exquisite erogenous zone. 'Spongy as jelly but shapely too.'

Chilled, Lisa panted and squirmed luxuriantly. *That's my sweet derrière.*

His pressure returned to the front. Under his vigour, her knuckle touched the tender stalk and she jerked up with a startled cry. A fiery spark jumped from her clitoris towards her anus. 'Now carry on. Show me how you do it.'

It's much too personal. I want you to take me.

'Excite me first.'

I can't. I'm not an exhibitionist.

'Your inhibitions make it interesting for me. Show me, now.'

Must I beg for it?

'Beg me, yes.'

Subsiding to the floor, Lisa became the tramp he wished her to be. Her nipples squeezed, her vagina pouted and she spread her legs, as she had on the bench, to offer him more. Expanding the outer folds, then the glistening inner membranes, she imagined an impossibility: that he could view the whole humid void to the depths of her belly. A woman's sheath; the softest glove, the deepest home his massive cock could ever find. And when she sensed his impatience, proof of his desire for her alone, he delighted her.

'Big tits and a juicy cunt.'

An invisible force propelled her upwards and her rounded eyes searched his face. He knew how crude language affected her mind, guaranteeing lasciviousness.

The man loomed above, brooding as a hulk, his steamy erection already tipped by a leaking drop. His attendance invested her actions with the dignity of participation; it was his smouldering gaze fondling her sex, not her own fingers probing these sensitive tissues. As he stroked the slopes of the labia, her itching mounted and her knees shook but he cruelly shirked the essential spot, not even stirring the apex. Lisa perfected her motions, tempting him by massaging slowly, but still he refused to accept the hint and there could be only one reason, and she yearned for that too: the dominating inward shove. *I need you moving inside me.* Quivering hot, her moisture seeped and her loins throbbed. It would take very little to come but she really wanted to contract on his glittering shaft.

Stray mental images interfered and his form wavered into a nubile satyr with flanks matted in curly hair, and a voice booming: 'Your cunt's been missing my young prick.' And there it stood, sleek and burnished as marble, poised to fellate eagerly. Floating, unbounded, she willed its gushing spunk and gripped her left teat, clenching hard, hurting herself, stretching her nipple into a grotesque taper to incite him more. All her different urgent perceptions fused into one inexorable tide. She tensed and relaxed, bucked and wailed, worked herself to a fine edge and the final orgasmic rush that blotted out the man, her studio, and all her consciousness.

Two

But when she emerged, reluctantly, Thomas Tadpole waited for his re-creation.

Fortified only by snacks during hours of unrelenting exertion, Lisa finished at four a.m. Nevertheless she woke after a few hours' sleep not only refreshed but exhilarated, which often happened at the end of an assignment. Two dark Colombians continued her revival and so did a long shower, soaking in the warm hissing stream of comforting jets. Then she laid out her clothes. For a visit to her agent, Miss Gibbs, it felt appropriate to dress in old style: a simple dress of silk, stockings and suspenders, sensible shoes. Lisa started with a satin suspender belt that fitted snugly, and straightened the clasps. Smoothing the stockings up her legs, she fastened the patterned bands. From the wardrobe she took a pair of shoes with heels much higher than Miss Gibbs would approve, slipped them on, and verified her appearance in the mirror's reflection. *Saucy*. Stirred by the dream of her body, she raised her arms and rotated her hips lazily, enjoying her abdomen's rippling and hollowing, and the way her pubic curls thrust into the light only to retreat bashfully. She bent her knees and leaned from the waist to emphasise her buttocks. *Very saucy*. So saucy, in fact, that the left deserved a playful slap, and a nice sensation, less than a sting, encouraged her to reprimand the right in the same way. The two strikes – pat, pat – suggested a rhythm that shifted her feet and she began to emulate a stripper for whom modesty is strictly forbidden. All over the room, in a resplendent public performance, she detached non-existent clothes and stopped at intervals to pose enticingly, proud of her swelling breasts and up-standing nipples which betrayed her passion and excitement for sex. *But I'd vary the roles.* At first pure and remote, she would hold herself aloof from the group of lust-sodden men but later, debauched –

Lisa came to a halt and muttered breathlessly, 'Behave yourself.' At the dressing table she tugged a comb through her short brunette hair and completed her basic make-up. Before applying her lipstick she held up the tube and wound the rosy tip until its indecent shape hovered above her face. 'Naughty!' she whispered. At the mirror she painted carefully, rubbed her lips together, and paused to admire the result. *Glossy as a coat of sperm I haven't wiped off.* She lifted a brush and hesitated. Up or down? It had to be down because upward stimulation exercised her tender bud far too vigorously. Even so, she gasped faintly at each delicious touch on her pubes. Now, tidy everywhere, the brush clattered onto the table. She checked her blue-grey eyes, items of beauty, though strangers were often unnerved by their remorseless inquisition.

Striding towards the kitchen she rushed too hastily and the heels, thudding the floor, vibrated her bosom unpleasantly. The force reminded her to adapt her walk and she changed to a slinky glide by placing each foot flat on the floor, enhancing the effect by rolling her hips. All her leg muscles came into action, making her aware of her movements. Her stockings expanded around her upper thighs and the suspender clips tightened insistently. 'I love it,' she murmured. She poured a refill and sipped, followed by more rehearsal of slinky gliding into the studio. There, draining her coffee, she put the mug on the floor. Empty, the mug had nothing to spill, and from there it had nowhere to fall. Satisfied by faultless logic and the elimination of all possible hazards, she glanced at the clock on the wall and noticed plenty of time for experiments.

On the levelled board she used a dry brush technique, mixing very little water into the colour, and scoured the

11

pigment in random daubs across the paper. Primary hues were brilliant and strong; ultramarine pulsed urgently; incandescent yellows gleamed as gold; and reds hinted at lakes of blood. With a spatula she textured the surface by hacking and scratching, with no recognisable plan, but when the last white disappeared she pinned the sheet to the far wall. Searching for clues, she could see several areas to develop further. 'OK, this works.' *So now I should –*

The telephone's shrill tone demolished her concentration. She lifted the receiver and dropped it with a crash into the cradle.

– isolate one of those parts and –

Again the damned instrument rang. Twenty, twenty-five rings drilled her brain. Its awful persistence eroded her final shreds of control and she snatched the handset to bellow, 'Yes!'

'There's something wrong with your phone. It's Ben.'

'Ben . . .' With a huge effort Lisa calmed herself. 'How's my favourite nephew? We haven't met for ages. What are you doing now?'

'I'm at college. Media Studies.'

'And your mother?'

'Off to Canada with her new husband.'

'From the way you said that I guess you're upset.'

'Well, it gets pretty lonely in digs and I don't get out much. I'm angling for an invitation.'

'That's inconvenient, Ben. I'm in the middle of a big commission.' *Liar!*

'Oh.'

The boy lapsed into an abrupt silence and Lisa smiled. He's only a kid, unable to pretend, and his clear disappointment altered her mood. 'OK. How about Saturday, two o'clock?'

'Great! That's one thing dad told me. "Lisa will always look after you," he said.'

'And what did he mean?'

'Dunno. I thought you would. 'Bye.'

Lisa replaced the receiver and switched on the answering machine. 'How long ago . . .' She and her brother-in-law,

Eric, had been joking and larking about, perhaps tipsy, while in the next room her sister prepared a meal. In the middle of a juvenile tussle she found both of her wrists trapped behind her, gripped by Eric in one hairy paw, arched backwards and off balance, for his kiss. *I was helpless.* He pulled away and – *I actually was, totally helpless.* For a moment, still binding her loosely, he studied her expression. Released, all she could remember was a baffling sense of loss. 'But if he hadn't sat in the chair and plucked out his . . . Or if only Barbara had interrupted.'

If either of these had been different Lisa might not have succumbed to the vile temptation and knelt to gaze at her first close-up view of an erect penis. Fascinated by the view of an alien object, she absorbed the complex form with abnormally sharp vision. A high stiff ridge ran the length of the underside; a triangular flanged crown, bulging and luscious; a mottled shaft and its veined bumps. All of these were immensely exciting but it was the erratic lurches and throbs which really captured her. Rooted in the base of his belly it reared independently. A live animal!

'Don't stare at it – suck it.'

His blunt instruction sent a cold shudder down her spine. The illicit – thing – belonged to her sister, her property as a marital right; it had fertilised her womb. And Barbara was there, beyond an open door, and might come in at any second: sheer madness. Inclining forward, Lisa had tentatively lapped the shining purple plum. Without knowing what she expected, her tongue relished the voluptuous curves and she almost fainted in the tangy aroma of an aroused male. Appealing for guidance, she peered up and he pushed her lower to envelop the bulky tube until it packed her mouth. She had been transfixed, stifled and panicky, her lips stretched by the alarming size. The intimacy of warm flesh! Eric raised her head, the blockage slid outwards, and she relaxed a little only to be stuffed again on the next shove. But she quickly adapted, bobbing to and fro, filling and emptying. How naturally she acquired the technique and how hot she had felt!

'Lisa!'

As she struggled to break free and respond to her sister's call, a clot of thick cream shot into her throat. The startling feeling produced a ripple, a tiny orgasm, but at the time she could not account for the new sensation. Savouring Eric's gift – an intoxicating drink for one adult to pass to another – she walked into the adjacent room. At the very instant she swallowed the emission, a curious metallic taste, Barbara glanced up. 'With all that horseplay you're flushed,' she said. 'And very pretty. Can you lay the table?'

During the elementary routine Lisa drifted hazily, aware of a wetness between her legs. Her emotions were elation and pride at having shared with her sister, secretly, her husband's fluid. How often had Barbara gulped his sperm? Hundreds of times? Wow! Lisa yearned for the chance to watch them do it.

Eric had simply used a convenient cavity but from that incident her sexuality sparked into life, an electric wire suddenly bared. The intensity burned her innocent notions of purity. It also led her to assume a virtuous mask as effective disguise.

Lisa crushed the memory ruthlessly and returned to the experiment. All the promising images, each one a potential picture, had evaporated mysteriously. Sighing with regret, she checked the clock and continued doggedly slopping paint onto the paper. This time, out of the runs and streaks she discerned writhing figures, quivering and imprecise, as if emerging from underwater. They were apparitions similar to those she had when half asleep. *Good, that's evocative.* 'Now . . .'

The telephone repeated its strident summons but she managed to maintain her focus through the machine's cut-in and then her recorded message. On the last bleep an amiable vibrant voice floated towards her.

'Lisa, how are you?' Following a brief delay it started to coax. 'You're there, listening, aren't you? I'm sure you are.'

A vaguely familiar voice, but conjuring no particular face or name.

'You're probably impatient to get on. The sooner you pick up the faster you can. Meanwhile, here's some

14

entertainment.' A flat tuneless whistle began, a horrible dirge obviously intended to drive her mad.

Lisa fought to resist the challenge but the melancholy noise grated severely. She grabbed the 'phone by the scruff of the neck and bawled, 'Go away!'

'Hello.'

'Who is that?'

'Have you forgotten me? Jon Bradley.'

Her temper melted in curiosity. 'Oh. I heard you were in the village.'

'I've been to Cambodia you'll be glad to learn, painting fabulous landscapes.'

'And the beautiful delicate women?'

'I did meet a few.'

'I also heard about your exhibition. I'd better warn you, I'm jealous as hell.'

'And so you should be,' Jon chuckled. 'I'm nearly famous.'

'Can I put that on my CV? I know someone nearly famous.'

'Certainly you may. But I've been told on the grapevine of your own growing reputation. I believe you're an expert in fluffy bunnies and rascally foxes.'

'You make my work sound trivial,' Lisa said icily. 'It isn't. As a pure artist you can do any subject you fancy but a commercial artist runs to tight specs and deadlines. There's far more to it than fluffy bunnies.'

'Of course – I'm kidding.'

Feeble jokes about serious things deserved a good kicking. But then Lisa recalled her previous assignment, Amanda the Panda, and rushed on. 'Why are you calling? If it's to offer me a slap-up dinner, I accept. I'm starving. I've just finished a big commission so I've been on my own for weeks. I could do with some company.'

'Yes, we'll do that, soon. But that's not why I called.'

'What a pity. So the reason is . . .?'

'Well . . .' He hesitated, and tried again. 'Well, I wondered if you would agree to model for me.'

'What? I did it once, as a young and naive student, who

needed the money. With your wealth you can easily afford a professional.'

'I could, and I'll pay you the going rate if you want. But –' he said hastily '– that's not meant as an insult. I'm asking because of that first session, one of my best early pieces.'

'Old Bennett called it "amorphous and radiant" and "a sensitive delineation".'

Jon laughed. 'Yes, he would. It sold recently at auction, in New York, for – well, for a lot.'

'So you're saying my splendour inspired you. In fairness you ought to give me some of the proceeds. I collaborated with you on that.'

'Unfortunately I sold it long ago for a pittance – the usual story. The big profit went to its last owner. But your comment's spot-on. As an artist yourself you understand what's required so I hoped we might collaborate once more.'

Collaborate ... Collaboration. Lisa rapidly tested the notion and its possible implications. Tempted, as any woman might if a man showed interest, she replied warily, 'I doubt that I could sit topless in front of a stranger.'

'I'm not a stranger,' he said indignantly. 'I'm a fellow artist, requesting assistance.' Lisa remained quiet, unwilling to commit herself. 'Anyway, I hoped we could move on to a full nude.'

'What?' She gazed down at her bush. On her mound its fronds seemed to ruffle as if stirred by a breeze to attract her attention.

'An artist?' Jon suggested optimistically. 'With sympathy for my desperation?' Bewilderingly he added, 'But it shouldn't be too hard – you've always been a rebel pretending to be a conformist.'

Disturbed by the intuition Lisa mumbled, 'I'll have to brood on this.' Two rings on the door bell interrupted. 'And there's my absolute deadline. I must go. Give me your number, just in case. Right now, I'm very dubious.'

Wrapping herself in her old coat, she welcomed her driver Baines and left him to stow her work, a bulky package, in the car's boot. In her bedroom she dressed quickly but sat on the bed to be thrilled by the control of conventional clothes. The fine material of her dress slipped like fluid over her skin. As she inhaled, her brassiere tightened across her back; she felt her breasts, cosseted in their lacy cups; the suspender belt constricting her waist; her tiny panties, airy and insignificant. As she placed one leg on the other her stockings swished together. The suspender strap's robust restraint pressed into her leg and she fluttered luxuriantly. *So much pleasure in being a woman*. She picked up her bag and a jacket for the evening journey home on the train.

The international publishing house for which she worked operated old-fashioned courtesies. Lisa settled into the passenger seat surrounded by the reassuring odour of polished leather as the car purred at a leisurely pace through the countryside and into London's outer suburbs. Lisa preferred the country but enjoyed her occasional visits provided they were short. Her thoughts turned to Miss Gibbs whose invariable uniform, twin-set and pearls, reflected her age and old-school standards. For one daredevil moment Lisa wished she had included her red file in the batch. She visualised Miss Gibbs lifting the cover innocently, then her sudden pallor succeeded by utter disgust. Lisa smiled, rejoicing in her double life.

The comfort, coupled with Baines's unhurried skill, filled her with confidence; even his rugged features and greying hair, revealed below his hat, added to her sense of security. As they reached the city's congested streets, their smooth progress was hindered, and Lisa sank into a light sleep. A long interval passed before Baines deliberately, and respectfully, raised the hem of her skirt to mid-thigh. Hazily she registered what he had done and there followed a second pause while he gauged her reaction. Taking her lack of protest as passive complicity, he shifted the hem higher, above the line of her stockings where he could see an area of soft pale flesh. Again he delayed, presumably satisfied by the sight, but with her eyes shut she could not be sure.

17

A large competent hand encouraged her knees to divide in order that he could hold her tense inner leg. That's all the scalding iron hand did, held her intimately. Its naturalness suggested she belonged to him, and she parted further. He interpreted that as an invitation and the heat and pressure eased upwards into her crotch. Lisa's throat dried as he started to caress her molten slit. *Ah, lovely! That's so good.* Sliding lower in her seat allowed dependable Baines to insert –

'Miss, we've arrived. You go on in. I'll bring the parcel.'

Jerking upright, Lisa found the car parked at the kerb. In one confused blur she pushed the door and staggered out. An on-coming vehicle screeched to a halt and she mimed forlorn apologies, rushed to the pavement, and into the doorway for sanctuary. In the outer office, waiting for Miss Gibbs, she gathered her scattered senses.

'My dear, do come in. It is so good to meet you again.'

Now in her seventies, Miss Gibbs treated Lisa with scrupulous politeness and sometimes an irritating or mildly amusing manner: fussy as a bird pecking at details. But as a connoisseur of children's illustration no one had greater expertise or sharper judgement. Her reputation caused Lisa to hover nervously, as she often did during the silent period of agony, while Miss Gibbs carried each picture to the window for close inspection. To distract herself Lisa gazed around, noticed an assembly of Victorian toys, and reduced her tension by examining them.

The essential, yet murderous, phase came to an end when Miss Gibbs chuckled. 'There is such captivating humour here. You have achieved a remarkable union of word and image. For that you have earned tea.'

Lisa's mounting stress of the past days drained away. With the assignment accepted, her life could involve more than work, perhaps a holiday sailing the Aegean – that intense blue sky and dark-flying sea – or anything else that would give her some ordinary social life in contact with people. Miss Gibbs's long-time secretary entered with a tray.

18

'Here comes Miss Dutton, bright as a button.' In need of mothering, Lisa took the tea and biscuits gratefully. 'You have a distinctive style,' Miss Gibbs continued 'as do all notable artists. But yours is far from static. I am fascinated by the way it constantly evolves.'

'I do lots of experiments.'

'On this one you have introduced these wonderful veils and skeins and tones of colour. How do you accomplish this unusual effect in the paint here? I am asking you to divulge your technical wizardry. Is that fair?'

'Of course. I washed that section in diluted bleach. This has been sprinkled with salt while the paint's still wet. There I dribbled ink.'

'And the result is magical! I want you to know that, in the country's long and extremely high reputation in this field, I am convinced that you are emerging as one of the best in your generation.'

Flattered by the opinion, Lisa admitted cautiously, 'As you say, it's a very strong tradition.'

'Already I have collectors enquiring about you. One consulted me recently, a Mr ... Johanes, if I remember correctly. A South African gentleman who –'

'He hasn't come to me!'

'Not yet perhaps. However, grounds for optimism, I am certain. Now, my dear, if you are refreshed, may I brief you on the next project? The story is entitled *Misfit Toys*. As you might predict from the title it is intended for a much older age group than Thomas Tadpole. I have been saving this – it could be your breakthrough. Your work has never been sentimental and this enables far greater scope for your own interpretation. You can let yourself go and explore your hidden side.'

Startled, Lisa glanced up, but her agent's expression conveyed no clue of an insight into her true nature.

Miss Dutton broke in with a letter. 'This has been delivered for Lisa,' she said.

'How thrilling!' Miss Gibbs raised her eyebrows in an obvious question. 'Don't stand on ceremony, my dear. You must attend to it immediately.'

19

Puzzled, Lisa checked the envelope, blank except for her name. Who knew she would be here, and at this time? She withdrew a single sheet of typewritten paper:

THE WALDORF BRASSERIE IN CROSS STREET. GOOD COFFEE. ENTERTAINMENT.

Lisa re-read the words. Why would anyone send her an advertisement? Or was it an obscure joke? Entertainment: what did that mean? The ambiguity, in addition to its unexpected arrival, gave her a disconcerting jolt and Miss Gibbs seemed to be watching. 'It's not important,' Lisa explained hastily. 'I'm meeting my sister.'

'Well, that's a relief. Let us conclude our business and you can be on your way.'

The remaining elements – fee, timescale, deadline date – were efficiently finalised. 'Could I borrow that doll,' Lisa asked 'and the spinning top from your display? I want them for the toy-box.'

'If you treasure them as your own and faithfully promise their return.'

Lisa put the items into her bag automatically, still disturbed by the message. Since her first recoil of alarm its mystifying words had begun to taunt her as a serious challenge. Abruptly she asked, 'Can you direct me to Cross Street? Is it far?'

'Oh, Lisa! Once upon a time that was a good address but now, I'm afraid, it is a most insalubrious district. If you must go there shall I ask Baines to escort you?'

'Unnecessary. Really, I'm quite confident.'

'Young women today!' Miss Gibbs spoke with admiration. 'So resolute!' The street lay only a few minutes' walk away. 'Take care, and good fortune with the work.'

Three

If this was my own fancy it would mean nothing.

But responding to a curious invitation or even, more seriously, to an unknown person's command transformed the visit into an adventure. Weighing the two concepts – invitation, command – Lisa could not decide which she preferred and shivered, excited by the anticipation.

Miss Gibbs's assessment of the district proved to be accurate with streets of degraded shops, either boarded up or derelict. Cross Street itself appeared a little smarter with a few modern shops and bright presentations. A lively market, a continuous row of stalls, packed the centre of the road and the congested pavements obliged her to barge a way through. In doorways she noticed ranks of cards and once stopped to scan the list: Karen, Ruby, Vanessa, Black Model. Nearing her destination she searched for any familiar face but without success. The Waldorf, one of the new businesses, had plush seating and a rich scent of coffee permeating the air.

From a selection of ten she ordered a simple cappuccino and sat on a stool in the window, gazing out at the crowds squeezing around the stalls. Time passed lazily and unproductively. She had a meal and afterwards nursed a second coffee together with growing resentment. The anonymous message had misled her. 'How can this be called entertaining?' Outwardly patient yet inwardly alert she waited for an approach, or perhaps a follow-up note. She distrusted her motive for staying, drifting in limbo and cut loose from her normal occupation with innocent creatures, and the traditional values of Miss Gibbs. Yet, earlier in the day, she had relished the idea of a double life.

She pulled from her bag the small pad and a pencil she always carried, and examined the fluctuating events outside. Her concentration burned everything else away and with a few strokes she established the busy stalls and their shaky canopies as sets of linked shapes. Cross-hatched diagonals formed areas of shadow on the flat surface, cheating the eye into an artificial dimension. Next she studied a tramp huddled in a doorway arranging his carefully hoarded property in plastic bags. Staring hard she absorbed his stooped posture, grizzled weather-beaten skin, his matted beard and furtive gestures. Swift lines captured him on the page. Elsewhere she included vignettes: a mother wheeling a buggy, a couple arm in arm, a stall holder expertly working his listeners. In a series of sketches she unravelled the scene and described the inhabitants.

By the time she finished the light had dulled towards evening. The number of people dwindled and one by one the stalls closed, leaving stacked rubbish to be removed overnight. Lacking the buzz of activity the street altered its character. Two girls emerged from a doorway and began a desultory patrol, already bored. On the opposite side of the road a sign spluttered, died, and flickered again. At the fourth attempt, in a blaze of neon it burst out above a cinema. Lisa considered the fluorescent letters, their fire exaggerated by advancing gloom. Lurid red, similar to her special file, associated with dire warning or actual danger. Stirring with interest, she read the film's title: *Wild Vixen plus Suppo . t . . . Progro . . . e.*

Had she been brought here for this? Nothing else unusual had occurred so that might account for it. And she definitely needed something – anything – as a change. 'But do I dare?'

She could guess what class of film *Wild Vixen* would be. It might provide material for the drawings but would they allow her in alone? A few men strolled inside but no women. Only the girls, leaning on walls at one end of the street, shared the men's solitude.

'Do I dare?'

Stifling all doubts, Lisa grasped her bag and crossed to the building purposefully. In the foyer, starkly exposed in garish light, she forced herself to ignore her discomfort and strode to the cash desk.

Behind the glass sat a cashier squinting through a plume of smoke. She regarded Lisa indifferently and mumbled, 'Card.'

'I don't have one.'

'Members only.'

Instantly blocked, Lisa crumbled and retreated as far as the door. There she paused, surprised by the strength of her bitterness; having committed herself she wanted to pursue the venture to its end. Retracing her steps as rapidly as her thumping heart she asked, 'Can I join?'

Impassively the cashier picked up a sheet from a pile at her side. 'Name?'

Lisa faltered. To give her real name – that she did not dare. *Frieda . . . Jane . . . Smith?*

'Bill Bailey, right? An' you're comin' 'ome.' The cashier erupted in wheezing laughter, cut short by a strangled cough. 'Signature.' Lisa welcomed the identity and concealed her true style in the looping scrawl of a confident man. 'Ten quid.' The note skimmed under the barrier. 'An' five for the film.' Supplied with a second note the cashier pushed out a ticket and growled reassuringly, 'We get all sorts.'

At the end of a narrow sloping corridor Lisa rounded a corner into the smallest cinema she had ever seen. Immediately her attention locked on a strenuous copulation of a kind that she personally – thankfully – had never had to endure, plus amplified panting and sighing, succeeded by sharp ecstatic cries. Distracted, she hunted for a seat among the rimmed outlines of a sparse and well dispersed audience until the shifting beams revealed a suitable place. Safely enclosed, she returned to the action, gripped by the novelty of a new visual experience, soaking up the details, crystal-clear. Later she focused on the women's fleeting expressions, and their hollowed cheeks sucking any available penis, always ready and willing to devour more. They sighed and moaned and faked their cries of arousal yet also, sometimes, sounded genuine. Lisa's next concern dwelt on the way they were used with little respect. Their grimaces and furrowed brows suggested punishment for their consent.

No wonder the men appreciated these nubile women; they all had perfect figures, fine hair, and flawless make-up. The camera dismissed all notions of privacy but they exuded an earthy eagerness to promptly service any demand. Lisa admired their courage even though they operated far from her own view of sensuous behaviour. Who, for example, would enjoy smearing her labia with an oozing cock-head? Lisa pondered the question: *Yes, I'm sure I do.* But only as the screen filled with an enlarged pussy, shorn of every shred of natural disguise, did Lisa wince, disturbed and offended.

Gradually, in some obscure way she did not understand, she recognised the pleasure of participating anonymously in the midst of male spectators. Relaxed, she slid down in her seat, noting the screen-men's well defined and sturdy physiques, bigger and stronger than any man she had ever met. As her critical edge blunted and the repetitions ceased to matter, she immersed herself in the vigour of the scenes.

Occasionally someone left the auditorium, or a new one came in but the most important arrival, a woman on the arm of a man, helped to protect Lisa from lurking fears of her own perversity. At the same time she could not escape from speculation. Had they come for advice? Were they holding themselves in? At home would there be an explosion of passion?

Even as a docile voyeur, the films' vitality inflamed Lisa's mood. How could she prevent it when a huge woman, flattened on top of another, gazed at a pool of spunk lying in the entrance to her friend's cunt? The top woman lowered, obviously fascinated. The tip of her tongue lifted the fluid but a random thread dripped and merged. She followed it, lapping the pool devotedly.

Retaining the aroma in her own nostrils, Lisa closed her eyes and rolled up her skirt to touch the super-soft flesh above her stockings. To accompany the noise from the screen she attached her own scenario and parted her legs. A damp patch on her panties stuck to her fingers. Tugging the fabric to one side, she found the tender spot that had to be soothed and unfurled her outer lips to release the springy inner tissues. A waft of air cooled the heat and a tight strain developed in her perineum. She taunted her clitoris sparingly, shuddering exquisitely, and imagined herself as one of those desirable and complaisant women. A stranger's incessant fondling urged her stage by stage towards a peak but she might easily die of bliss before getting there. Her agitation quickened and she desperately hoped the liquid squelches were inaudible. But wouldn't it be incredible to sit here with the men, watching herself up there, magnified to vast proportions? She floated inwards, rising on waves inexorably. A distended organ, a thick shaft of exceptional length, loomed directly out of the screen. Her upper thighs were suddenly blotted by wet semen. It spurred her on to the point she loved, when frantic stimulation had done its job and her body took charge.

Is anyone looking?

Teetering on the very brink of orgasm, she peered through a fog of whirling sensations. One man on her right seemed to be more interested in her than the film. Lisa stood clumsily, grabbed her bag and stumbled to the exit. Jittery, heart pounding, she crossed the foyer in to the chill of the street.

Now she realised why Miss Gibbs had been apprehensive. Beneath the ordinary activity of the day a night-time population transformed its character once again. The Waldorf Brasserie appeared as blackened as the shops on both sides. Clusters of girls, a few bundles in their arms for warmth, flitted about, transient as shadows, and shops had opened in what Lisa had supposed were derelict shells. Intrigued, she had no inclination to rush away; perhaps, from this valuable resource she could learn many things.

Slipping between people, invisibly thin, she hesitated at the first shop and glanced inside at racks of videos and magazines. Mannequins displayed scraps of provocative clothing, a few similar to those in her own wardrobe, and she noticed a range of flamboyant adult toys. Poised for a bold decision, Lisa asked herself: *Do I dare?*

But the whole interior, much too highly illuminated, provided no discretion, nowhere to hide. Moving on, she loitered by a second shop, jostled within a gaggle of men: bees hovering around a hive. She concluded reluctantly that a lone female should not risk entering an arcane world reserved for the male species alone. Instead, she dodged through a line of cars to the opposite pavement. The girls glared, mistaking her for competition and Lisa did compete, but only vicariously, offering herself in silence to clients who passed by on either side.

Later, aware she had stayed too long, she managed to hail a taxi and spent the journey recreating those fading moments of recklessness. Masturbating among men! *Am I mad?* But it was such consolation to be wrapped in the dark. In the dark you can do anything.

The taxi reached the station in time to catch the last train and Lisa slumped in the seat of an empty carriage. Now, with her ardour diminished, she could analyse the films properly. The positive aspect lay in their basic and raw appeal, undermining prissy pretence. But they had also taught her a negative lesson: errors to avoid. They had no mystery and did not portray sex as she preferred it, with further and far more subtle dimensions. One day, perhaps soon, her own work would show them.

Four

But not on this particular day.

Lisa woke, almost with tired jaws and swollen lips from the night's rampaging cocks, and stewed aimlessly on the questions of who sent the note, how they knew where to find her, and whether she had been enticed to the café specifically for the cinema. These churning anxieties combined with the films which seemed to have become a layer of her own past. The women had not been actresses performing a role but real people behaving frankly. In refusing to be confined by convention they became successors to the numberless courtesans of previous generations. But how could she feel bonded to them, as if she had actually joined in?

You're comin' 'ome, the cashier said.

During breakfast Lisa pondered the situation again. Those brave women were uninhibited even with an interfering camera and crew. If they could do that, surely she could pose for a fellow artist in private? In contrast to them she would not be active but simply engage in a normal and essentially passive routine; her figure, all of it, bartered for Jon's work.

'Another service that women, including those same courtesans, have done for centuries.'

And Lisa had recruited models on countless occasions, usually craggy men or children. Nevertheless she delayed until, refreshed by her shower, she made the call. 'Jon? It's me. I'll do it.'

'Great! Come this afternoon.'

Lisa rocked in surprise. 'So quickly?'

'You've finished your commission so this could be a good time. Two o'clock. Come in the old way.'

'Jon –' The disconnection buzzed in her ear. Expecting a few days to prepare, she now had only a few hours.

In the studio she persisted with her experiments of the day before, a set of evocative marks suggesting many interpretations. But the attempt lacked any strength. She over-painted to improve a poor start and predictably the pristine colours swirled, corrupted, and puddled to mud. Discouraged, she abandoned the mess and restlessly picked up the new assignment. She began to read the story, a crucial stage to absorb the key events, understand the characters, and establish the general tone. Unfortunately her concentration insisted on flying away, pursuing odd fragments of the films and their constantly changing perspectives. Unlike the lineal story she was trying to read, films broke up a continuous sequence by taking shots from different angles and distances. As cinematic narratives, graphic novels and cartoons did the same thing. And strobe lighting too, when each flash locked various arrangements in space.

On a pad Lisa rapidly drew six rectangles, then composed carefully. In the first box a tall slim woman walked forward. A luxuriant white wig, held at the back with an elaborate bow, framed her slender features. Lisa paused and sketched a dramatic cat mask to encircle her eyes. She drafted the woman's mouth as parted, to imply her mounting excitement. 'Your name will be . . . Jacqueline. What should you wear?' A broad ruff enclosed Jacqueline's neck and fell as a thin band between a pair of splendid globes, rather large in terms of ideal proportions if compared to her tiny waist. *Extreme décolleté, a symbol of youth, beauty and fertility.* The costume's skirt draped to the ankles and two extra lines at the top of her legs indicated a ripe pudenda. Lisa revised the precise shape of Jacqueline's breasts as pert upright pears, added prominent nipples to the upper slopes – the kind any girl would wish for – and shaded their areolae.

The next illustration showed the gown from behind. Hitched by an easily unravelled knot on both hips, it drooped below a deep buttock cleft. Supremely confident, Jacqueline advanced towards a row of men who stared lasciviously, with the same obvious thought in all their evil minds. In a spirit of revenge Lisa fixed them, coarse and repellent.

The pencil flickered over the page, striving to keep pace with teeming ideas. In the next frame, a lateral view, Jacqueline was sandwiched by two of the men and one had spread her skirt's side split, baring the full length of her legs. An ornate garter gripped one thigh halfway up and the gap revealed that she wore nothing beneath. The second brute, his member already proud, pulled back her arm – *that hurts* – while his warm tongue licked the nape of her neck, sending cold ripples down her spine. But the expanses around the edge reduced the impact and Lisa replaced it by close-cropping onto the action. This time, flushed and panting, under her skirt she could feel him, *touching my* –

Lisa's heart pounded as she glanced at the clock. Her time had run out. Shunning all premature judgements – these would follow in a quieter mood – she stored the work in the bottom drawer.

After a snatched lunch she rushed to the shower and emerged swiftly, smothered in a thick beach towel to consult the mirror. Her only direct experience of the nude came from student life-drawing classes and for several minutes she toyed with an urge to throw off the towel and sample a few positions. But she gave it up impatiently; the effort to see herself as a man did would be utterly futile. Lisa accepted the fear that many women shared concerning the notorious male gaze which turned them into mere objects, but she also knew that an artist must begin with hard observation. He would look at her in the same way as he would an apple or a chair. Anyway, it must be a compliment to be recorded in her prime.

Rejecting a brassiere, she dressed in a baggy T-shirt and flimsy panties, a scrap of material. Jon, a professional, would ignore any unsightly lines from tight underwear but she, as the model, could not. For her own reassurance she had to present herself unblemished. Shabby jeans and trainers were a sensible choice.

Her destination, Jon's vast pile discreetly located in acres of meadow and woodland, lay on the far side of the village, beyond the final houses and into the country. Soon she pursued a narrow winding path and in a few yards arrived at a wrought-iron gate in the high boundary wall of old weathered brick. Unoiled, the gate squealed in distress as she pushed through into an airy wood of hazel and birch. A breeze in the canopy disturbed the sun's rays and spots of brilliant emerald speckled the ground. Slowing her speed Lisa examined the modulations of yellow-green, the colours of youth and optimism: a day would come to paint that effect. At the top of a grassy knoll appeared the imposing house that Mr Bennett described as a mansion. What did Jon do with it all? Most of the rooms must be empty and gathering dust unless the upper floor contained something exotic, a harem perhaps. Approaching the door, the rapid climb up the slope could not wholly explain her breathlessness. She rang the bell, hoping for a long respite in order to calm down.

Jon opened the door. He had become handsome since they last met, lean and tanned as if he had spent years travelling in tropical countries. Lisa felt unsophisticated, even gauche; a student again in awe of the successful practitioner.

Smiling, he pecked her politely on both cheeks. 'You've grown into beauty,' he said admiringly.

'So have you.'

A modern hallway had a number of rooms leading from it, all with their doors wide, scattering sparkling light into the area. From an adjacent room came a telephone's shrill call. 'I'll just answer that,' Jon said. 'We're in there.'

His ample studio, typically masculine, was disappointingly functional, lacking flowers or bright textiles or anything else to promote cheerfulness. On the plus side Lisa gave him credit for a well-planted garden filling the window view. In front of it stood a shabby armchair, incongruous in the modern setting, but a smarter low couch occupied the centre of the floor by an easel, similar to her own but far more expensive. These barren surroundings had only one decoration: a sizeable hanging photograph, an automatic attraction.

Lisa immersed herself in a composition of dense blacks and clean whites. It showed an oppressive room stuffed with items. A dado of dark polished wood bordered a florid and sombre wallpaper, and pedestals supported embellished clocks or small bronze heroes wrestling with goats. Higher on the wall to her right a hawk and an eagle, and there on her left a snowy owl, were poised on the verge of flight, wings unfurled and talons clawed, their eyes glinting as pin-points of fire. She noticed the head of a doe and a brace of rabbits held by the heels, horned skulls of antelopes, and a powerful boar with nasty tusks.

In the foreground, on a couch of black crepe, sat a topless woman with a giant wig of crinkled hair. She had an extraordinary doll face, guileless and gently rounded, flawless alabaster skin, and lips strangely curled to resemble an alluring rosebud. Her name must be – *Angelique*. Her eyes, ringed in kohl, gave her an expression of constant surprise though she seemed oblivious to the impending violence about to explode. To comfort her Lisa caressed her milky flesh and discreetly nuzzled her tender pink tips. Pleased, the woman stirred briefly then resumed her passive state. Lisa peered apprehensively past Angelique at – *Griselda* – whose reflection in a mirror glared malevolently at the younger woman. At the top of the mirror's gleaming ebony frame perched a carved raven, dangerously alert, and Griselda's hair flared in a huge fan suggesting that she, with the hawk, was about to fly; flying hair stretched as a wing to summon the birds. *But if wild creatures – all raptors – are brought to life they'll be unpredictable and –*

'Lisa?'

– their malice, erupting in sharp beaks and stabbing –

'Lisa! Are you ready?'

31

Jon's voice wrenched her out of the scene and dumped her back in reality. She quivered and blinked and to gain time she asked, 'Who are they?'

He scanned the photo cursorily. 'Just girls.'

'What girls?'

'Girls!' He dismissed them as of no importance.

'Where was it taken?'

'Uhm . . . Venice. Maybe.'

'And who is this?' Lisa indicated the doll-faced woman. 'Does she have a name?'

Again Jon shrugged carelessly. 'Don't know. Can we make a start?' Abruptly he walked to the easel and attached a sheet of paper.

Why display the picture if it had no meaning? Lisa's speculations cushioned anxiety as she unrolled her T-shirt. This much he had seen before, but she discounted the uneasy thought that she had now blossomed to maturity. Unfastening the buttons at her fly, she tried to kick off her trainers but the awkward jeans restricted her struggles and she cursed herself for not choosing a loose skirt. Stifling the image of other women undressing for a client, she reminded herself of the serious purpose. As she tugged at her panties, they fell to her ankles unexpectedly and she inhaled deeply to steady her nerves. Stepping out, she glided to the couch, hoping to subdue her bust's natural momentum and sat primly, knees together, arms crossing her chest.

'Come on, Lisa.' Jon weakened her resistance by coaxing amiably. 'This isn't your first time.'

'How do you want me?' Too late she realised how he might mistake an innocent question.

'Up.'

She complied, hands at her side, while he surveyed from a distance. His presence strayed over her body like a smouldering flame on a surface of oil.

'Of course,' he said, coming closer 'the convention is to avoid touching the model. But I haven't done a complete figure for years. I need more data than sight can give me. I'm sure you appreciate what I'm saying, so with your permission . . .?' He began to explore her belly's soft undulations. His warmth, combined with his slow advance, amplified the intimacy.

'Oh, god!' Lisa recalled one of her own illustrations.

'Hold still.'

With his eyes shut he visualised her form through tactile sensation. This, a perfectly reasonable notion, helped her to accept his fondling. Curving around the firm swell of her right thigh he investigated her crisp cushion of pubic hair. At the incitement resting on her mound she became rigid, feeling a shameful impulse of moisture. His fingers slid away, hugging her posterior's slopes, and entered the cleft. Safely now, he traced the ridged muscles up her spine to the outcrops of shoulder blades, and when he continued behind her neck he sent a prickling stream down her back. He moved to her front and raised and nursed the silky pulp of one breast, as if assessing the resilient weight. Her nipple erected spontaneously and pressed into his palm. Lisa trembled, indecently stimulated.

'Are you enjoying this?' she muttered grimly.

Jon broke off in a curt rejection. 'Thank you,' he said and retired to the easel, briskly efficient. 'Pivot to the window but don't shift your feet. Look out at the garden.'

In presenting her profile Lisa could only guess his progress by the sleek stroke of a pencil, succeeded by the coarse scratch and brushed lines of charcoal. Jon drew in silence with no sighs of frustration or the angry ripping of paper to signify poor results.

'Excellent! You have superb proportions.'

Personal comments also violate the code.

'Would you lie on the couch?'

Lisa decided instead to confront him, sitting with her wrists in her lap to hide her pubes. She adopted the position deliberately to watch him at work, tightly focused but without a photographer's cold calculation or mechanical lens. Jon observed scrupulously, registered fluently, and checked to confirm the line's accuracy – plotting which guaranteed the validity of each mark. He had obviously planned the session and knew exactly what he wanted to take from her. At no time did their eyes meet.

He fixed a page and requested a new pose. Snared by his rapt attention that required nothing else, only her, Lisa surrendered a layer of self-defence to offer him more. Swivelling onto one hip she twisted her torso, crossed her legs, and draped one arm in a languid gesture on the top of the couch. Half-turned to the easel her boobs now hung asymmetrically in an interesting way for him to record. His brooding study – the insistent dreaded male gaze – reduced her to a set of planes patterned by light and shade. She had often subjected her own models to the same cruel analysis in order to extract any tiny clue. But the remorseless interrogation also accentuated their true relationship; she had relinquished any control of her own to his authority.

On the next change she amended the balance through provocation. Hoisting one foot onto the seat she permitted her leg to sag outwards, knowing he would follow their lines into the apex of her crotch. Jon drew urgently, now that her appearance had grown familiar. Soon everything she had to supply would be lodged in his memory.

Another sign from the easel. Mimicking one of her own drawings Lisa lay flat, keeping one foot on the seat, the other on the floor. He would spot, peeking shyly out of her hairy bush, the pouting blushing lips of her sex. He devoured her, gathering information but also appeasing his lechery. A mist of perspiration, beads of aphrodisia, clung to her skin. *Now we're both breaching the code.* Protecting herself from his sadistic intensity, she spread the rubbery folds to add spice to her petting. During a long absorbed period the studio faded away. Floating in reverie, she missed his approach.

'It's good to see you so relaxed.'

Jon loomed above her as Lisa fumbled to a halt, brightly flushed and so disgraced she could scarcely breathe. Laughing, he helped her to stand and nudged her towards the armchair in front of the window. 'Let's try the last one with you leaning on that.'

If her arousal had been less acute she might have refused but raw excitement propelled her forwards. The easel stood directly behind and the films had taught Lisa how revealing a rear view would be; a lewd posture that might encourage a carnal response. She propped her weight on her hands and parted her legs, just a little. The beat of her heart slowed as if she acted within a dream and she inclined further onto her forearms. The pendant drag of her quivering bosom emphasised her vulnerability. Even so, she brazenly hollowed her back and splayed to the full extent, emulating her mentors, the filmed women. Now the pose, flawed by the absence of aesthetic taste, lay far outside the normal code. She heard approval, then the measured scrape of graphite on paper, and concentrated on the garden's foliage beyond the windows. Gradually she lost all track of time.

Suddenly, out of nowhere, he smashed all pretence of artistic convention. 'You're showing me a beautiful sight.' Jon paused to let the idea sink into her mind. 'Someone wise, presumably male, once said that between her legs are a woman's jewels. Do you have any faith in that?'

Lisa's dried throat prevented an answer. Her own audacity had titillated and made him horny, leading to this flagrant liberty.

'Jewels ... that's certainly what I believe them to be.' Only faint scuffs from the easel reassured Lisa that he was still at work. But how appealing to think of them as attractive jewels, far better than messy anatomy. The area under discussion started to ache and swell.

'Have you examined your genitalia in the mirror? If not, I'll amuse you with a brief description.'

Lisa's heart thumped so hard it hurt. No one had ever treated her in a manner remotely resembling this. Why was she frozen, unable to break the binding spell?

'I'll begin the tour with the high curves of your haunches and your fine thighs that provide an immaculate frame. At the top of their broad valley your small anal ring is puckered with the rays of a sun. They all converge in that one dark aperture so they're very enticing. Below are the slack puffy curtains of flesh shielding your cunt. They meet near to your charming anus and from there they droop, a buckled diamond, all tints of coral. I'll paint them in oils the next time you model.'

35

The next time?

'Your modest rim of hair, more oval than the lips themselves . . .'

He went on and on, quietly trickling the images into her brain. Lurid, lancing words produced their usual effect and he, in contrast to Lisa, may have been pleased at the moisture shining on her labia. A moment came when, giddy with euphoria, she pictured him kneeling, her cheeks covering his face like a pair of moons and she wriggled slightly to flaunt –

Strong grips clamped her waist on both sides and a pulsing bulge settled against her yielding entry, which was soft and wet and willing to give way. 'Uhm,' Jon murmured, 'the perfume of a woman on heat.' A thick girth widened her creamy passage, advanced and veered its course, and Lisa surged with elation and lust. The entire session, a prolonged and potent foreplay, had ignited her senses. The penis inserted fully and prickly pubic hair crushed into her bottom. At first he glided deliciously, very slowly, letting her feel its whole length and shape, and she cried out at such an expert lover. The position allowed him to bore in deeply, sparking nerve endings that had never been so stimulated, while a robust tension anchored her to the floor. Vibrated by each impact, swinging her dangling globes to and fro, Lisa groaned deliriously. She hadn't appreciated how much she needed the real thing or how good a base animal coupling, with no refinement or false seduction, could be. On each thrust his testicles compacted her clit which stiffened so much it must be in pain. The liquid pumping mounted in devastating speed and force, and Lisa feared his imminent come would leave her stranded. Under her belly she massaged her throbbing bud, circling frantically. Her own vigour, allied to the plunging shaft, opened and closed and clenched her body in a fierce ecstatic release at the same instant his gushing ejaculate burst inside, time after time.

He retained possession of her drenched hole, diminishing steadily, and Lisa's own turmoil dwindled down to a single perception: her warm receptacle held a soothing balm of sperm. Later he pulled out and her channel contracted.

Naked, and with no embarrassment, he remained still. She inspected his pectoral muscles and his limp glans, richly gleaming with her own lubrication, nestling over pendulous balls. His masculine aura exuded virility and passion, and affected her powerfully. She kissed him but broke it off to complain, 'You should have asked my permission.'

'Rather unnecessary. You gave me a clear invitation.'

'Bastard!' Lisa protested. 'You know damn well what you were doing to me. That's twice you've used me and for that I deserve a peek at the stuff.' For one of them she already had the evidence, feeling loosened and pacified.

Jon lifted the sheets one by one. In all of them he had created a confident and desirable woman. But professional jealousy spoiled her admiration. These superb drawings conveyed vitality and strength.

'You're an amazing draughtsman.'

'Inspired by a beautiful subject.'

Dazed, she kissed him again. 'What about the last one?'

As Jon flipped the page Lisa clutched his arm. Swift lines caught her slim calves and also a pattern of upward bands on stockings that melted away mysteriously above her knees. She had assumed her bold hemispheres would be the most distinctive feature with a discreetly indicated fig beneath. The picture ought to have matched his inflammatory words but instead, in a grotesque exaggeration, an immense vulva protruded outwards in a flabby gaping O. Her dear pussy had been transformed to an exotic corrupted flower and the elegance of exquisite detail increased the shock. Lisa stared, appalled by gratuitous exploitation; a betrayal, a disturbing obsession, or some type of fetish.

'You've made me obscene,' she spat angrily. 'Why have you abused me?'

'Is that what you actually think?'

His reasonable tone impelled her to reassess. In a period of careful reflection she recognised the effrontery gave her a new perspective. His concept proclaimed her sex as more than a flower; rather, it was a complete garden, luscious and erotic, soliciting massive or multiple penetration. 'I hope you're not going to exhibit these.'

37

Jon looked surprised. 'Why? Don't you want immortality?'

'Not of that kind.' Lisa pointed to the erotic garden, then gave him a vengeful warning. 'I have a better plan for next time – I'll do you, in the buff.'

'Uhm, that could be dodgy. Suppose I get an erection? Hardly aesthetic.'

'Very rude is better still. Or perhaps I'll give up on the rest of you and spend all my time on this gross appendage.' As she weighed his member, slumped across her palm like a fat version of Dali's limp watch, its odour wafted up in a wave and she fought the urge to drop to the floor for a suck. 'Naturally, I'd have to be right up against it to see properly.' Her voice sounded annoyingly husky.

'You would,' Jon agreed.

The tempting flaccid tube waited for rejuvenation but a second – organised – fuck could not equal the spontaneity of the first. Lisa consoled herself by rubbing her teats on the raised plateau of Jon's chest. His skin was as smooth as her own. Smearing her body to his – a silky, full-of-intent, provocative cat – she let his penis fall with a thud. His smile of anticipation died away. She put on her blouse but before she could reach her panties he snatched them away. Silently she held out her hand.

'I'm keeping them.'

'What on earth for?' she asked, bewildered.

'A souvenir.'

'Are you weird? I can't walk through the village without them.'

He laughed mockingly. 'Are you telling me you've not done it? Except for us who could possibly know?'

Lisa struggled to understand the motive. His determination suggested that losing her panties meant there was no going back. Abruptly she abandoned them, stepped into her jeans, and pushed on her trainers. 'When shall we have that slap-up meal you promised?'

'As soon as I return.'

'You're going away? Where to?'

'Oh, round and about.'

She noted the vagueness. 'Here and there?'

Jon acknowledged her teasing but refused to explain.

Reluctant to leave, she protracted their kiss for her own satisfaction. As he accompanied her to the door he demonstrated their shared belief in dressing, or not, just as he wished in his own house. After a few yards in strong sunlight Lisa glanced behind.

Swinging her panties as if he had captured a valuable trophy he called, 'Beware of bad bunnies.'

Declining the bait, and trying to forget his cocksure condition, she followed the slope towards the distant wood, drifting in a squishy decadent haze. *Physical love makes me shine.*

In the wood, approaching the gate, she noticed a black object draped on a branch. Curiously, she dragged off an impractical female thong. Exploring further, she inhaled a sweet scent impregnating the fabric. How could this be with no sign of anyone? Again she buried her nose in the faint diffused aroma.

Breathless at her own behaviour, as errant as Jon's in stealing her panties, she took off her jeans and hauled up the thong, shuffling for adjustment and gasping as the narrow string pressed her sphincter. Lisa had no experience of such a garment, especially one that might recently have snuggled the intimate parts of a stranger. *Pervert!* But in a deserted wood this was merely a private act, a simple experiment. The covering was so tiny! She observed untidy threads of hair splayed outside the boundaries of the pouch and hastily smothered the nasty sight in her jeans.

As she moved homewards her strides magnified the unusual confinement of her crotch, and the constant goading revived Jon's final picture. *Why did he put me in stockings?* Perhaps as a personal fantasy. And why in an out-of-date style with vertical bands? Puzzled, she walked on.

Did those stripes represent something else? What are they? Tenacious lines, or straps, rigid things that enclosed her limbs. And Lisa knew beyond any doubt.

But a fantasy, by definition, is not a fact.

Even so, it might be wise to keep away in future.

Five

Escaping Jon's powerful effect proved far more difficult; along with his fluid emission he had also planted a seed in her brain. The extreme liberty of reconstructing her genitals as erotic enticement acted on Lisa all night and the next morning, half asleep, a fresh perception jumped into her mind. For these gifts of serendipity, which often happened, she had a pen and pad always ready on the bedside table and before they could fade a number of rapid sketches combined and doubled her visions.

During the morning routine slugs of caffeine boosted the sequence, and with plenty of time to spare she padded to the studio without bothering to dress. Wedged on her stool she visualised the illustration while rotating her wrist clockwise, then the reverse and wringing her shoulders, loosening up for the fluency needed. Her pencil hovered above the page – ghost-drawing, shadow-drawing – searching for the correct scale. As her instincts crystallised the pencil produced its first mark. Lisa worked automatically, dropping finished pieces to the floor so the series continued with no interruption, and when the flow dried she avoided the error of attempting to squeeze out more; they might arrive by chance later. She peered about, dazzled by the scattered hoard that had come so easily. It confirmed the force of imagination to make her dreams materialise. At one turn of a secret key they poured out.

Sliding off her stool, she looked at a woman leaning forward. Curving over her back were the outline of fingers stretching apart the lips of her cunt. The digits had no thickness at all and lay flat on the surface, as if they belonged to a phantom species able to open her body at will.

Another example showed a stern erection with its spade-shaped plum fully exposed, and its stem tattooed with the form of a woman whose entire head surrounded the sperm slit.

And how had this come? Stooping, Lisa picked up an image of anonymous legs sprawled in opposite directions. At the centre, below alluring pudenda with a thin veil of pubic hair, voluptuous dilated labia held the enlarged sphere of a staring eye.

Lisa gathered the sheets together. On top of the pile a different vagina, fashioned as a sea anemone, floated in tidal currents. Within its fluttering web, hardly visible, lay rows of arrowed teeth duplicating a shark's mouth.

The collection joined the earlier work in her red file. Lisa shut the drawer deliberately and checked it twice. In her bedroom a novel decision – panties or thong? – delayed her preparation. In brief experiments the previous evening she had relished the strict control of her thong. She had squatted, knees widened to their maximum, and found an almost-hidden sodden strip. On the floor in front of her a man had gazed into her fork, transfixed by the flimsy material crumpled and stained in her crease.

Regrettably it must be discarded. Lisa's errant bush on either side made it unrealistic unless she shaved but that would upset her natural appearance. Quite simply, it could not be done. She fitted a pair of fine white panties cut high at the waist whose delicate embroidery revealed her thatch through the sheer mesh. Confronted by a well-framed view she paused. 'Not a total shave, only a trim.' What would suitable topiary be? A heart, or perhaps a diamond, a flame, or a feather. These lovely experiments would have to wait but, in compensation for losing her thong, she chose a filmy lace bra with half cups that scarcely cloaked her nipples. This was a better choice for meeting an impressionable boy than to go unsupported. An ample

T-shirt, printed with a cartoon, concealed the harmless vanity. Legs and feet could remain bare but a skirt of good length would be advisable.

She answered the doorbell dutifully. Her nephew smiled, kissed her cheek, and offered a bottle of cheap plonk. 'Nice to see you, Ben. Go into the garden and I'll get this uncorked.'

On teak chairs by the lawn she caught up on family affairs of only mild interest. They both used formal politeness to keep the other at a distance and, as the initial flood of conversation dried, they sought refuge in the wine. Lisa examined the floppy-haired youth who had good basic features and dark liquid eyes; an appealing subject to paint. But his edgy manner of talking to the ground, flashing impulsive glances at her legs, urged against the idea.

'How's college?' she asked. 'Lots of parties? Queues of girlfriends?'

'A bit of that,' Ben admitted. 'No queues. Mostly getting drunk in the Student Union.'

'Tell me about the girlfriends.'

Her bid to lighten his mood had unfortunate consequences. He launched into a morose account of disputes with Gail who refused to take him seriously, flirted with his mates, and so on and so on. It was a thoroughly boring whinge that Lisa crushed irritably. 'OK, so extend your horizons. There are plenty more and at your age you should be exploring.'

'I know,' he replied. His calculated stare conveyed the kind of notion a nephew should never have about an aunt.

Lisa's offence boiled into rage. How could this – boy! – be so impertinent. She had, of course, witnessed all his developing years and now, on the verge of manhood, he had the gall to think of her in a wholly inappropriate way. For a quiet period she lowered the mellow wine and calmed gradually. She understood he had come for help.

What would be easier than to ignore the unspoken desire and bury the awkward tension in bright chatter? An aunt should always behave responsibly. But good conduct competed with a far more intoxicating, sneaky thought: the kind of notion she should never have about a nephew. His lust had communicated itself to her. *He's come for assistance that only I can provide.* She broke the silence cautiously. 'Perhaps what you should have is ... an alternative. Maybe –' Lisa gave a casual shrug '– a mature woman.'

Ben's startled gaze anchored her face. 'That would be great.'

Lisa flared with excitement. Steadying her voice she asked, 'Are you a virgin?'

'Yes,' he mumbled sheepishly.

'A young man,' she mused aloud, 'who needs to experiment and learn a few things.' She kept him dangling, then repeated, 'Perhaps with the aid of a mature woman.'

His dumb nod gave her a giddy sense of mastery. She could lead him anywhere but first his resolve must be tested by fire. 'Let me be clear about this,' she said crisply. 'Is that why you're visiting? What did you expect – that I would let you fuck me?'

He blanched at the brutal attack, delighting her; at least he could still be shamed. 'Sorry.' He jerked out of his chair as if she had scalded him. 'I shouldn't have come.'

'No, you should not! Am I no more to you than a common street-girl, ready to lie down and open up on request?' Good – there was so much pleasure in seeing the brat squirm!

Her nephew departed across the lawn and Lisa scrambled to clarify some of the issues. A virgin boy, not yet a man who could exercise superior strength, could be trained how to treat a woman properly. Perhaps that would save others later, in his adult life. A noble motive!

And her collaboration would permit it to happen. She would be allowing it.

One advantage of such an outrageous situation would be to dispense with the feminine wiles. All that tedious foreplay of repulsing the male's advance, giving way, and tempting him again. None of these strategies, intended to enhance the value of what a woman eventually yields, would be required. What a relief!

As Lisa called out her voice croaked. 'Don't be in such a hurry.'

The boy returned, pitiful with hope in his eyes.

'Sit,' she ordered severely. 'I am appalled at you. How did you persuade yourself that I might agree?'

'I didn't. I just . . . fantasised.'

'About me?' Her reaction registered genuine alarm at discovering herself as a character in someone else's fantasy. What disgusting acts did Ben use her for? She challenged him stridently, 'Do you masturbate?'

Her nephew studied the grass diligently.

Lisa envisaged his ungainly sprawled position and the vigorous pumping. Mentally, as he reached the last frenetic stage, he had her locked in something vile, and for that scandalous licence he would have to bleed. 'Tell me what you imagined.'

'Oh – usual things.'

'What things!' Lisa snapped. 'If you wish to experience a mature woman you'd better start acting like a man who is worthy of her.' She watched him struggling to gather his nerve: he must want her very much indeed.

'You, undressed. And . . . your tits – sorry! Er . . . how they'd feel . . .' He coloured and grimaced in desperation.

'I'm waiting.'

'And . . . inside you . . .' Tormented, he added, 'That makes me come.'

That random spurting and splashing. Lisa discounted her dear pussy's encouragement and kept him suspended. She had the authority of a judge about to declare a verdict, but a decision that satisfied him condemned her. In the garden's tranquil atmosphere, she considered the rights and wrongs, despite a growing ache between her legs. After much hesitation she murmured, 'You don't deserve anything but you may give me a kiss.'

She regretted the result immediately when he rushed at her with too much enthusiasm. Disturbed, the laboured beat of her heart matched his own and she insisted on a slow pace. 'You must be discreet,' she warned. 'Can you manage that? Or will you boast to your friends about what you did to your aunt?'

Ben flushed resentfully. 'No. I respect you.'

'And so you should. Now you can touch me. Women enjoy being tactile.' She arranged his hands to hold her buttocks as a docile platform while she taught him how to sustain a kiss. But in a short time the palms and the individual fingers came alive and ranged candidly, bunching and squeezing, and pressing into her crevice through her skirt. That sensitive area yearned to be fondled but she had given no permission and he had no right to privilege. The agile tongue searching her mouth stifled her protest and his knee widened her crotch. Too quickly the boy assumed the role of a man and Lisa pulled away hissing, 'You're a cocky kid who presumes too much.'

From excessive command he flipped over to instant defeat. 'Sorry,' he blurted.

Lisa paused long enough to scare him about losing his opportunity. At last she said, 'OK, what's the next thing in your dirty mind?'

'Taking your clothes off.'

In her bedroom's mock-striptease she had become used to undressing on demand but to be pawed by a boy would be new, and not necessarily entertaining. 'And I'm passive, I suppose, letting you do what you want.'

'How did you know?'

'Do it,' she mumbled.

At the loss of contact with his body she wavered, but before she could change tactics he lifted the hem of her shirt. Fearing impending doom, she raised her arms for the garment to be hauled higher, revealing her provocatively tiny lace brassiere that was not meant to be on display. And with her head enclosed in a fabric balloon she had no defence: he could freely ogle her curves and glimpse her areolae. The material snagged her wrists and even its feeble constraint recalled his father, binding them. As the shirt fell to the grass she avoided appraisal by resting against him, and it reduced her embarrassment at the inexpert fumbling to unclip her bra. The support finally sagged but its loose behaviour only equalled her own in lowering her arms to drop the straps from her shoulders. Ben gaped at a view prohibited by normal convention and Lisa flamed; her vulnerability reversed their relationship of all the years past. *But he's already pictured me – and used me.* Her loins grew heavy and the mere brush of his skin caused her nipples to tighten urgently. In the suction of his lips one of her buds elongated, sending a tingling shock throughout her system. She fed him the second but writhed in the painful scrape of his teeth and by the time she jerked away, both projected as vivid stalks. 'They're throbbing with desire,' she groaned.

With no invitation he unfastened her skirt and pushed it over her hips, gawping at her briefs and the visible dark smudge. He petted the swell of her mound, dragged off the panties, and moved apart to admire her nudity.

How could I let this happen? Ferociously Lisa answered her doubts: *Because he needs me.* 'Is this what you visualised?'

'Better,' he croaked.

As in her modelling she protected herself from the male gaze by playing upon it, swivelling from side to side. Humiliation mixed with her lust in confusing eddies of passion. For herself she rejoiced in the supple weight of her breasts – she always had – and used their trembling gestures to provoke him. His trousers lurched eagerly. Not since her teenage years on the beach, adoring and afraid at the same time, had she cast furtive glances at a boy's intriguing bulge. A cold chill shivered her spine as she realised how much she wanted to try that virile tool.

She delayed for a fraction too long when he came behind and trapped her arms. His clothed shaft flattened onto her rear and rubbed up and down in her cleft. Seizing her boobs, he hoisted both and rotated them in opposing circles. 'Ooh, god,' Lisa moaned. *That's wonderful!* Her back arched, not to resist but to increase the force, relishing the slight addition of pain to spice the pleasure. On the occasions she did this herself it was tenderly, but a man's grip was so hard! This must be one of Ben's fantasies and Lisa almost allowed it but, if she did, she would lose her advantage to unbridled masculine dominance. Wrenching out of his grasp, she turned to unbutton his shirt but he grabbed her silky triangle to agitate her clit and her concentration dispersed.

Bewildered by his knowledge and fighting arousal, she managed to strip him in small steps. Caressing his warm bare chest affected her peculiarly. It seemed bizarre and far more intimate than if he had been a strange man. In kneeling to take off his trousers the awareness magnified. As she grappled them off his feet his genital package nudged her cheek. Awkwardly, mesmerised by a wet patch, a leak of pre-ejaculation fluid, she levered his pants over the end of a rigid pole. His turgid member, remarkably large on his slim physique, oddly blended a boy and a man, though the virginal stem had none of the gnarls and veins of maturity.

'What a beautiful sight,' she said, her voice shaking. As she gently eased the slack envelope to and fro she felt, beneath the fine buckling tissue, an iron bar. It took her breath away. She loved having the chance to stimulate a man and continued very carefully. This time she must be sure to prevent premature –

'Ah!' Ben strained, 'Aunt . . .'

A convulsive streak spewed up her wrist. More chaotic bursts flew up her arm and others embedded in her pubic hair. The boy looked dismayed.

Blaming herself, Lisa remembered a scene in the films. The tip of her tongue picked up the viscous web. Caught in a mesh of brazen excitement, she let him watch the seed creeping into her throat and then she swallowed. On savouring his spunk she shuddered involuntarily. An appalling connection, never intended, had just occurred: first the father, now the son. Ben wiped his knob in her bush and smeared the stray threads as if he knew it would glue them into a solid mass. 'You enjoyed that,' he said. 'Sucking . . .' Curiously he enquired, 'How does it taste?'

'You do not ask that sort of question!' Her anger shook his complacency. In a similar way to the girl-woman she herself had once been, he might be capable of an adult performance but emotionally he remained a boy; that's why he needed her guidance. 'It had a delicious flavour,' she admitted. For one awful moment Lisa dreaded he might ask: Like dad's?

'So that's it,' her nephew said regretfully, 'my one shot. I really, really wanted to come inside you.'

Of course he did – to feel his cock held in a cavernous and pliable swamp, the most welcoming gift a woman could grant. Her punishment for indecent haste would be another stage of initiation.

'I'm sure a young man has plenty more where that came from,' Lisa muttered thickly and pulled him to the ground. His knee, again pressing into her crotch, would sense a spot of radiant pussy heat, even more intense than that of the sun. Entwined in his arms she lay quietly as beads of perspiration trickled into her cleavage. His resurgence arrived quickly and his next words ignited an equal reaction.

'Can I see your –' he hesitated but finished boldly '– your cunt?'

'That's an impolite word,' she warned him but his fluttering breath betrayed an unmistakable appetite. She twisted onto her back. The sun's glare, shading his eyes, made it easier to raise her knees and open her legs. She had no call to be so audacious. Perhaps she did it to shock him, or perhaps the justification was her own salacious thrill. As she covered her matted hair, the sides of her arms down the length of her torso bunched her breasts, their teats stretched out as sun-starved blooms. With both hands she spread the outer cushioned flesh, and reached further to unfold the succulent inner membranes, ripe as a glistening fruit. His sultry flush made her alert to the blatant display: closest to him her wide diamond aperture, in the middle distance her alluring globes, and furthest away her own expression.

'Let me . . .' His voice quivered fervently.

His fingers in a single wedge – a sudden rapier – thrust into her clammy passage, sampling what his penis would find. The digits separated, exploring her creamy walls independently, and lunging deep. Ignoring the loss of her mastery she melted into a carnal glow, and when he shifted above her he blocked the sun. Shiny and sleek, the broad crown settled into her portal but now, at this irrevocable point, she felt crazed: *My own nephew!* Not for years had Lisa been ashamed of her sexuality but his crude shoves demonstrated that her own sluttish behaviour had led to this. Fully impaled, her struggles were far too late; the motions captured her and his animal thrashing cancelled any lingering scruple. Her hips lifted to meet each glorious plunge.

'I can't hold it for long.'

'Pump me,' she whimpered. 'Flood me.' Half an instruction, half a plea.

He clutched her wrists and pinned them apart on either side. Her mind blanked, conscious only of three strong pressures: two on her wrists and the remorseless jarring shunts, much too frenetic, into her belly. Under his power, persecuted by raging passion, she vibrated heavily. Her channel grew hot and sore, despite its copious lubrication, and her sharp protesting cries begged for mercy. He stopped, tense, his glans twitching, shedding its load in fierce blasts, and collapsed on top of her, the side of his face against her own.

During the afterglow Lisa supported him in her arms. Her swollen labia troubled her but that was incidental to her main response: the absence of guilt. She had merely supplied the experience he lacked – and needed so badly. Uneasily she dwelt on the inexplicable joy when he clamped her onto the grass but that dissolved in idle speculations. How would they appear from the house, linked together on the bright lawn? Or, up there on the ridge, a voyeur might be staring, binoculars focused, on the lean form embraced in the junction of her splayed thighs. But no magnification would show his dwindled organ clinging tenaciously, its shrunken helmet nestled among her outer pleats. She loved the touch of it slumbering there though the boy, desperate for his own relief, had left her marooned on a jagged edge. And Lisa hated this post-coital period. Nature restored their virility by drowning them in a stupor while the poor woman, sweaty and crushed, resented the burden. She wriggled for comfort but stirred him to life unexpectedly. He started to advance and swell agreeably in her smooth sheath. Elated, she eased her pelvis to accommodate the growing size and whispered, 'Slowly this time.'

With his leisurely drives she forgot her earlier distress and sighed contentedly. He controlled his urges for longer, sometimes pausing or skewing the inward stroke, leaving her gasping and shaking in delight. Her delayed rise resumed gradually and mounted towards a sublime peak, her hungry body bounced by his force. Seizing her wrists, he wrenched them to the ground beyond her head to achieve his maximum satisfaction but the extra compulsion also worked for Lisa. A rippling flow unravelled all her pretence of being the older and wiser partner. She was simply a woman, nakedly exposed, susceptible to ecstatic release through patient command. In the midst of her own delirious threshing she gladly received the pouring tributes from deep in his loins.

'Well, you've lost your virginity now.'

'I'll never forget your orgasms,' Ben murmured. His smile had a faint suggestion of male superiority. 'Thanks, aunt, you're a good person.' He walked a few yards up the gravelled path, then retraced his steps. 'Can I come again?'

'You came three times, you greedy boy! Don't ever consider me as a regular date!' He flinched at her vehemence and Lisa, savagely pleased, relented. 'Give me a call next week, after my convalescence. There, another boost to your ego.'

Exhausted by youthful zeal she meandered lazily, the hair on her mound stiffened with sap as if starched. In the shower, soothed by the water's caress, she assessed the unforeseen events of the afternoon. Absence of guilt mingled with gratification. Why shouldn't her nephew observe her climaxes? He gave them to her – and she repaid him like the women in the films. 'I must be a wanton.' For a moment she thought of her 'bound' wrists, and how restriction could generate a peculiar freedom, but in the spray's warm consolation her lassitude allowed the anomaly, and the excitement, to fade.

Wrapped in a dressing gown and snuggled into an armchair nursing a coffee, she listened to her favourite tracks on the stereo. Her throbbing diminished steadily until, completely relaxed, she drifted to the studio and from the doorway contemplated her equipment in the centre of the space. On top of the plan chest lay the brief for her new assignment and below, the series of closed drawers – except for the lowest where a narrow rim caught the light. *It was shut!* She ran across the room, located the red file and expelled a sigh of deliverance. But on shuffling the pages she discovered them in the wrong order. A burglar must have examined them! Lisa panicked and screamed, 'You bastard!' She tried to comprehend the calamity. First, her privacy had been invaded – again. Second, crippling anguish at losing her secret. Third, the consequences; would there be any, dangerous to her reputation? Fourth, tomorrow, too late, she must fit locks.

To pacify her shattered nerves she reinstated the proper sequence. Though she was familiar with every detail, the drawings exerted their fascination and by the time she placed the file beneath a stack of paper she knew, more clearly than ever before, that these images excluded all other concerns. They were crucial; far more important than commercial success.

Six

Yet in two hours *Misfit Toys* fell into place.

By an automatic process she had digested the story and identified the prime incidents for development as full-page spreads, another seven for a smaller scale, and the main spot – the front cover. All twelve had notes describing the characters, types of action, and objects to include. The next stage would be to rough-out each design with appropriate drama. On a side table Lisa arranged the articles she had borrowed from Miss Gibbs: a ceramic doll and a top, together with its string whip.

Such rapid and painless progress should be celebrated and she sat at the kitchen table, cradling a Colombian in both hands. A distorted blur on the glass panel of the door announced the arrival of the morning post, a single item. From her chair Lisa appreciated the imposing size and quality of the envelope and its lilac colour. Its powerful presence demanded attention. She answered its call and scanned her name and address in lilac ink. At the table she withdrew a sheet written in confident flourishes:

My dear Lisa,
I have been advised of your exceptional pictures and immediately looked you up. You may guess at the depth of my surprise at finding you listed as a children's illustrator. It is quite extraordinary that from your specialism you could have anything of relevance to my particular interests. I admit to initial scepticism of my

informant's judgement. He remains adamant, however, that your red file –

Lisa jerked upright, her heart thumping painfully. The repercussion she had dreaded had come so quickly! What would it be, a threat of disclosure? Blackmail? She forced herself back to the letter.

He remains adamant, however, that your red file contains remarkable work. If this opinion is correct it would be significant to me, and to those I represent. I should add that it could also be of generous financial benefit to you. That is the first inducement I can offer. The second, perhaps of more value, is entry to a community of similar individuals. In my experience people attract to themselves the life they imagine so perhaps, in your file, there is a clue. Could your work be explained as psychic invention?

I am mortified by the manner in which this knowledge has come to me. My only hope is that you can forgive the invasion of your privacy; I would hate it myself. Yet means can justify ends if those ends are potentially as rewarding as yours could be. If you are bold enough – if you dare – contact me on the number below. The offer is available for the next twenty-four hours.

I urge you to think carefully.

Pauline.

Lisa read the whole thing again. The woman's informant – he. It was a man who had twice sneaked into her house, not stealing money or possessions but worse, to violate her concealed file, her hidden self. 'You bastard!' she muttered bitterly. But he also reported her efforts as remarkable: a strange kind of thief.

Generous financial benefit. *Nice to hear*.

Think carefully. *What about?* The second inducement 'perhaps of more value' could be worthless.

People attract to themselves the life they imagine. *Is that what the work is?* Could it really be something she wanted for herself?

If you are bold enough, dare.

The letter stayed on the table as a reminder or as a provocation while Lisa, in the studio, concentrated on her assignment. Using white layout paper she mentally constructed the composition and its necessary scale, greater than the size of reproduction. After shadowing, ghost-drawing, her pencil made its mark and she continued longer than usual, with no breaks, as if under the menace of a strict deadline.

By the time early evening dimmed the illumination she had grown weary and stiff. In the kitchen a lilac page – reminder? provocation? – waited for her. *Do I dare?* 'Twenty-four hours ...' From when? Lisa decided to calculate from its delivery provided, of course, that she wished to reply. A job for tomorrow – maybe.

The following morning sunlight bounced off the finished roughs pinned to the wall. Nursing her mug of coffee, she studied the contrast between innocent expressions and lewd twists at the corners of mouths. One picture, obscured in deep shades, suggested dismembered limbs lying at grotesque angles to their normal position. The next showed an ominous doll, strongly lit from the side, with half-open pouting lips. A third, an abandoned splayed form, resembled a carcase curved round a stair-post.

Do I dare?

Neutralising her thoughts, Lisa examined the front cover. Three giant dolls lurked beside the toy-box. Half of Hermione's face had broken off and the twin sisters had been joined at the hip. Behind them were four decapitated and grinning heads, though their eye-sockets were blind. 'Definitely – a bunch of misfits.' Lisa peered at the clock. In a fluent sequence, merely engaged in a routine task, she picked up the 'phone and dialled the number written in lilac ink.

She paid the fare, clambered out of the taxi, and lifted her portfolio onto the pavement. The large thin case brought back memories of the days when, as a raw graduate from a school of art, she had struggled off and onto lurching buses carrying samples to the agencies. Lunch-time crowds rushed past as she surveyed the blood-red facade of a well-maintained Georgian house. Stone steps edged by wrought-iron balustrades led to a portico framing a highly polished mahogany door. A brass knocker gleamed in the sun but the entrance lacked an inscribed plate and only 'Eighteen' confirmed the address. She climbed up to the door, rapped on the knocker and eased her arm.

A graceful woman appeared, taller and older than herself. A smoky grey suit packaged her figure with expensively tailored precision and its tight narrow skirt sculpted her thighs. Lisa noticed an aquiline profile, perfect make-up, grey pupils and fine ash-blonde hair pulled back severely, held by a plain metal clamp. The woman radiated clear sensuality, sure of her worth, and her shrewd appraisal weakened Lisa's self-assurance.

'Thank you for coming. I'm Pauline. Come this way.'

Along a carpeted hall they passed a row of mahogany doors and from several came vague but muffled noises difficult to classify. They arrived at a comfortably furnished room. 'My sanctuary,' Pauline stated and gestured towards a desk with a shining burgundy leather top. 'Put your folio there and we'll start by getting acquainted.'

Sliding off her jacket she hung it on the shoulder of an upholstered chair. Lisa sat opposite and quietly regarded Pauline's slim legs crossed elegantly, then her stylish minimal sandals. Resting in her lap, her fingers had manicured nails like scarlet shells. Her blouse, of sheer white silk, had parted in the centre to reveal the inner slopes of a smooth cleavage and Lisa caught a glimpse of small buds moulding their shapes in the material.

'Do you always scrutinise?'

'Sorry! ... Yes. It's second nature to look hard at everything.'

Pauline laughed. 'Well, I trust you approve because, to speak frankly, I find you very appealing.' She paused and collected herself. 'First, let me repeat my apologies for the way I learned of you. I assume that, in coming here, you have forgiven me. But I've never met a children's artist before – you are not in the world I inhabit – so I'm intrigued. How do you manage to encompass the extremes of naiveté and adult pleasures?'

'I suppose it comes from different aspects of my character.'

'A split personality?'

Lisa shrugged silently.

'Tell me about your private work. Why do you do it?'

'Probably as a bid for freedom. Escaping from the dictates of an author and simple linear stories – striking out on my own path.'

'Try again,' Pauline gravely advised. 'Drawing and painting are very slow activities demanding intense commitment to a subject for a long period. Who knows that better than you? There must be far more to it.'

'Because the best sex is in the head?'

'I see – it's a question you do not take seriously. Don't you need to fathom the basic motive?'

'I simply show fantasies that –'

'Yes, of course,' Pauline said impatiently. 'That is the field. But fantasies run very deep in our psyche and are, therefore, inestimable. Are you curious at all about why I, and those I represent, might treasure your work?'

'No.'

'How disheartening to be so unreflective. Allow me to explain. Even if conducted ingeniously, sexual events last for a relatively short time. We constantly rehearse those delectable pursuits in a variety of ways – why would we not? – but also seek to expand and enrich the persistent impulse. Erotic illustration – and our lesser cousin, photography – are a way to relive and renew the experience. For centuries, succeeding generations have bequeathed visual evidence of their practices so, if we replenish that stock, we help to refresh a profound and complex piece of our culture. How many artists of this kind are familiar to you?'

'Well. Er . . . Aubrey Beardsley, Egon Schiele, Hokusai. The Surrealists, of course.'

'A tiny range, nearly all men. So that is one reason why I, and those I represent, have such aspirations for you. We are interested in what might emerge from a female sensibility.'

'You keep saying "those I represent." Who are they?'

'I have contacts with connoisseurs in many countries who pay ample amounts for publications of outstanding quality.'

'But I couldn't rival those I've mentioned.'

'Ha! A good example of misplaced modesty. Yet that is the promise I have been given – that you are, potentially, just as good –'

'By a sneaky informant,' Lisa interrupted stridently 'who burgled my house. What's his name?'

'Frederick Johansen. That's j, o, h, a, n, s, e, n.'

'What? Who's he? I've heard a similar name recently . . . do you mean Johannes?'

'In my business I cannot afford to confuse names,' Pauline replied frostily. Relaxing, she added, 'Don't condemn him. His recommendation may provide an opportunity that is rarely available. We are a select group who consider the best episodes as a mystery. After all, enigma releases fundamental emotions. But to endorse his judgement I must examine your portfolio.' Scanning Lisa's face she asked, 'Do you feel exposed? I shall be invading your sexuality.'

Lisa blushed. 'I don't know,' she mumbled.

'At least you have dared this far.'

The woman's manner was so formidable and her standards so intimidating! Pauline returned to the desk and Lisa trailed apprehensively. As a stumbling beginner in exacting territory she would certainly fail. The zip rasped, abnormally loud, and the case flattened onto the desk.

Pauline murmured a commentary, more to herself than to Lisa. 'A wonderfully expressive line.' Later she said, 'This one is good. A woman on the verge of discovery – a delicious, tense situation. And that sequence of open doors denoting that she's no longer virgin. A nice touch.' Reaching the pictures of Jacqueline she exploded suddenly. 'No! This will not do. I am not in the market for cartoons.'

'They're scraps of a larger narrative,' Lisa said defensively.

'I realise that, but there is great power in the single image – a moment suspended in time. We can play mentally with what preceded that moment and what will follow, and that lends an extra frisson. It is the small meticulous idea that seizes our attention.'

Immediately Lisa recalled her own response to Jon Bradley's distortion of her dear pussy.

'And your technical skill lends enormous impact.'

Something else I learned from him.

At the next sheet Lisa clarified the intention hastily. 'I did this series to demonstrate that drawing can go far beyond photography.'

'By superimposing the inner view on the outer. Yes, that notion is valid,' Pauline conceded. Then, holding an illustration of a standing woman, she froze. Lisa had produced the figure in coarse striations of Indian ink resembling the grain of bark on a tree, and twisted the woman's features in desperate torment. The rigid shaft and testicles of a giant erection – or those balls could be interpreted as a man's rounded arse and its shaft could be his slender back – rammed upwards under her ribs, rending her body. 'A gigantic wound. That's a remarkable concept of penetration as wholly consuming.'

Scanning the sheets as carefully as Miss Gibbs had ever done, Pauline held up a page. 'This!' She indicated an ambiguous woman, seen from the rear, leaning forwards with her hands on the floor. In the foreground her buttocks quivered high in the air and further away dangled her heavy boobs. But then, within her conspicuous haunches rested the tip of an upright stem in the precise position of the woman's genitals. 'Clever. Her pendulous breasts are also his balls. Her torso becomes his prick. And their fluid portions are entirely merged. So we have a neatly combined male and female – an original type of hermaphrodite.' Later she said, 'Ah! A Vagina Dentate arranged as a shell with shark's teeth.'

'Are you saying this has a name? I meant to suggest a form of ravenous desire.'

'Search the literature. You'll find this described as a male fear of castration. But I agree with you – from our perspective it could be interpreted quite differently.' At a quiet click from the door Pauline glanced behind. 'However, since you refer to desire let me introduce my assistant.'

A young woman had entered the room and Lisa gasped, appalled yet fascinated. A horse's bridle enclosed the woman's head and across her jaw she clenched a bar gag. From the ends of the bar red leather straps ascended in a vee to join a silver ring above her eyes. A thicker tie passed from the ring over her cranium to more straps linked to a neck band elevating her chin.

'I believe that's charming, do you? We won't ask for Kim's opinion – the poor girl can't speak.' Pauline invited Lisa to the chairs they had earlier occupied and called out, 'Walkies!'

Kim drifted, completely poised, as if no harness impeded her vision or gag hindered her breath. Through a dark translucent blouse shadowed areas glimmered and its high knot at the front revealed her abdomen's shallow curves. The purity of her skin gleamed luminously. Below the summits of her hip bones a tiny skirt consisted merely of a broad leather belt supporting a minuscule screen of black lace. The blend of materials created a distracting opposition of girly and butch. The lace hem flicked to and fro at the very top of her legs and disguised her slit – just – but the flurry also beguiled Lisa's gaze to the spot where, with certainty, she wore nothing beneath. High-heeled shoes stressed her calves to narrow cords and, in moving away, she offered the swerve of supple cheeks and frisky muscles compacting and lengthening at each step.

'What a scandalously impertinent bottom she has. A pretty symphony in black and white. Do you think so too?'

Lisa felt trapped by the candid allure, a clear incitement to improper thoughts.

Kim finished two circuits before Pauline pointed to her lap. The girl sat, and groaned and tussled unconvincingly, while her employer fondled her left tit, pinching and stretching its nipple under the blouse. Pauline subdued her lust to unfasten the buckles and detach the harness.

Finally, as the gag came out, Kim shook and tossed a wild mane of hair.

For the first time Lisa saw her natural face, white and glossy as an eggshell. She had the unblemished innocence of a Barbie doll except for odd rosebud lips that gave her a constantly lewd look. This, unmistakably, was –

Angelique! – from the photograph in Jon Bradley's studio.

Ignoring Lisa's presence, the women kissed passionately until Pauline grasped a bunch of hair and tugged backwards, tilting her assistant more steeply over her lap until she was thoroughly arched. A dusky pool of hair settled on the floor. Maintaining her grip, Pauline flipped up the skirt to bare the sleek contours of a shaved mound. Nestling in the upper folds of a deep padded crease glittered a silver ring. The only shaved pubes Lisa had studied were in the films and none of them were pierced. Enthralled, she noted how, with the loss of a mature thatch, the girl appeared adolescent and terribly vulnerable.

Pauline's gentle caresses encouraged Kim to part her legs, displaying her split pouch. It received a cupped palm, stroking and teasing the yielding pleats. The ball of Pauline's thumb began to rotate on the tender bud, stirring the silver ring to pursue its path.

As in the cinema Lisa observed passively, but spellbound by a scene actually happening in a hushed room on an ordinary day. Pauline's physical actions and the girl's reactions were genuine, and they were unembarrassed to be doing these intimate things in front of a stranger. Yet how nice it was to watch the respect that one woman had for the feelings of another.

Two digits, a single brutal rod, drove in to the hilt. The normal groove spread to a gaping incision. Pauline thrust steadily, performing a well practised routine, and rising moans accompanied the slick, slick, of abundant juice. The women's carefree behaviour forced Lisa's attraction which made her own, in safe privacy, seem childish by comparison. Yearning for her own self-induced ecstasy she itched to staunch the trickling secretions but inhibition prevented her.

The assistant fumbled for her ring and raised her labia's hood to a fleshy gash. Frantically she agitated her clitoris, augmenting Pauline's vigour, and delivered a climax that shuddered her delicate frame violently. Pauline pulled out, sniffed her fingers in satisfaction, and ostentatiously wiped the liquid on the girl's open thighs.

Kim lifted, panting and flushed, and Pauline murmured, 'In contrast to the poor men, orgasm's only function for us is to give pleasure. So I want you this evening.'

'If you go easy with that whip of yours. I'm a submissive, not a masochist. I need floods of arousal not floods of tears.'

'I'll curb my inclinations. I'm doing courgettes.'

'I hate courgettes.'

'Peeled to form unusual dildos.'

Kim giggled. 'Cold but already wet and slippery.'

'Instead of the lump of ice.'

'Ugh! That really makes me squirm.'

'Yes, it does.' Pauline's tone had a trace of nostalgia. 'Well, Lisa, I noticed how alert you became. I expect you wish to join us?'

'Er . . . no,' Lisa managed to say. 'Thanks, but I'm strictly hetero.'

'Oh dear! A censorious streak. We too are heterosexual when we choose to be. You may resume your duties, Kim. My visitor has no use for you.'

Her assistant stood and straightened her rucked clothing. Her peculiar little mouth widened in amusement. Loose tumbled softness transmitted joy and a promise of pure delight.

As the door shut, Lisa rued her decision. 'Perhaps she could model for me sometime?' The girl's breasts, resilient as spongy springs, would lie warm in Lisa's hands.

'She is yours to use in any way – assuming, of course, you can summon the nerve. Now, let's return to your portfolio.'

Standing beside Pauline Lisa could smell a female odour, a startling enticement, accentuating the reality of the events she had witnessed: definitely not a fantasy.

'These dolls,' Pauline was saying 'they're weird, damaged. Their faces are no more than bland shells yet they are sexually precocious. Decadent too.' She had missed the resemblance to Kim that Lisa remembered, as Angelique, from the photograph; Kim had been their model. 'They're just as erotic as Bellmer's dolls and that, as I trust you appreciate, is lofty praise.'

Pauline skimmed the remainder superficially. Recognising the signs of impending refusal, Lisa waited for the verdict with a familiar sensation of shrinking in size.

'Technically you are highly accomplished and that much verifies your reputation. I shall purchase two. However, an essential quality is missing from most of them – that of true emotion. I guess that is due to your limited knowledge. On this evidence I would say you are operating solely from imagination and in consequence your work lacks authenticity. To enhance your sharp vision you should record perceptions from within the experience. No man can possibly do that. Your subsequent efforts will be unique and for that reason eagerly sought. If you are dedicated you might achieve fame.'

The value of this advice subdued Lisa's disappointment.

'I have a proposal,' Pauline continued. 'I can arrange a few . . . shall we call them encounters? From them you may produce whatever appeals to you in the medium of your choice. If your work contains that missing ingredient I shall give you a substantial commission.' She paused. 'However, I see you are unconvinced.'

'I'm anxious. It's tempting, obviously, but too risky. I could be getting involved in anything.'

'That's the second invitation you have rejected. How depressing that you have ceased to explore. Even if new ventures prove unfortunate they can also be liberating. At the minimum level they act as an antidote to boredom.' Pauline searched Lisa's expression and asked abruptly, 'Do you intend to illustrate our little Sapphic entertainment?'

Unaware of the fact, Lisa had identified the elements of a composition: the girl's helplessness with her legs splayed and her arm flung out; the elongated belly on her mistress's lap and the downward drag on her hair; in the foreground, her unprotected channel invaded with callous masculine strength. The pair would be in a darkened room, isolated in slanting light, and casting huge misshapen spectres on the wall. 'Yes, I probably shall.'

Pauline's cool manner suggested she had predicted the reply. 'At least you have gained that. In what medium?'

'Well . . . Conté crayon might be appropriate.'

'I hope you show it to me one day.' Pauline replaced her jacket and linked all the buttons, a simple way to emphasise their separation. She added physical distance by moving back to her desk and the intercom. 'Please call a taxi.' Extracting the two for purchase she packed the surplus in Lisa's portfolio. 'We'll speak later to negotiate a price.'

Eventually ending an awkward silence, Kim reported, 'It's here.'

'My final comment,' Pauline said to Lisa. 'As women we are conditioned from birth to censure our conduct. If you change your mind give me a call.'

Kim escorted Lisa towards the entrance. Dressed as before, her lithe form exulted in beauty and stoked Lisa's sense of loss. Stopping at the main door, the young woman said, 'I'll leave you here.' She bubbled with laughter. 'I'm not in a fit state for the street.'

'Answer one question. Do you know an artist called Jon Bradley?'

'No, should I?'

'Have you ever been photographed in Venice?'

'That's two questions. I've never been there.'

'Is she actually going to whip you this evening?'

'That's three. She promised.'

'Won't it hurt?'

'How many more? Yes, a bit – but the way she does it turns me on.'

'She said I had no use for you. If I had, would you come?'

Kim sighed dramatically. 'Sure, she often lends me to clients.'

'And you don't care?' Lisa could not disguise her incredulity.

'A girl's gotta have fun, every chance she gets, isn't that so?'

A taste of excitement now and again. Or even more often.

'Pauline has a saying. "If we're driven by our nature we should regret nothing."' Smiling ambiguously, the girl retraced her route into the building.

Lisa watched her twitching tail and the tantalising glide of her calves. To quell her riotous thoughts, she rushed across the pavement and ducked into the taxi.

If we're driven by our nature –

In the studio that evening Lisa repeated the phrase. Pauline had conveyed a potent authority in the casual way she treated Kim/Angelique. They would be together now. Absently, Lisa picked up the Victorian child's top and wrapped its cord whip around the upper section. A neat flick of her wrist unwound the cord and sent the top spinning, precisely balanced, on the wooden floor. *Together now, and Pauline is whipping –*

The string kissed the top to maintain its impetus. Is Angelique tied? Flick! Snap! An erratic stroke staggered the toy, it lurched drunkenly. She must be tied but in what position? The gyroscopic force weakened, causing the top to lean and lose momentum in a lazy curve. 'The ropes are tight but how is she doing it?' Flick! Snap! The top jumped and flew and crashed into the far wall.

A loud impact shocked Lisa awake. The whip clattered to the floor and a feverish glint faded from her eyes. Ripped wood, pale flesh, split the toy from tip to base.

Seven

In the heavier drawing the two figures materialised from dense shadow but their vague boundaries no longer resembled Pauline or Kim. Lisa struggled to understand how the substitution occurred. Out of a subterranean will of its own, a different scene had emerged. And she remembered, throughout the whole process, a feeling of virility. But what would it really be like for that poor woman?

She sprayed fixative on the sheet then left it to dry. In her bedroom she applied make-up, brushed her hair and patted perfume at her ears, her wrists and into her cleavage. Squatting, she spread her knees and had just anointed her dear pussy when an innocent angelic boy approached timelessly, noiselessly. She knew his desire and widened more to reveal her pink fig, its fresh bouquet wafting upwards. He gave her a bottle of cream and she held it high. The fluid poured into her gaping mouth, and out to join the smooth stream caressing her bosom, tunnelling down her belly, and drenching her pubes. As the warm river possessed her body she reacted with a low moan and time passed, soothing the cream over her full and supple globes, relishing her own fondling. He reached out –

A piercing ring from the door-bell demolished the boy. Lisa instantly considered remaining nude but her confidence crumbled and she rushed to the kitchen, threw on her gardening coat, then opened the door.

'Ben, come in.' She gave him a peck on the cheek but quickly stepped away in case he detected her secret. 'I'll be with you in a minute.'

In the bedroom she wondered how to clothe herself seductively in a way that would provoke his interest, stiffen his cock and – 'Jerk out his spunk,' she concluded, her face flaming in sudden heat. But given his immaturity would anything special be required? 'OK,' she muttered 'I'll do it for me.'

She selected a pair of lace panties and adjusted their fit to secure all the errant strands of pubic hair. She covered her chest with a large scarf knotted with a bow; this brilliant idea would eliminate all the tricky fumbling with a brassiere's clasp. *I can do that again.* Immediately she tore off her panties and found an alternative with bows at the hips. Sling-back shoes completed the outfit and she made a final check in the wardrobe's glass. Eager nipples poked-out the delicate silk. The minute triangle, far below her navel, dived to her crotch leaving, above it, a daring band of enticing curls. Lisa's imagination started to play. 'Dressing for sex is having sex. What do you think,' she asked the mirror 'am I erotic?' She waited expectantly, maybe for a wink of light, but gave in with a shrug. 'No answer came the stern reply.' As a temporary measure – probably – she screened the sight with a loose summer skirt. Shoes were unnecessary.

Ben had been in the kitchen but the room was deserted. Gathering herself, she amended her course to the lounge but that room also lay empty. There were only two other possibilities, one of them fearful, and Lisa ran along the corridor and into the studio. Her nephew, hunched by her board, had the desk lamp spilling a bright disc onto her recent illustration.

'Don't look at that! It's not finished yet.' Scarcely able to breathe, she reversed the page, knowing he had already studied every detail.

'I was told you did children's books.'

'Don't be so nosy! It's a private commission.'

He pulled her into a vigorous kiss, neither asking

permission nor needing her guidance. He seemed to have come prepared to take what he wanted.

At risk of losing control, Lisa withdrew. 'Lounge,' she ordered.

'What about the bedroom?'

'This is my house and that's off limits!'

She noticed he had gained a sign of masculinity: an alarming, wholly unconscious, flowing power in his gestures. Settled onto the couch, he gave her no time and smothered her in greedy kisses. Upset and confused she panted, 'You've changed.'

'Why don't you demonstrate the gear?'

Good. Anything to slow him down. As Lisa stood, she recalled Kim and began to patrol the room as calmly as that young woman had been. In her attempt to glide, serene as a swan on still water, the narrow split of her skirt unveiled her legs' shapeliness to the top. Beneath its shield an impulse of moisture tickled her pussy.

'Up with the skirt,' he called.

How far should she go? Blindly grasping the hem, she bunched the material high on her waist and persevered on the journey. The bold decision taught her a lesson: that sluttish exposure felt more humiliating than losing the garment altogether. Competing, perhaps foolishly, with her nephew's appetite she thought of herself as offering bait and allowed him to revel in the image she presented. Eventually, returning to the couch, she posed by swivelling slightly, permitting the weighty mass of her breasts to bulge the scarf on the left and then on the right. Roused, Ben tugged her close to unclip and drop her skirt. Pressing into her groin he announced triumphantly, 'You're wet.'

Numb, Lisa cursed him silently but without her skirt her condition could not be denied. His glazed attention focused on her line of curls and he unfastened one of the bows. The fabric slumped, releasing a faint but unmistakable aroma, and his eyes glittered with a darkly ecstatic light. In exhibiting only a portion of her bush he strangely hinted at using a whore. 'Damn you!' she spat angrily.

'More circuits.'

At least that provided a short reprieve from intensity. The frail panties draped from the bow and gradually the dangling incitement, stroking her leg, influenced her mood. Intoxicated, she unravelled the second bow and the panties sagged but did not fall away; they flapped like a tail, gripped in her crease, blatantly swinging from side to side, enhanced by the sassy sway of her butt. Dimly she understood that she wanted whatever might happen and on her next arrival at the couch she flung them, scattering her scent, straight at Ben's lecherous smirk.

Standing, he took her in a long challenging kiss, unwound her scarf and rubbed her paps, shrieking with lust. 'Your tits are fantastic,' he gloated. He sat to indulge himself by kissing and licking her fleece, ending low on her pubes immersed in her hair. 'I can't get enough of your cunny smell,' he mumbled.

Her loins quivered as she gasped, 'How did you learn to treat a woman this way?' He leaned back to examine her in a cavalier fashion. 'This is getting to be a nasty habit. You enjoy having your aunt naked while you're fully dressed, don't you?'

'So do you,' he grinned.

Lisa's heart beat furiously as she straddled his lap. She teased herself by flicking her amorous teats on his lips, savouring the ripples that chilled them both. Ben stopped her and sucked on the left, drawing in the whole front of her pulpy flesh. At the rigorous suction Lisa groaned desperately, fumbling to unzip his pants and a solid erection sprang out. *He's loaded.* She wrenched away to shove him into the couch. 'Don't move,' she hissed, and set about teaching him the bliss of steadily building sensations. Holding the vertical shaft, she lowered a fraction to give him a taster, prodding the crown in her soft furrow. 'Don't you dare shoot off,' she warned and sank in small stages, hot for each dilation until his length embedded to the hilt. Packed full, she dismissed the memory of who it belonged to.

Rotating her pelvis, she nudged the rod around her resilient walls before sliding up and down. As he grimaced she wondered if he could last but he lay quietly, content for her to take the lead. Elated at a new experience – screwing a passive male – she regulated the speed and depth to discover the sensitive spots within her vagina's sloppy heat.

His palms spread out possessively over her splayed rump. She paused, thrilled by the touch, but a rude fingertip investigated her anal rim and tried to penetrate. To stimulate a quick climax she mounted the pole and fell violently, the swift impacts wobbling her spheres onto his thighs and matching the heavy bounce of her boobs. Her action froze in mid-flight at the sharp sting of a slap on her right haunch. The reprimand prickled her skin as she started again more patiently, dragging out her labia as a broad elastic band constricting his stem. Nurturing her own upward climb, her features sealed in concentration. More slaps burned on her left and Lisa choked but persisted, too far on to complain. One, more severe this time, cracked on her right and she yelped but continued to pump tirelessly. Surprisingly, the stinging spurred her orgasm and she squeezed urgently to extract his milk. Deep inside his member twitched and delivered its sperm in a flood.

She collapsed on his chest. His beautiful organ shrank away leaving, in her fork, a gaping dank hole in contrast to her bottom, which glowed comfortably. Subsiding, half asleep, she drifted away.

Dulled by lassitude, Lisa woke to find her wrists clamped. Unable to escape, her throat dried and she croaked, 'Ben . . .' He prevented her protest by levering her body off his lap and onto the seat of the couch where he pushed her down. *What's he going to do?* Absurd possibilities swept her brain, she throbbed with crazy ill-defined longings, and the map of her face revealed the conflict.

'Dad told me about this. He said, "A little bit affects Lisa a lot".'

'Have you been talking about me?' She struggled but her nephew's strength sapped her resolve. 'What do you want?' she whispered.

'That's the wrong question.' Ben released her and kissed her briefly. 'Your picture showed me what you want.'

Lisa's belly gave a sickening lurch. *'Could your work be explained as psychic invention?'*

'Stand up.'

She hesitated at a frightening boundary. She would be at his mercy and vulnerable, but forbidden things had compelling allure; dimensions beyond the ordinary. Meekly, as required, Lisa positioned her arms behind her back. Ben wrapped her wrists with the scarf and knotted it firmly. She welcomed the bondage which excused her from a fate she dreaded more: the tyranny of guilt. Fever blended with cold anxiety in a complex state, betrayed by a husky tone in her voice. 'I might scream and alarm the neighbours.' Inconceivable, of course. No one lived close enough to hear.

In slow motion, far away, Ben lifted her panties and wound them into a taut string. The material flattened her tongue and when the gag stretched her mouth at the corners she reeled in unexpected pride.

'Walk about.' Her nephew began to undress.

Recording the fresh sensations for future reference detached Lisa from his scrutiny. With her arms tied her bulbs stuck out and the improvised gag did not stifle, although it led her to inhale through her nose. Its constraint almost duplicated her binding. Another degrading leak moistened her crotch but there was nothing she could do to help herself. Recalling Kim, who endured a harness but retained her dignity Lisa, in a surge of elation, realised that Pauline was right. It was liberating to give away her own control. She decided to take this role to its end regardless of outcome: how does anyone know the consequences of anything? Ben gave a wordless command and Lisa humbled herself over his lap, her forehead settled on the floor. Her bust hung unnaturally towards her chin and his restored penis compressed her ribs as she flaunted her intimate parts to his gaze.

His gentle caresses, soon accompanied by kisses and wet licks, dispersed delight from her upended rear. With past lovers she had sometimes demanded having it worked over in this way but, at the same time, it created a rising mental conflict in permitting her nephew so much licence. Just like being a virgin again! He clinched her fears by widening her legs and petting her undefended anus and cunt. When he entered the damp folds and dipped in her honey her hips writhed and the gag muffled a despairing moan. His free hand pressed on her neck and she waited breathlessly, anticipating the first –

Slap! The flash on her right was so all-consuming that her mind blanked. More jolts set her ablaze and she squealed and yelped at each fiery strike. Using her well-anchored form for his own satisfaction meant that she had to strive alone for crumbs of pleasure but even during a rest she clenched her muscles, predicting the next awful shock. A staccato attack injected bolts of lightning, drove the air from her lungs, and in the following break she wriggled frantically to shake off the white heat. Distress rivalled increasing desire as he invaded her channel, drilling fast, and it felt good, coupling her tenderised flesh to a yearning ache in her pit. In her portal's puffy ridges trickling secretions wetted his palm which carried the evidence of her arousal around her buttocks and thighs. Shamed by her own excitement as much as the smacks, whirling perceptions clashed and chased, and muffled in the gag she yelled, 'Fuck me!' Dazed by the sudden change, she knelt on the floor and pitched forward as Ben's ruthless cock, in a single lunge, crammed her passage, impacting against her inflamed derrière. His rapid rhythmic strokes, eased in her abundant liquid flow, brushed on her diamond-hard clit and she panted harshly in exquisite pain. She sensed his come about to explode but he reined himself in and thrust leisurely, maintaining her rise. Governed by his remorseless vigour she bucked in the midst of crashing waves – his generous gift – and drowned, swirling in dark caves of oblivion.

The revised drawing had a far greater punch than the original. Lisa used ink as impenetrable as soot, applied with a scratchy pen in short stabs, and the figures were larger, one more dominant. Curled over a man's lap, the woman's hair screened her face. Disorientated by the loss of her vision, the slightest impression would magnify. She would fight the length of shining rope, cursing and relishing her hopelessness at the same time, but with no reprieve she had no choice but to bear whatever he gave her. The imprint of fingers already blotched her soft spheres, ripe as tomatoes. Lisa knew how unforgiving those slaps would have been; her own spanking pulsed with a regular beat. The man's sturdy build and his tough evenly paced smacks would have jarred those cheeks constantly. Wailing to distract herself, the woman would brim with tears, but if he attended to her crucial needs the unimportant tensions would fade, expelled by euphoria. 'Orgasm affects her whole being,' Lisa murmured. 'Sex for a woman isn't only physical. It takes us onto a higher plane.' So, even spanked, she has an erotic reward.

The strength in this version came from Lisa's knowledge of how it felt, quite literally, to be in that situation.

She locked the lowest drawer and withdrew the key. On her way to the kitchen she tottered past the illustrations for *Misfit Toys* pinned to the walls, almost completed in jewelled inks and gouache colour to make them more subtle without losing clarity. One essential job remained, always the final task; to clarify the pupils of their eyes by adding a small patch of directional light. Before that stage only a silhouette existed: afterwards, a person with life. Magic! As soon as they were delivered Lisa could organise that deferred holiday.

She poured a coffee then lowered herself cautiously onto the chair with a squab cushion, but even that spurred her residual pangs. She wrestled again with a complicated question. How would she cope with Ben in future? A line had been crossed into a far more dangerous world which prevented them from resuming a normal aunt-and-nephew relationship. She was teetering on fragile ground, having started something beyond her power to discipline in allowing – no, inviting him – to treat her in that way. Why?

Lisa forced the admission pitilessly: *Because humiliation is a potent aphrodisiac*.

And he had obliged, all too readily.

How had he grown so quickly from a boy, a novice, into an exacting adult? A horrible thought chilled her blood: his father advised him. Unwisely Lisa had given favours to both and a truly appalling illusion erupted: of the father, behind, cradling her breast while, in front, his teenage son dropped her skirt and pulled off her panties. Their dual fondling in every aperture eroded her –

'Stop!' she howled, scandalised by her imagination.

As she stood too swiftly she winced at a sore jab and shuffled carefully into the studio. Beside the telephone lay a sheet of writing paper and she dialled the number written in lilac ink. To the answering voice Lisa blurted, 'I understand what you said about feeling and . . . authenticity.'

Pauline chuckled ironically. 'What happened?'

'I accept your proposal.'

'Good. Are you free of commitments?'

'A few days, at most, to finish an assignment.'

'You can have one week. I'll post the details on how to get there.'

'Get where?'

'Keep your packing of clothes to the minimum, and one more case for your kit of materials.'

'Where am I going?'

'To an estate in Scotland. My agent will meet you there. You must obey all instructions faithfully if you wish to benefit.'

Lisa hesitated. This crazy notion might substitute a single problem for many more, perhaps even less welcome.

'Do you want to reassess?'

Casting away a blizzard of doubts, she gulped and whispered, 'No.'

'Take your contraception.'

Dimly, far away, Lisa heard a click as the connection broke.

Eight

The clicking continued monotonously and when the train entered a wood the tree canopy shaded the light. Lisa snapped the pad shut and glanced at her watch. Half-an-hour to go. At least the waiting, each day and hour by hour, would soon be over. Luckily Miss Gibbs had lavishly praised *Misfit Toys* and called it a brilliantly disturbing series. Then she lobbed a bombshell. 'I'm going to submit this work for the Kate Greenaway Medal.' For a moment Lisa basked in a warm glow of achievement; nominated for the most prestigious prize in her field, worth several thousand pounds!

Again she squirmed. The seat's contours pricked her sensitive pleats and she vibrated into the cushion, faintly simulating her bounces onto a rigid shaft. That distinguished man sitting opposite could not suspect she had hoisted her skirt or that her bare pussy, fiendishly provoked by the stubby fibres, seeped its juice. The raised skirt with no panties had been the first order Pauline had given. But Lisa delayed for a long time, afraid of tampering with her natural appearance, before she complied with the second. Summoning her courage, she pursued an earlier idea and trimmed her unruly pubic bush to a neat shape. For the next stage she laid a mirror flat on the floor, sat, and spread her legs. She gazed at the softness of her skin and its fine glinting fleece. Doubled in the mirror's reflection her split gash created a queer erotic jolt with her own face looking down. A voyeur of her own vulva! She had never made a link between them but now saw the vertical line of pouting labia contrasted with the horizontal lips of her mouth. Leaning strenuously, she tried to bring them together and visualised the two coalesced; hot breath blending with sexual fragrance and lapping her own spicy pool.

Impossible, unfortunately.

To compensate, she had examined the wrinkles and textures that her fingers had often explored. With great reluctance she agreed with Pauline's view that a screen of hair sullied her purity. She assembled the implements and her stress began with the shaving cream, soothing but also obscuring the site in foaming snow. For exquisite minutes the razor eased and separated the delicate membranes in a hunt for stray threads. The feathery yet menacing touch in defenceless tissues sent tremors rippling but even so, her sex urged upwards to meet the blade. With the last traces of cream washed away she savoured her succulence, captivated by carnal beauty. In the most private area the inner folds boldly pushed out, and she shuddered at the enhanced response of the silky dimpled flesh. Now, truly naked and wholly alluring, she had an explicit bond to the women in the films. A new lover whose tongue discovered this sweet spot, could play –

As the train curved towards a distant viaduct the carriage tilted.

Lisa recalled the raging ecstatic fire in her bottom caused by Ben's hand. Had she been wicked to let herself be bound and chastised? Or was she bound and chastised for wickedness? Whatever the true explanation it led her here.

Pauline had ended their conversation by saying, 'At Balmayne you must not refuse, nor make any protest. You will learn there is much to enjoy in obedience.' Lisa contemplated the implications of being alone among strangers. Normally she exercised her own will with someone she chose. But now her body would be an open invitation to anyone, at any time, for anything! A sliver of ice ran down her spine. She tested the man opposite stealthily. Could she volunteer to go with him? No, and why? Because his cold blue eyes transmitted no lively sparks, indicating interest in her as a person. But suppose they did? Without knowing him, or meaning anything special to him, could she give herself? Her heart gave a nauseating thump: what if he didn't fancy her at all but simply used her to gratify his own urge?

The friction of coarse fabric emphasised her abstinence of the last few days, also one of Pauline's requirements. Lisa yearned for – needed – the energy of a real cock but, denied even her own stimulus, she had no outlet for bottled-up frustration than to pour it into a sketch. In her pad she started with the table in front and included herself in the gangway, bending over. What next? The pencil hovered indecisively. *My skirt's up.* Her pale arse, fully exposed, curved into the taut lines of stockinged thighs. More certain now, she quickly drew the man, trousers loosened, jammed in hard from behind. Lisa trembled, but then something awful occurred. At the top of the seat came a row of ugly mugs, gawping lustfully while she was hopelessly compromised. The pleasing fluency of her lines rescued the scene from erasure but she ripped out the page and halved it with a sharp crease just as an on-coming train thundered past. Turbulence rocked the carriage and she pitched to the side away from the blow.

Considering the sequence of events that brought her to this journey she wondered if they were random accidents, or co-ordinated. If the latter, then who could be organising them? Miss Gibbs, who was there when she received the first message? *That's stupid!* The hateful man who invaded her privacy? What about Pauline? But Pauline had not even heard of her at that time. Her own nephew? Impatiently, Lisa stifled her speculations.

The train reduced speed at the edge of a town. Relieved, yet nervous, she stood to pull her cases from the rack which allowed her skirt to fall into position. The man glanced up, innocent of how she had just made use of him, and met Lisa's disarming smile. As they arrived at the station she humped her cases into the gangway and stuffed the pad into her pocket. In a hasty scan she caught sight of her drawing. *Do I dare?* Impulsively she placed the sheet on the table close to the man, grabbed her cases and shuffled briskly down the gangway. From the platform, through the window, she glimpsed him reaching forward.

In the station forecourt a taxi driver stowed her bags in the boot. She gave the address and settled into the rear seat, her skirt lowered this time. *I'm incorrigible!* That man on the train; probably the most shocking thing he's ever –

'You're happy,' the driver said.

Quietly the vehicle purred onto a coiling forest road, swinging confidently into the corners and over successive peaks. Discomforted by his stare in the mirror Lisa asked, 'Is it far to the house?'

'About twenty minutes, lassie. I take quite a few out there. He's generous with tips.'

'Who's generous – the owner?'

'The owner, yes . . . Mr Johansen.'

Lisa bolted upright. 'Who?'

'Frederick Johansen.'

That detested man! For the remainder of the journey her smouldering anger focused on what she would do and say when they finally met.

A sweeping bend led to a gateway and a sign, carved into old brick, half hidden by shrubs: BALMAYNE. The car crunched gravel to the front of a large Victorian house. A figure waited on the steps and as Lisa stepped out into still, clean air she gasped aloud. *Griselda!* The woman's narrow features and the wild hair were unmistakable though the hair, black in the photograph on Jon's studio wall had, in reality, a lustrous auburn colour. 'Where's Johansen?' Lisa demanded.

Griselda showed mingled boredom, wisdom and weariness. Without saying a word she turned away to re-enter the building. Thwarted, Lisa paid the fare, picked up her luggage, and pursued the woman along a dismal corridor and into a snug old-fashioned room. As the woman beckoned to join her she left her bags at the door.

The woman's self-possession, coupled with obvious indifference, stressed her authority. 'My name is Imogen. Mr Johansen is away at this time.'

'When is he here?'

'That's impossible to say – he comes and goes at odd times. Now, repeat to me Pauline's instructions.' Imogen's malign expression resembled the photograph.

To Lisa, saying the words to someone else seemed to give them the status of a fixed contract.

'So why had you not raised your skirt in the taxi?'

A man of medium height came into the room. Supple and lithe, he moved like a predatory primitive, an untamed animal wearing clothes. He looped Imogen's waist and tilted her backwards levered over his arm. His free hand fondled her during their kiss. Lisa recorded their silent ardour with a sense of having seen it before – almost a Pauline and Kim – and noticed the man's abundance of wavy hair, similar to Imogen's. They finished and the man said, 'I'm Max, and you must be Lisa.' He coolly appraised her body from top to toe. 'Nice. I'll have you – soon.'

Lisa glared distastefully, hating his sardonic manner.

'Haven't you told her the rules?' he asked Imogen.

'Leave now!' she barked. 'You can meet her this evening.'

As he departed Imogen rounded on Lisa furiously. 'Never do that again! Do not divulge your true feelings. Be led by the prostitutes' example – tolerance and detachment at all times. Now, I'll take you to your room.'

Lisa collected her bags and abandoned herself to fate. As they clambered up three flights of gloomy stairs she detected no sounds of activity. At the top they arrived at a spacious, austere room plainly furnished with a chest of drawers, two wardrobes, and a single mirror attached to a whitewashed wall. Beds occupied opposite ends of the room.

Imogen pointed to the bed nearest a window. 'Sleep there. That's your wardrobe and there's the bathroom. As Pauline told you, masturbation is prohibited. If you are fortunate enough to orgasm at all it will be induced by others. Unpack, and rest.'

'Who sleeps in the second bed?'

'I do. You are a guest in my room.'

Alone, Lisa began to worry. She must give herself to strangers even if she had no desire for them. Now, according to Imogen, she must take lessons from prostitutes about tolerance and detachment. 'Can I actually do this?' she fretted.

She hung her clothes and claimed a portion of the bathroom shelves. Sitting on her bed she filled idle time at the window, contemplating thick undulating woodland illuminated by silver-grey light, modulations of pearl. Breaking away, she hunted for a working surface, chose a card table propped by the door, and with nothing else to do resumed drawing in her sketch pad.

An hour later Imogen returned. Placing the tray containing a meal on the bed she glanced at two portraits, of herself and Max, captured in a few exact lines. 'Pauline warned me about this. They're completely accurate yet you saw Max for only a few minutes. Do you memorise everything?'

Lisa shrugged. 'Not really – I just catch all the detail. It's a process I can't regulate.'

'And a potentially dangerous gift. Here we ban all photography so that none of our guests can be inconvenienced by kiss-and-tell, or worse.' Imogen took both portraits and ripped them to shreds.

'Hey!'

'In future I advise you to disguise all identity.' Imogen threw the torn pieces on the bed then concentrated on a third picture, in pastels. Arched over Max's arm, her blouse had been dragged down and his grip distorted her flesh. 'But you're also casual with the facts – he didn't handle me with my tit hanging out.'

'I go where my fancy leads.'

'Well, I prefer to stick to facts. I'll bring your clothing shortly.'

After the meal Lisa, anxious about the evening to come, showered thoroughly and more empty time elapsed while she watched the landscape drown imperceptibly in purple dusk.

Imogen appeared carrying a nondescript item of dull grey which might have been a prison uniform. 'Get ready,' she said curtly. 'I want you in the buff.'

Blasé, with a vision of herself as daring and bold, Lisa dropped her clothes but her bosom's rapid lift and fall betrayed her tension when Imogen circled ominously. Lisa had never been manipulated by a woman, nor had ever wished to be and steeled herself, hunched forward, trying to bear the loss of her self-control.

'At least you obeyed orders and shaved your pubes to show those fanny creases.'

Imogen fluttered the compact nub of her clitoris. Lisa stretched upwards with a dull ache. In a fugitive dream, distant and vague, she recognised Kim's flawless figure as a wraith gliding in thinning mist, and a sonorous voice echoing Pauline: *Once a pledge is given there is no going back.* Men surrounded her, taking their pleasure. Wriggling to evade or to meet their clutches she dissolved in a warm –

'Smooth and clammy,' Imogen murmured and Lisa accepted a lingering kiss. As they separated Imogen understood her confused state. 'Do you love your imagination, or fear it?'

'Love it, of course. Why should I fear it?'

'It makes you too easy.'

The garment she had brought was scattered with dull blue feathers. The cloth in the armpit had been stained by sweat and a faint waft of perfume gave something more of its history. Curiously, the fetishistic effect did not seem repellent. Lisa stepped into the dress, hooking its thin straps onto her shoulders.

'Look at the mirror,' Imogen said. 'In my experience we often take on the persona conveyed by our clothes. So what does this trashy article say about you?'

Lisa studied a new version of herself. A low neck disclosed the slopes of her bust, and the ragged hem crossed her upper leg. With so much exposed and bare beneath this was the most scandalous frock she had ever worn. Since her first boyfriend blundered to strip her naked she had realised that the female body exercised a tangible power over men. Regrettably, they usually countered its provocation, or subdued its power, by their own domination. And that's what her clothing, a slinky appeal to indecency, encouraged! Swallowing nervously she whispered, 'That I'm some kind of a . . . plaything.'

Imogen chuckled. 'And don't forget it. You're an amusing love object. That's your role.'

Descending two flights of stairs, Lisa deliberately blocked her thoughts. She could not rationalise or plan ahead to manage the situation but simply followed, dreading what might occur. They entered a corridor and into a room where a group of men and women clustered around a dining table with the remains of a meal. To Lisa they were only blurred shapes.

'Here is a guest,' Imogen announced 'who has come to introduce herself.'

The blurs, intent and silent, twisted in Lisa's direction. In the security of her bedroom she had often pretended but now, in the beams of attention from real people, she froze. Gradually her mood stabilised. Lightly clad and swathed in the gaudy feathers of a frivolous bird she did, uncomfortably, resemble a plaything. And it was better to do this in front of strangers than among her friends. She had to let go.

But in my own game.

Hesitating, she balanced the merits of whether to conceal or reveal, but in the end shadowed her instincts. Fondling her breasts languorously, rotating and bunching, she defined her nipples. They stirred with excitement and led her on. One strap dropped from her shoulder and the fabric clung attractively to the top of one up-surging curve as she pressed her groin. She flicked up the hem of the dress in fleeting waves, submitting her vulva to glimpses. The second strap fell, this time below her ripe globe: much more erotic to present only one! As she began to spin, the skirt flared, her loins and heart pounding simultaneously. When she stopped, the hem swung erratically and again drooped as a shield. Those brief views would be quite enough for the unmoving men with their shuttered eyes. The women, in contrast, responded with nods and smiles of active support, as if they envied her opportunity. The material slithered, bundling on her hips, and sagged suggestively. In a few more spins it would be on the floor but what would she then do with nothing else to use for enticement?

One of the men beckoned and Lisa danced towards him sinuously, maintaining the skirt's momentum by swivelling and lewdly swaying. He picked up the hem and she raised her arms, leaning back, defenceless in offering her dear pussy to a brutal stare. Her modest protection plunged to the floor, giving alien hands access to every part, groping and screwing her buds painfully. Gasping she jerked away, but her legs were spread and searching fingers pawed her sex and into her cleft. Women as well as men reached out, used her as they chose, and passed her along. Her mood switched capriciously. She had started out with her own game but now discovered herself as a pawn in a different game, governed by them. The men and the women kissed her, or pinched her bottom, and occasional taps, almost slaps, vibrated her buttocks. She knew how much they invited and even welcomed such treatment but each delivered a dazzling shock.

At the end of a journey, unlike any she had ever known, Lisa arrived at an imposing woman who cleared a space among the mess of plates and surplus food. Guided to lie down, the woman grasped one of her wrists while another pinned her on the opposite side. Lisa squinted awkwardly at her torso and her crests angled outwards; the high wings of her ribs and beyond, her hollowed abdomen. And furthest away her bulging pudenda, bald as a plucked chicken. Spectators gathered to peer at her splayed form. Lisa lowered her head and gazed at the ceiling sightlessly. At a sudden sharp sting on one thigh she contorted and cried out. The women holding her clamped hard as she wrenched – 'Ouch!' – at a smarting strike across her belly. She struggled to see her tormentors and the short thongs they wielded haphazardly. Alarmed by the aimless pattern, which magnified the burning within, she wrestled with the fierce grips on either side.

Caught by the ankles, her legs were hoisted in a high V. She squirmed hopelessly to resist the public display of her genitals. Max, fully erect, loomed in her crotch and Lisa stiffened expectantly. His formidable rod opened her in taunting raids, his girth expanding her inner walls. Soon he thrust hastily with no concern for her own satisfaction. From both flanks the smacks continued, distracting her mind, torn between the unpredictable fiery jabs and the virile fuck. One flying thong crashed into a glass. A deluge of white wine pooled in her navel and dripped from her pouch.

With no warning her vagina emptied and she wallowed desperately, feeling abandoned.

Imogen approached wearing a tight leather costume with thin gold chains joined to long boots. Her small pointed tits projected through cut-outs and from her mound jutted a rigorous black stem, jiggling and tilting clumsily, smeared with uneven streaks of gel. Lisa moaned as the ovoid crown, as large as an egg, nestled into her soft tissues and pushed forwards tentatively, little by little inserting the whole length. Instead of a man's organ throbbing with life, this inert cylinder felt unnatural: a violation.

One of the women slopped a mush of pudding on Lisa's left breast. From her right a man squirted chocolate sauce and they both mixed the pulp to hideous multi-coloured blobs. Residue slid over her ribs to puddle beneath.

Imogen lacked a man's pelvic strength but even her faltering lunges shoved Lisa backwards. Then, grabbing her waist, Imogen drove emphatically and Lisa writhed, gabbling pleas for mercy. All the witnesses could hear the bar squelching in her abundant flow. But when her channel, void once more, interrupted her rise, her emotions lurched in the opposed direction: deserted and futile. Again Max hovered in her fork and the slippery amalgam of her lubrication with the dildo's gel allowed his hot shaft to glide easily. As the strikes resumed and overlapped, Lisa jolted and groaned, deflected constantly from her scoured limbs to Max's arduous punishment. Ejaculating, he pulled out immediately, spurting his last spunk to curdle and blend with the wine.

The rigid column took his place in Lisa's boiling depths. Jittery, near to her own peak, she strained upwards to meet the invasion. Bewilderingly, the artificial version brought her as much delight as it did to Imogen who panted with exertion. Lisa's cries lifted to a shrill crescendo. A warm rippling climax ascended from deep inside to her tingling teats until she collapsed in a come, all her senses consumed.

She scarcely noticed the random stings had come to an end and her arms released. Nor the splashing dregs from wine glasses and the mushy food squeezed as a poultice into her churning cunt. Later, alone and neglected, she stirred warily to inspect her soiled condition.

Nine

That disgusting mess – the worst part of a bad experience? Perhaps it was, now that the swelling caused by the unyielding strap-on had subsided. So too had the flushed lines marking her skin.

Lisa's useless worries haunted her but why regret what lies in the past? Like the repellent coating it deserved only to be washed away. The abiding gift would be her pictures, and five or six already existed as mental sketches.

Imogen's bed lay vacant, its counterpane straight and neat. A breakfast tray, with the tempting aroma of coffee, had been laid on the card table and a piece of paper held a brief message:

A good start. The soreness will soon be gone. Take a rest. Explore the grounds if you want. Imogen.

Ribbons of windswept rain thrashed the window. With the luxury of unstructured time, Lisa followed her meal by a lazy routine, though she applied her make-up fastidiously. At last, settling to work, the scenes she had visualised emerged on the page: a woman wearing a false cock smudged with come, and a second woman supine on a table, immersed in piles of succulent fruit which presented her as an exotic ornament.

Drawings succeeded effortlessly and Lisa took care to hide all identities. She lost track of time but finally stretched and yawned. The sun had burst out and glittered on the sodden foliage of trees. From the wardrobe she picked out a few ordinary clothes, dressed sluggishly, and left the room.

Outside the house, chilled by the crisp air, she gazed at a hill of russet heather, decorated by the shapes of sailing clouds. She considered the different paths and selected one which led, on a stony route, into dense pine-woods saturated with a fresh resinous tang. In one isolated clearing a large bird occupied a stone base. Further on she found a carved badger, and another clearing contained a stone fox, all in frozen action on plinths. Skirting a number of lodges she discovered a trickling fall of water, its drops exploding in flares of light. The pungent fragrance of geraniums and honeysuckle drifted from the damp scrub, combined with animal scents. Lisa stooped to examine a group of mushrooms whose delicate velvety undersides resembled her own supple pussy. As she made the unexpected link she realised that in this remote location there were no rules. She could indulge in any behaviour here because licentiousness was permitted, even required.

As she stood her attention latched onto a pale figure, perhaps naked, crossing the space at the far end of an avenue of trees. Its head was no more than a blob, perhaps wrapped in a bag, or bandages. And the arms did not swing freely, as if they were bound to the sides. From Lisa's position it seemed to be led by someone with an abnormally small physique – a dwarf or a child – using a neck chain, implied by a narrow steely glint. Unable to ignore the intriguing possibilities she hurried towards them but the distance ensured that by the time she reached the spot they had long gone.

Pursuing the path they might have taken, she passed beyond a screen of shrubs and decided to investigate one of the lodges. She advanced cautiously, observing the decayed stone, grey and black with age, and the chipped and crumbled carvings around an oak door. On the right, uneven panes of a window shot with gold, reflected a sparkling sun. Lisa mounted three steps onto a meagre terrace, crept to the window, and shielded the glass with her hand.

The barren room had one item of startling interest: a kneeling woman with her shoulders flattened onto the carpet and her wrists extended between her feet, clipped to a bar separating her ankles. The cramped pose elevated her buttocks, immense spherical balloons, high in the air. In disbelief Lisa stared at a dark crater in the centre of huge thighs with a creamy wad in the moist reddened circular rim. The wad teetered, then crept down in a glistening flow into her sex lips. Lisa's horrified survey came to an end as a man knelt behind the woman, aimed his erect member, and plunged in.

'It's rude to do that, uninvited.'

Swivelling guiltily, Lisa confronted a ruddy-faced, heavily built man. His bearing of authority suggested command and impatience with fools. As he came closer he said in surprise, 'Ah, it's you.'

In a futile attempt to regain her composure she asked, 'Do you know me?'

'I mashed some of that revolting mess on your lovely elastic flesh. I'll have to sample your tits again.'

'You saw me –'

'Being given a royal shag.'

'Helped by you all.'

'Oh, yes! We enjoyed having a share of you. I'm Michael, by the way. Are you still feeling the effects?'

'No. But I've never been taken that way.'

'They always operate as a pair. One gets jealous if the other entertains a third party.'

'Why?'

'They're family. To be precise, brother and sister.' Climbing up, he joined Lisa and inclined to the window. 'Ah, yes, that's Marion getting it in her preferred manner. She offers her arse regularly.' He added, 'Anyway, it's you I was coming to find. Are you prepared for your next challenge?'

'Challenge?'

'Your striptease. You'll have a sizeable audience to fascinate with your charms.' Michael waited for her agreement, plainly unwilling to accept refusal.

'I have no experience of that,' Lisa replied shakily.

'Maybe not, but to judge by your taster I'm sure you've imagined it – and practised some of the moves. Tell me I'm wrong.'

Lisa hesitated. After modelling for Jon, twice baring all for her nephew, and the events of the previous night, no one could take away anything, simply by looking. A sickening twinge deep in her belly betrayed her excitement.

'Come with me.'

Michael led the way on a grass path lit by the sun in brilliant daubs of exceptional green. Trunks of trees altered to silhouettes with distinctly etched patterns of bark. They approached an old building the same as the first, and branches cast their shadows over mottled walls like permanent stains. Even by Lisa's keen-eyed standards all the qualities were unusually intense: hyper-real.

They entered a vestibule where a patch of pure abstraction, a brightly defined rectangle, coloured the wall. Their footsteps drummed along a musty corridor until Michael stopped and said, 'Here's the changing room.' He scanned her proportions. 'Choose suitable gear. I'm sure there are pieces of the appropriate size. And a musical accompaniment is all prepared. When you're ready come out of the red velvet curtains. At the end of your fun, having driven us crazy with lust, we want a particular type of finale.'

'What do you mean?'

'Don't worry. By the end you'll need it.'

The curtains were obvious and so too were the racks of clothes with accessories arranged on shelves. With stark decisions to make Lisa wavered uncertainly. What could they do if she didn't appear? Nothing, probably. Running away would be a disgrace, intolerable to her pride, but the opportunity to enact a persistent fantasy came with a fervent hope to do it well; the worst kind of failure, damaging her self-esteem, would be ineptitude. To enhance the mood, in a wall mirror she watched herself undress and realised how she could explore new and thrilling transgressions. The notion of acting seductively filtered through all her nerves and tissues, quickening her rising heat. *So – who shall I be?* Everyone in this sort of trade used an attractive name.

Searching a variety of underwear, she rejected panties in favour of a tiny white lace thong and adjusted its narrow cord into her crotch. Its presence, a thorn, would goad her constantly and would also be a perfect adornment, giving an alluring view of her sweet derrière. Its string, hidden in her crevice, would create the impression of a single large unclad buttock. Bending with her rear to the mirror, she squinted at the fabric hugging her pouch firmly enough to see the mark of her slit. Stay-up stockings in the same hue were an easy complement. As the lacy bands grasped her swelling upper legs, she decided to keep them on.

From the brassieres hung on hangers she chose one of white lace with embroidered holes in the middle of their cups. Her choice fitted neatly and she pulled her nipples to peek out of the apertures as luscious berries. Their pinnacles provoked her, as strongly as her thong's constriction, to adopt the role. It also influenced her selection of a short skirt, split on both sides, to show off her legs and provide tempting flashes of her groin. But her chest and shoulders should be toned. A transparent black blouse – a reminder of Kim – allowed her bra and pale skin to glimmer, and its row of pearl buttons would assist leisurely unveiling. She finished with stilettos with glass heels as thin and sharp as pencil leads. *I'll be Chantelle.*

A thread of music wafted from the adjacent room. The style and beat fitted her motions excellently. Anticipation caused her to moisten. A hasty check in the mirror endorsed Imogen's opinion: Lisa had ripened to a sleazy street hooker, similar to those she had once wandered among in Cross Street.

Chantelle parted the curtains and found herself on a carpeted stage. The instant volume, together with blinding lights blotting out the crowd, and a vertical object on the central table almost crushed her resolve. They wanted far more than conventional striptease! Gathering shreds of courage, she glided to the table and leaned on the edge to shield the column from sight. Before coming back to it she would have to travel a long way. In widening her legs the skirt rode up above her stockings to reveal broad ribbons of creamy flesh. When it scarcely covered the vital spot, she lowered her head and remained still.

They would have to wait expectantly for the tarty hooker to begin. This had to be a controlled performance. Instinct would guide her all the way.

She began by tracing her pussy's outline. Her fingers drifted lazily, emphasising her curves and fondled her eager crests, lurking beneath a thin layer. Gazing out at the glaring void, she slowly unravelled a few buttons. In time to the music she bucked in a clear imitation of intercourse then flowed from the table, dancing sinuously. Spinning, unfastening more buttons, the material gaped to present her whiteness in a billowing cloud of black foam. She contorted rhythmically, and with the final button her blouse sailed extravagantly in a swirling arc. Even in the midst of her dance she glimpsed the menacing static item, her ultimate goal, and circled, sliding the flimsy material down her arms. In a slipstream it poured from her wrists and flew away.

She turned to the auditorium, oscillating, her arms raised. She wished them to admire the flagrant exhibition of her berries. *So sexy!* Gyrating, she released the bra, revolved to the front, and supported her breasts to exaggerate their soft bowls. Chantelle projected her teats in a frank invitation and stroked them affectionately as they doubled in length.

Surging with lewd joy, she tracked the music, her flesh spilling and falling, rotating and bumping spontaneously. Blurred in her actions she detached the skirt, let it droop enticingly and wriggled the garment to her feet, stretched to simulate the bondage bar she had recently seen. She clasped her pudenda and pulsed emphatically, snap, snap, right on the beat, and kicked away the skirt to coil her arms in the air, willowy, writhing, smooching crabwise, rolling her hips in supple waves.

Knees bent, she stuck out her tail to disclose the taut thong deep in her cleft, dividing her lips. The feeling activated a fresh idea to introduce if the time came, and the chance arrived after another snaking routine. Her dance subsided to follow the quietening music, dallying with a partner tenderly. Slithering out from his embrace she faced the audience to lever the chords of her thong from her waist, lift and force its string hard against her pubic bone. As the sides of her labia bulged she prolonged the pose, satisfied by the unusual provocation of her natural features, and squirmed delectably to make them envious of her sensations.

Shaking the redundant fabric to the floor she kicked it away, chased by her shoes, so that at last she could dance free. Smiling and fully aware of her value, Chantelle blazed through a raunchy display. Propelled across the stage, her limbs flickered with electric detail, twisting voluptuously, fluent and precise. Exuberance brought a state of ecstasy and she revelled there to block out her fear. Nevertheless, when the music altered to a tranquil phase she accepted her cue. Dancing, dwindling towards the table, her manner resembled a slut with a solitary raw need.

She filled her mouth with a shaped dildo, a gruesome cock. Bold and wicked, she rested on the table's rim to show the observers, then applied the saliva-coated device to her erect nubs and down her belly for the tip to enter its home. Her pliant folds moulded around the fat bulk as she pushed to and fro in a private reverie. On squeezing the stem, her back arched immediately. Snatching the tool from her soaking pit, she sucked avidly, staring straight out at the hidden spectators. Again she nudged in to play with herself but soon halted, panting, demented, unable to endure the pretence. She lay flat on the table and spread her legs high in the air to betray her self-penetration. Faster and more brutally in and out, the blessed agony swept in a fire and she came with a strangled cry, undisguised.

Chantelle levered upright drunkenly and paused, trembling. Opening her legs, she delayed for a moment to expose the stub. Deliberately she contracted her internal muscles, expelling the rod a short distance and left it dangling. Tightening, committed and trapped in brazen behaviour, she discharged more. The dildo's weight started to drag and she gripped feverishly to hold it inside. Resuming command, she evacuated very slowly until, smeared in her lubrication, the shaft fell to the floor with a faint vapour trail spiralling upwards.

Pencil lines successfully captured the curling strands. *How could I have been so outrageous?* Lisa had relied on instinct but perhaps it all came from intuition, derived from the countless times she had imagined her way into a scene.

To distract her thoughts she reviewed the first illustration, of a kneeling woman strapped by the wrists and ankles to a bar. Centred in huge rotund moons a dark circular hole rivalled the size of her crinkled gash. Once again, as if for its own reasons, it deviated from the real event. The word SLAVE in neat letters had been printed along one meaty thigh, and from her anus protruded the handle of a whip, its thongs bending onto the floor.

For the next picture Lisa roughed the drawing in pencil, as a template for a draughtsman's pen loaded with ink. At the end she considered an exhausted woman ejecting an implement from her cunt to applause. Perhaps that's where the whip came from as a variation on a theme; a different type of insertion for the pleasure of others.

That earlier image troubled her and she uncovered the problem in the word slave. What could have spurred that medieval notion? Perhaps it came from the woman's binding which compelled submission to any treatment. Pauline had said that, in obedience, there was much to enjoy, but if obedience resulted in such an extreme outcome the price to pay was too high. Cold repugnance rippled Lisa's spine, tingling the base of her neck.

However, Pauline had been right to say there were many lessons to learn here. The public striptease had acquainted Lisa with a new sort of power, previously unknown to her. Emotionally drained, she fell into sleep.

She awoke with a jolt to whispers drifting through black air. Only the window could be vaguely discerned. The whispering stopped, replaced by muffled adjustments and a few coarse creaks. Lisa's hearing sharpened and she registered sighs from Imogen's bed, then the rustle of sheets cast aside. Sometime later the springs began a regular protest.

Imogen would obviously be relishing it but the couple's intimacy accentuated Lisa's neglect. Louder moans combined with the harsh creak-pause-creak sequence. Gradually the springs complained more rapidly, and discretion came to an end in garbled animal cries. Suddenly, as every sound abruptly ceased, Lisa visualised the entwined figures and the spermatozoa shooting out of one into a cavity seizing it gratefully.

For several minutes she waited for him, all her senses struggling for clues. She deserved her own turn for gratification, anything else would be unfair. At any second a silhouette would loom above. It must happen! After furtive comments, bare feet padded away. Anxiously Lisa rolled over to glimpse the man's profile dimly lit in the frame of the door and collapsed, dazed, onto her pillow.

Her own brother!

Ten

Did I really perform to an audience?

The question popped into Lisa's brain at the moment she woke. Having been told there would be an audience, she acted as if it was there, but at no time did she see any people or hear their response. At the end she had merely walked off, leaving her clothing scattered on the floor. Her conviction strengthened: she had, undoubtedly, been deceived. All the time she been alone, indulging an erotic dream, a more elaborate form of her bedroom play. Good! That meant her scandalous conduct would go unreported.

Relieved, she noticed the opposite bed lying neat and tidy, as if Imogen had not slept there at all. The smell of coffee brought her attention to the card table, a breakfast tray, and another message. She gave priority to the meal, assuming the sheet of paper would again suggest a leisurely day, but when she casually picked it up the words leapt off the page:

Mr Johansen returned in time to catch your entertainment. He liked what you did and said you showed a genuine talent for displaying yourself in the sexiest way. He had rarely seen it done with such innate artistry and particularly approved of your last trick.

Lisa's scrupulous logic disintegrated. So she had been observed and, worst of all, by the one she hated the most. Her resentment boiled. He always acted secretly to keep the advantage, and his praise could only be ironic or aimed to insult her. Enraged, she read the remaining paragraph:

I have received a special request for you. Wear the dress in your wardrobe and be outside the house at ten.
Imogen

Half-an-hour. Shoving her anger aside, Lisa rushed to finish her morning routine. In the wardrobe she found a simple rustic garment and blanched at the lightness. By twisting awkwardly, its loose fit enabled her to tie flamboyant bows at her shoulders. Beneath the sheer gossamer her aeriolae blushed conspicuously, and the contours of her legs were fully visible up to her pubes. Strangely, following her striptease, the exposure worried her less than it should have done. Her normal shoes were suitable for walking outdoors.

Just in time, Lisa stepped out of the house. Wondering who would ask especially for her, she wrapped her arms to her chest and stamped her feet, shivering in the hard mineral air. In the distance a man emerged from the trees and her belly tensed in anticipation as she stared, trying to decipher his features. Glinting silver hair. Brisk loping strides gave him a determined aura of purpose. As he came nearer, Lisa groaned despondently and clutched herself. The man from the train!

'I'm glad you remember me,' he called. Beside her, he added, 'Because I certainly appreciated your amusing gift. For a quick sketch, executed in difficult conditions, it was very stimulating and that, I expect, is what you intended. A pity about that crease, though – the drawing deserved better treatment. I shall have it mounted as an agreeable after-dinner anecdote. And if, as I believe, it indicates your preference for copulation the requirement is duly noted. But first we have some essential stages of preparation.'

Lisa, numbed at being in his control, fretted about what he might mean. His self-confidence disturbed her too; his candid inspection and familiarity implied that he knew all about her. A germ of disquiet planted itself in her mind. Appalled, she reeled and blurted, 'Are you Johansen? Frederick Johansen?'

The man's poise weakened. 'No, but you're surprisingly close. My name does begin with a J.'

'Tell me what it stands for,' she demanded 'or I don't budge from this spot.'

'Are you unaware of the rules? We don't normally give our true names. As with photographs they are banned to save us from . . . shall we say, embarrassment.'

'You know my name. Why shouldn't I know yours?'

'Lisa is your real name? That's interesting. There's an illustrator, a very good one, with that name. As a matter of fact your graphic quality bears distinct similarities. And that row of ugly creatures at the top of the seat reminds me of her humour.'

What a bloody fool! In one impetuous moment she had forgotten that even a sketch could betray an identity, as clear in style as a signature. Vehemently she repeated, 'Tell me your name!'

'Well . . . OK. I'll bend the rules, once. The J is for Johannes.'

Miss Gibbs had mentioned that name. A South African she had said, and this man spoke with a clipped accent. Her agent had regarded him as a potential buyer!

'And that's all you're getting,' he said. 'Let's go.'

His arm pressed her forward and its warmth on her waist, filtering her fragile envelope, hinted at more unwelcome intimacy. Lisa recorded nothing of the path they were on, or any surroundings. The hem flicked her ankles and the material sighed, and below its veil her breasts vibrated, emphasised by the clench of her chilled nipples. When the frail fabric settled to a single thickness over the tips, or indented her crotch, they were moulded transparently. As the process reversed, bunched layers disguised them until the next thinning presented more enticement. Defying her own wish, the dress blatantly advertised her figure and the man, whoever he was, appeared to take these involuntary accidents as deliberate solicitation. With a huge effort she wrested away from the grip of his eyes.

In the past Lisa had enjoyed the collision between outward respectability and a louche inner life, but now they conflicted. If this was the same Johannes who might purchase her work, how could she possibly meet him again? But that concern paled to insignificance at a truly devastating idea: that, whatever he claimed, he could actually be Johansen. And she had virtually invited his penetration!

He watched her face, reading her bitter recriminations.

They arrived at a lodge where he steered her into a hallway and from there into a room, as hushed as a library, with a long table covered by a startling collection. Lisa glanced at Johannes who gestured encouragingly. From the table she inhaled the alluring aroma of leather and rubber, and gazed in awe coupled with fascination at a range of instruments, precisely aligned to aid their selection. The nearest, constructions of matt black leather or glowing red, had segments combined with studs, shining bars, rings and buckles of steel. These were far more complex than the harness that Kim had worn, perhaps composed for the whole body. Lisa admired the leather's stitching and polish, and its firm yet supple elegance produced a chaos of vague urges. At her own pace she advanced to a hoard of coloured dildos in many sizes and shapes. A few had thin chains attached to the ends.

'On a different occasion I might stuff you with one of those.'

Shuffling about with a bulky object buried inside! Shuddering, Lisa continued. She came to new bindings of sparkling metal, clawed Velcro, and more leather with tough surfaces which had no flexibility; severe evidence of futile resistance. The man – Johannes? Johansen? – joined her and took a long time, filled with dire suspense, to choose one item. Her heart jumped and her throat dried as he tugged her arms behind, fitted her wrists in broad leather cuffs, and fastened the buckles.

His next choice, a narrow band positioned above her elbows, dragged them inwards. She winced at the power, her breathing constricted. Her nephew's binding could not be compared to this stern cage which banished the slightest exercise of her own will. The constraints hollowed her back and pushed out her boobs, and she revelled magnificently before her pride collapsed at her captor's icy appraisal.

Horrified, Lisa realised he had propelled her into a world resembling her recent drawing, only lacking the word 'slave' printed onto her skin.

Her steps drummed in her ears. She paused apprehensively at articles that were inert yet capable of terrible domination. One of them, a long tawse, had three stiff prongs.

'Only for the very experienced,' the man muttered. He unravelled the bows of her dress which slithered down, and only her bound arms obstructed its drop to the floor. Lisa scarcely noticed the rapid rise and fall of her chest.

Another tawse, lighter and shorter, had been divided in two strands. Across the table were riding crops of dulled leather. Densely wound, they were compact and far more serious than the straps, alongside, that had nipped her flesh on the first evening. An assortment of paddles, of solid hide and rubber, recalled Ben's burning stings but those were the result of a human hand, not a cold device.

Further on, she found the type of bar gag that Kim had so proudly worn. The man nudged her towards a rank of canes in austere lines and Lisa dutifully studied their variations, some of them whippet-thin. Colourful leather whips, differing in size and number of thongs, filled her with less dread than the grim chastises. Their pliable threads would surely embrace sympathetically, just as the string whip had wrapped around the Victorian top. A slim tongue of leather would singe the moist tissues of her sex. For once imagination was too remote, she almost wanted to feel it for confirmation. How would they bind her to receive the remorseless whacks? On the wall hung costumes of glossy PVC, and hoods with zips for hideous mouths. Lisa's senses flared, needle-edged.

She would have quickly passed the surgical group if the man had not prevented her. Among the bright metal some of the implements appeared graceful, even seductive, and a few were frightening. The man smiled reassuringly and kissed her, his grip enlarging her soft pulp. He began to screw her tender crests and Lisa moaned, inflamed by the loss of her own control. He pulled away to examine her glazed expression and murmured, 'You have to walk and for that reason I won't clamp your cunt.' In the end he let her go and she slumped, quivering, against him.

As he turned to the table for a new selection Lisa stared, panting convulsively. Widening a pair of curled jaws, he fitted them accurately to the base of her raised nub. They were ready to snap greedily and on their release she answered the bite with a cry of alarm, rigidly tensed. Undeterred, he teased its twin with the jaws of a second clamp. Tightening, it stabbed both her delicate buds and she jolted violently, her eyes rounded in shock. A thin chain, linking the two, dangled onto her belly. It lifted, levelled, became taut, stretching her teats. A barbed wrench compelled her to move and in the adrenaline rush her lubrication flooded at once.

By the final section he saw her telltale gleam matched by a heavy blush. 'I guessed as much.' From the table he picked up a thick fabric. 'Now you're acquainted with the instruments you will never forget them.'

No, she would not. They were permanent, branded into her memory.

'But from this point on, you will see nothing in order to feel everything.' The mask shut her lids decisively.

Deprived of sight, her primary sense, Lisa forfeited the last shreds of autonomy. She waited anxiously, suspended in limitless black. As the chain elongated her throbbing studs she gasped explosively and lurched forwards in despairing attempts to lessen the jabs. Echoing air thumped and jarred each time the unrelenting clenches forced the pace. A fierce doubled pinch created the raw centre of her consciousness – 'Ah!' – and generated an image of slicing blades to replace her blinded vision. Even so, for a few moments she drifted serenely, aware of nascent exhilaration, until the next awful flash shattered complacency. During an endless journey the dress sagged loosely from her rigorously cramped arms, and she cried out piteously as a pierce in her left nipple signalled a shift of direction. At last, brought to a halt, she rocked unsteadily in a calm space.

'The gear suits her well. Bring her here.'

The words came in a rusty grating voice that had lost the resilience of youth. Appalled, Lisa caught her breath. Was she being given to an old man? The impassive tone conveyed no hint of pleasure, as if she meant no more to him than a delivered parcel. *He must be the real Johansen!*

'You've obviously worked her up a bit,' the voice rasped disagreeably. 'What's your name?'

'Lisa,' she croaked, ragged with nervousness. She struggled to relax but the chain vibrated, snatched her globes, and the jaws dug into her swollen pips. She yelped and contorted.

'It's a pity these have to come off but we must restore the circulation.'

She loathed the calloused fumbling and pulled away. But as the clamps freed, a swirl of gratitude engulfed her. Horny palms rotated her stalks, big and hard as pebbles, and she could only cringe even if the intention seemed to ease gently, and soothe. Led – somewhere – she stumbled to the rim of a table, bent at the waist, and settled down. Her blazing tips hit the surface. She reacted instantly with a startled yelp, then tried again more carefully, her face to one side, her breasts flattened to pads beyond her ribcage. The hem of her skirt fell onto her arms and shrouded her head. Dismayed by her telltale leakage, Lisa flinched as tough claws travelled familiarly around her rump and probed the length of her slit.

'Flawless. Luscious targets begging for attention.'

'What's your preference?'

Johannes had asked the question. *Is he Johannes?*

'Let's try her with three feet of flexible rattan.'

They knew her name yet, to them, she had no existence as an individual person, only as a naked arse and genitals for their use. Lisa shuddered in distaste, visualising the old man's unshaven stubble, his drooping lids over rheumy eyes, and his thinning fibres of iron-grey hair. The wrinkled hide on his hands revolted her. She reconstructed him as a monster using scaly pincers to violate her dear pussy, expert in opening her labia and trapping her clit while she trembled, unable to defend herself. Quiet groans revealed her stress but gradually her disgust for him, being old and ugly and covered in scales, gave way to disgust at herself for getting involved in this. She could hear her own animal cries emerging as drawn-out sobs.

'You're a fine piece of cunt.' His severity clashed with the praise.

Coerced by his skilful caresses, she bucked and twisted. Her body's independent and shameful response contradicted her mental revulsion. Her channel liquidised and her protests, confusingly, altered to resemble sighs. On the verge of a climax, an atrocious idea ravaged her brain: *I must learn to accept, even enjoy –*

Approaching footsteps grew louder and her skin itched. Thwarted efforts to extricate her arms bolstered her anguish. At the same time her haunches pushed outwards, as if inviting their first marks. In one corner of her mind she relished what was about to happen though the conventional side of her nature recoiled in horror. About to be caned by a stranger, she writhed desperately. What gave him the right? Her reply came unbidden, implacable: *The fact that I'm here.*

A thin cold line compressed her sex, smoothing ominously back and forth between her lips which rucked and buckled under the pressure. An alien, in such an intimate place! As a mild portent of stern command came a series of small raps on her proffered hole. Keen-edged flickers radiated out from her groin and she craned up, complaining resentfully in petulant whimpers. She pictured the heated change in her frail membranes from oyster pink to fiery red, displaying them as a glowing halo. Wet with her juice, the unmistakable sign of arousal, the cane rested across the broadest expanse of her cheeks. Shrivelled by the touch, she partially yearned for the new ordeal yet also dreaded what was to come. The contact withdrew and she imagined the cane poised high in the air. Ravenous for flesh it quivered, animated by a leering smile. As she waited for its fall, strangled and jittery, all her surroundings dimmed away and every noise faded to silence.

Out of perfect stillness ripened a low swiftly building whoo –

Crack! The stroke exploded a fury, a searing knife deep in her buttocks. Stunned and incredulous, she jerked upwards and howled, roaring and swelling in pain. Mercifully the old man allowed her time to adjust but when she rested, pulsing in waves, she did so spiked with anxiety. A long low whoo – crack! Higher than the first, the second landed with the same force. She jolted helplessly and without any respite the next crossed her lower curves. Just as the agony arrived at a peak, another strike set off a renewed electric surge. At each viper bite, rolling within it, she rose and fell – a wired puppet – her features screwed to a tight ball. Countless more followed – whoo, crack! – blotching their locations on her tender thighs.

The torrent ceased, leaving her consumed in flame and beaded with sweat. Immediately a bony cock slipped through her sore folds and into her molten funnel. Its drives prodded her forward, chafing her raw nubs to and fro on the top, and she gasped in rhythm with the harsh thrusts into her depths. A throbbing crescendo of lust built up in her loins. Competing sensations expanded and burst, and she scarcely registered the stream of spunk spewing inside. As soon as her passage emptied, a fresh penis took charge and fast impatient ploughing continued. A new climax began to build. Rushed inexorably into new convulsions, she choked on screams of ecstasy just as the invader pulled out. Jets of fluid drenched her anal cleft and dribbled down.

Perched uncomfortably on a cushion, she finally gave up sketching. Sighing, Lisa arranged the scattered sheets in a pile and lay supine so that her weight subdued the residual twinges.

The episode had introduced her to an advanced, intensely serious dimension she had never suspected. It had left her drained, wonderfully scoured and gravely fulfilled. It also brought the belief that an orgasm induced by pain could have an extraordinary power, making others seem minor by comparison. The man who called himself Johannes had loosened her bindings stage by stage, her mask at the end. She had blinked away her tears, but the old man had gone and Lisa's disappointment persisted, even now. In a mirror the man from the train had demonstrated her patchwork of stripes, all vividly etched, white in the centre and suffused to dull red on the outer fringes. They had cut, profound as incisions but since then, as their authority slowly declined, she had fluctuated in a radiant haze. Now, back in her room, Lisa shuffled the batch for the incident: a woman clutching her dress to her hips, presenting the etched pattern to a pair of suave men. She had used watercolour rubbed with pastel and had only to look at the livid welts for her own to flare and prickle again. At least the traces of the straps on her arms had now bleached.

She could not even guess at the accuracy of the next illustration. In a close-up of the metal vice its jaws were now serrated with pointed teeth. It was clamped to the base of one stalk, which was swollen and purpled, thick as a thimble, and further deformed by the extension of a chain. Drawn literally out of her raw perceptions, the image had far greater strength than a scene merely observed.

A new page showed her delivered to the old man but in different circumstances. Here the woman, obstructed by her bound wrists, toiled to get out of a car in rain at night. A fur cape, held at the neck by a single button, gaped at the front and the pitiless light of a street lamp exposed her pale belly and dark pubic bush. She struggled onto the glistening pavement, eyed by men who had gathered, subjecting her to a heartless inspection. Lisa empathised with the woman's plight. The first evening had taught her how humiliation magnified if witnessed by a group.

At the mirror the man had asked, 'Have you nothing to say?' His hand glided unerringly into her wet furrow, coating his fingers to anoint the hot blemishes with her own lubrication mixed with their sperm. Lisa had kissed him and whispered, 'Thank you.'

She wriggled to ease her muscles. Taking pleasure in pain would obviously be a dangerous, or even destructive, path. Restlessly, she twisted sideways.

But I feel so alive!

In small doses? A special kind of occasional satisfaction? Would that be so bad?

Eleven

Anything, if it supplied new experience, would be infinitely preferable to a vacuum.

For the past two days Lisa had been alone, even crying a little, frustrated by inexplicable neglect and thoughts of what she might be missing. There had been no further notes from Imogen nor hints of activity, except for her meals on trays routinely delivered and collected. Glancing up from her pad she found it increasingly difficult to wait for instructions. For a while she subsided into a tranquil state only to wake again, longing for any variety of action. Her grip on the pencil tired and her concentration splintered. She prowled the corridors and listened at doors but detected no sounds. On the bed she appeased her frustration in the familiar way despite Imogen's rule. In compensating for lost time, her masturbation helped a rich seam of creativity to unravel and merge in overlapping dreams.

By lunch-time on her last day, stifled by the prison, she decided to escape. A weak sun glittered fitfully through thin cloud. The cool air revived her spirits and from all around swirled confusing combinations of aroma. Shots of silver light on sheets of water dazzled her. She discovered more clearings with carved stone animals on plinths. On one, attached to the base of a proud stag with enormous antlers, a glass bottle, mottled and pockmarked by age, had a label: EJACULATE OF DEER.

Revelling in her own licentiousness, Lisa detached the stopper from the dome. The smell was pungent and she sampled it twice. Replacing the bottle, she fixed the site in her mind. She could use these hidden spaces as settings for sexual rites, somehow connected to their statues. In a few more steps she stooped to inhale the sense-tingling bitter-sweet tang of wild garlic. As she did so an eerie thread of song floated towards her. She peered about and noticed a shred of white some distance away, obscured by the glimmering trunks of birch trees. The stark colour, in the midst of woodland tones, was entirely wrong. Lured magnetically but attempting to avoid disturbance, Lisa began treading cautiously among fallen leaves. In the forked trunk of a tree she recognised a woman's alabaster skin above and below a tiny white corset. Filaments of rope lashed the immobile figure and angry scratches inflamed her buttocks, scraped by the sharp-edged bark.

Beyond lay an empty glade. Only the tree canopy's rustling caresses broke the peace. The woman had, apparently, been abandoned to fate. Moving carefully, Lisa progressed to the side for a plain view, then realised she could take as much time as she wished: a mask blocked the woman's sight.

Ringlets of glossy black hair hung to her shoulders and scarlet lipstick outlined her mouth brilliantly. *Her name is ... Mary.* On her wrists and ankles loops of buckled leather, with embedded rings joined to ropes, secured her to the tree. Her upright arms, tied to branches, raised her breasts and gravity drooped their weight in distinctive pears. Her corset, if such a minuscule thing could be given that name, had been tightened brutally to narrow her waist. Suspenders supported white stockings high on her plump thighs. In the centre, framed by the white fabric, glowed her raw shaven pouch.

In her bindings she's very attractive. Unintentionally, Lisa stirred the leaves on the ground.

'Who's there? Is that you?'

For a second, Lisa contemplated going away but curiosity guided her on.

'Who are you?' the woman demanded. Her voice trembled nervously.

'No one to fear. How long have you been here?'

'Hours ... I don't know. He'll come for me when he's ready. At least, I hope he will.'

Why did he dress her in this manner only to desert her in isolation? Intrigued, Lisa enquired, 'So you didn't volunteer for this?'

Mary recited her answer. 'A slave trusts her master. She is strong and prepared to accept his treatment.'

Here was an actual slave, in the real world, not a fantasy in one of her drawings! And the slave had a master. Somehow, Lisa had only considered the idea of submission, not another actual person to enforce it. Curiously she asked, 'What sort of things do you have to accept?'

'Whatever serves your desire.'

Lisa jerked in surprise. Mary assumed that she would substitute for her own master. 'Why did he put you here?'

'So that you can use me in your own way.'

'Have many so far?'

'Five.'

Her master permitted anyone, who came upon her by accident, to share his privileges. On his return he would savour her docile behaviour and resume command. Cold shivers ran down Lisa's spine. With unlimited power, what would he do?

Surely he would begin by studying her. He would note the minute dimpled texture of flesh, changing from her neck and upper chest into her cleavage, and again on the swelling masses of her pendulous globes. He would admire the tiny pebbles on her aeriolae and their low quiescent humps. Certainly he would want to define their beauty so that they jutted majestically. Lisa reached for the pulp, expressly designed for squeezing, nuzzling and providing drink; several kinds of sustenance.

'Ah,' Mary sighed.

He would lick his thumb and give the responsive studs a moist rotation. As he roved ceaselessly between the two, pinching and rolling their firming peaks in the hollow of his palm, her faltering wail would amuse him. In provoking her he would excite himself and to set her on a fresh course he would let the heavy bulbs fall to produce a sudden bouncing shock.

'Ugh!'

That cry would agitate him more and recklessly he would lift the mammary by using its engorged nipple as a small handle.

'Ah!' Mary protested, squirming away from the pressure. The sheer thrill of that reaction would lead him on. Lisa dragged her nails up the delectable curves to the areolae, delighting in the instinctive reflex and bright lines that flushed the surface.

'Ugh.' The woman mumbled and slumped, and her pelvis lunged forward.

The long teats, hard as rubies, emulated, modestly, his own erection. Perhaps he would pause to appreciate the reddened marks. Starting once more, he would trickle over her belly's silky pillow to declare an unmistakable aim. A master would glide under the pubic bone to stroke her sex, warm and damp. He would arrive at the point where a leak betrayed her entrance and with no hesitation – which, for a master, would be unbefitting – dive into the deep resilience.

'Oh.' Mary panted and strained.

To be able to feel a woman ripening – incredible! The fluid would amuse him and he would follow its internal track as far as he could, up to the knuckles. Lisa slithered in and out of the rubbery tissues, pleased by her slave's quivers and gulps. Buried in this glorious heat, so smooth and wet, his fly would bulge impatiently. Perhaps he would rip it open and lay his hot member against her fleece. He would be tempted to kiss this soft willing mouth and enjoy the gentle explosions of breath as he pushed inside. It was easy to fathom why men loved to dip their tools in these supple yawning recesses. His loins would kick lecherously. He would taste her lipstick and smell its perfume. Maintaining three stiff digits within her cunt his unoccupied hand would undoubtedly repossess her boob. His thumb would massage her clit candidly. Surging with lust he would drive and twist –

'Uhm.' Immersed in their kiss, Mary moaned desperately.

From one side came the sound of crashing through bracken. But Lisa had never manipulated one of her own gender and persisted obstinately. She refused to break the marvellous spell or relinquish the liquid passage embracing her fingers in boiling and slimy walls.

'If he catches you he'll make you join me,' Mary gasped. 'Go while you can.'

Lisa crushed her regret and pulled out, ran across the clearing, and sank behind a screen of foliage. She clamped her ears to block out the gabbling cries and occasional shrieks, concentrating on locking all her impressions in memory. Much later, when the disturbance had gone, she risked a cautious peek. In the empty space the tree looked normal and also, bare of its ornament, unnatural. That must be corrected. Almost in a dream Lisa drifted towards it and located herself by hoisting her arms and widening her legs. She visualised the upward tug of a rope and the low grip on divided ankles, stretching apart. A snatching breeze chilled her skin, in contrast to her unprotected rear, smarting from the abrasion of blades of bark. If she jerked her wrists or legs the reminder of helplessness would add a tremor of guilty joy. Silently and hopelessly she hung there, available to the whims of unpredictable strangers.

And one did emerge noiselessly from the trees' edge. Thongs of a dangling whip shuffled and flicked the leaves aside. Lisa's naked torso arched, ready to meet –

'I envy you!' A fervent cry reverberated around the glade, fading into the crisp air.

In the latest compositions, simple domination had been greatly amplified by a master's deviant sensibility. Absorbed, Lisa failed to notice Imogen's approach before she peered over her shoulder and gave a stab of brittle laughter.

'You've obviously spent some time exploring. However, I would suggest that, while our own gender may be congenial as passing fun it can, in no way, beat an efficient shag.'

'And you get yours from your brother.'

Imogen scanned Lisa's face, searching for resentment or hostility. 'None of us can afford self-delusion,' she replied coolly. 'Subversion increases the spice. Am I much different from you, fucking your own nephew?'

Lisa recoiled, ashen. 'How did you know?'

'From Mr Johansen, of course.'

Sickened by this further evidence of his spying, Lisa whimpered pathetically. 'He gives me nowhere to hide.'

'Again, the same as me – everyone's heard of my arrangement with Max. He's had me in public many times.'

'Aren't you concerned about that?'

'Not now. Especially if a spectator has me straight after. All that feeble cock can do is watch me spasm on the end of someone else's prick.'

'Until he takes you the next time.'

'Illicit things are irresistible bait, as you well understand. Now, get up.' Lisa complied reluctantly. 'Who teaches you about tolerance and detachment?'

'The harlot.'

'And that is your role this evening, but don't plan on getting paid for it. Laid, yes. Paid, no. How should I dress you? In what style?'

'I suppose . . . sleazily.'

'Suitable to the slut that you are?'

The new challenge might change her irreparably, losing the person she had always been. Lisa controlled her looming fear by taking refuge in the shower and pampering herself luxuriantly. The hissing jet and the lining of condensation enclosed her in welcome solitude and security. As the cubicle door swung open she swivelled hastily, expecting Imogen, but in stepped a slim white form. Through curtains of spray Lisa squinted at Kim's innocent doll features, her refined pencil eyebrows. Amazed, she asked, 'What are you doing here?'

Kim smiled, a bizarre twist of her pouting lips. 'Pauline's sent me all this way to be with you.'

'Don't you care?'

'Do you?'

Lisa blinked as if slapped. She realised suddenly that with this confident young woman accompanying her she had no anxiety at all.

'We'll be a lovely prostitute pair,' Kim said. 'Marion's coming too because there's lots of randy guys who need us.'

Kim's milky flesh had the texture of soft glove leather and revealed no marks or blemishes. Her breasts, perfect cones, had, at their glorious summits, pointed pink nipples so delicate they appeared raw. 'You're beautiful.' Lisa's voice quivered with undisguised fervour.

When they dried off she observed Kim's full nudity, as she might if drawing her from a distance. In the taut narrow vee of her loins her slit, higher than Lisa's, had greater distinction. 'I want you to pose for me.'

'Sure, any time.'

As Kim turned away Lisa gazed at flawless bunched curves separated by a vertical chasm as deep as her own. The girl wiggled her rump enticingly and Lisa, excited, knelt to kiss her vertebrae one by one. Her tongue investigated the valley between Kim's thighs, rippling with unbridled desire. 'Wider,' Lisa requested huskily.

Without demur Kim did so and murmured, 'I remember the first time a guy fingered my anus. It felt heavenly.'

Lisa used a warm towel to dry the bursting seam of her sex, stroking sensuously up and down. Later, as sisters, they helped with make-up and alternated, thrilling each others' tempting nubs.

They left the bathroom glowing and sleek, and met Imogen who indicated clothing laid on the bed. 'Put these on. They should fit.'

Lisa attached a thin suspender belt, midnight blue in colour. Kim wore a similar belt in blood red. Held by clips at the side their sheer stockings, in the same dramatic hues, emphasised the whiteness of their skin. Matching high-heeled shoes completed their lower halves. The only garment they were allowed, a filmy negligée, descended to their ankles. Nipped at the waist, the light fabric ballooned amply above and below.

111

'I adore this old-fashioned gear.' As Kim circled the room the skirt of her negligée flowed as a tail of seduction and brought her bare vulva into clear sight.

'If clothes do their job properly,' Imogen instructed Lisa 'you will have less to do. And don't forget this. Let your clients look at you but don't look at them.'

As they walked the corridors, cool air wafted over Lisa's groin. She disciplined the pounding of her heart by concentrating on the task ahead. *This brothel clothing is working for me.* And: *Be tolerant even if –* Imogen stopped outside a double door, panelled in oak. 'Are you ready?' she asked.

Kim nodded eagerly.

'You are both charming – thoroughbred fillips. Be proud!'

As soon as they entered the room Lisa rocked with surprise. In seconds she confirmed the details: an ancient florid wallpaper; embellished clocks; the bronze figures on pedestals; higher, on the wall to her right, the group of raptors – hawk, eagle, the snowy owl – all with their wings and talons outstretched; the doe and a small rabbit. This, unmistakably, was the room photographed in Jon Bradley's studio where she had first encountered the girl at her side. And now she was actually here: *With Angelique.*

Lisa tightened her grasp on Kim's hand and her dear pussy twitched in a signal of anticipation. Moving together, their gowns unfurled, permitting their potential clients to sample them briefly as they wove in and out of the chairs. Some of the men regarded them sombrely – perhaps as a threat? – and alarmed Lisa. Whatever could they be brooding upon? Unlike her striptease she had no control on events and instead, by hustling, solicited favours. And she knew immediately which she preferred.

The women had not proceeded far before a pair beckoned. Kim, with the attraction of a magnet for its missing half, settled onto the lap of her client. Lisa followed, adjusting to her own client's kiss as he loosened her gown, and valued the unhurried pace of his foreplay. Struggling to reciprocate, she nurtured his bulge, unzipped him and gently, with difficulty, pulled out the swollen shaft while he explored her dewy folds. Intuitively she understood his wish to sit squarely across his lap, her back to his face. Bridging his knees the plum-shaped cap nestled within her aperture and by sinking little by little, her creamy passage swallowed the length. On the first evening she had been a passive recipient but on this occasion her own flagrant actions would cause her client to come. Lisa checked Kim, impaled in the same manner and squirming her hips, her ring gleaming in the fork of her legs. Kim's client prised the ring and dragged her membranes up into a grotesque band. Jointly, levering on the arms of the chairs, they mounted and fell on the straining rods. Lisa's client released her gown to unwrap her globes, heaving and flopping in synchronisation with Kim's. The men nearby leaned closer to study Lisa's motions and her spreading gash. As if watching her own mirror image, she fixed her attention on her friend's transient expressions resembling flickers of pain or ecstasy, and hoped their clients would come at the same time but not yet, not yet, for her own rise was building fast but needed more time. Exhilarated and panting deliriously, she lifted high in order to fall, driving the loaded stem fully inside. Repeated endlessly, the manoeuvre drained his jetting fluid too quickly and she eased to a halt, attempting to smother her jittery nerves. Hauled upright, she swayed giddily, just as Kim's climactic cry came in the midst of her client's convulsions.

Clamping down on her disappointment, Lisa walked to a bar at the side of the room. She sipped a drink slowly, aware of a clammy leak. As her tension ebbed away she marvelled at her own composure, clad only in stockings and shoes and with men on either side, chatting amiably as if they had met in the street. 'Be proud,' Imogen said: *And that's liberating*. Lisa began to savour the sedate atmosphere of a gentleman's club in which three women had been summoned to serve, with no connection to censure or shame. And that too was liberating.

Kim floated towards them and sipped her own drink, as relaxed as when they stepped through the door.

'Lucky you,' Lisa said.

'I am lucky. I come easily.'

Lisa draped herself in the filmy gown whose single layer presented no barrier to prying hands, and waited as Kim finished the last of her drink. On the next parade she envied the girl's natural naked flirtations, a sign that she had no fear. What a compelling authority to have over men! This time, copying Kim's lead, Lisa glided provocatively, posing here and there to offer herself. Some men reached out and groped them as they passed but their teasing progression came to an end with the approach of two clients, both with livid erections poking out of their zips. Kim corrected Lisa's dismay by a friendly grin and gave herself hungrily to the one she fancied.

Lisa's client led her behind a couch where she inclined forwards, her hair sprawled on the seat. He brushed the gown aside and the bite of suspender straps in both thighs reminded her of the way they framed her genitals, a pleasing view for him to enjoy. But he would be staring at jewels that were now soiled, just as Marion had been when Lisa gazed at her. Quivering, Lisa succumbed to embarrassment and guilt until a new association filled her with dread. This, a posture perfect for spanking, recalled the impacts, the fierce stings, the deep pink coloration. In consenting to exhibitionism she had not considered public humiliation and billowing panic began to sap –

Kim rescued her by sliding down to match her position. In gratitude Lisa kissed her awkwardly.

Separated roughly, stiff cocks demanded their mouths. Lisa conscientiously performed her role even though it could not pacify her own longing. A few moments later the organ unaccountably slipped away and she slumped forwards, confused. Uncoordinated shifting and shuffling occurred, then she was levered upwards to receive a solid member insistently nudging her lips. Lisa glimpsed the bloated phallus and tasted its difference, warmed and smooth with Kim's saliva. She accepted the substitute willingly but this one shortly deserted too and she drooped once more in the cushioned dark.

A swift raid tested her anus and she jolted up in consternation, scaring away the predator. Kim clutched her for reassurance, just as a gloriously strict pole pierced Lisa's vagina and fast effective drives continued her stimulation. Her gasps coincided with each virile plunge and the astounding fuck would undoubtedly bring the relief she craved.

Abruptly her channel emptied. With the domination removed she floundered helplessly, unable to believe it, or comprehend why her client had not even discharged. She waited apprehensively, all her senses alert, for a gruff command or some kind of contact. '*Seeing nothing, feeling everything.*' Without warning a thick column rammed to the hilt and its heavy testicles banged her clitoris. This one had altered proportions and a varying rhythm and Lisa realised their clients had switched. They were using them both and Kim's lubrication would be mixed with her own. Elated, Lisa swelled in flame. A few more delicious strokes –

When they ceased, her emotions lurched in chaos. Her cunt palpitated with the force of a heartbeat and she yearned for only the briefest interval before the first penis returned, this time carrying her friend's internal heat. It came, widening her sopping depths, and rocked her to and fro, dissolving rapidly. She belonged wholly to him, this stranger who ruled her imperiously, who coerced her onto an exquisite edge and a shuddering fall, a surging annihilation, blinding her from the erupting semen.

Through a muted time the women regained their composure. Curved over the couch with their cheeks split like halved peaches, Lisa knew that once again their flushed parts were exposed to any inspection. When they stood she embraced her friend ardently, attached to her in a nebulous way. They had, after all, exchanged their secretions.

'Using us both,' Kim giggled. 'That's very naughty – but nice too.'

Arm in arm they wandered dreamily to the bar for more welcome refreshment, but having taken only a few sips Kim put her glass on the counter. 'There's a guy calling me.'

Impressed by her insatiable appetite, Lisa delayed to examine the old-fashioned room. On the wall she noticed a further detail from the photograph: a mirror with a carved ebony frame, and at the top a malevolent raven with unleashed claws. In the picture the bird had frightened her but now, curiously at home, she relished the situation. She and her sisters were here to be used in a simple break from calm conversation. Did that betray the mentality of a whore? Untroubled, Lisa embarked on a leisurely cruise, brazen and potent. Her enchanting gown fluttered, randomly veiling and revealing her figure. It translated her to a seductive vision, shedding light and confidence as she circulated among her clients. Some of them idly fondled between her legs and it amused her to deposit a trace of fluid on their skin.

In a small anteroom she discovered Marion, a queen bee in her own space, surrounded by huddled spectators. Marion lodged on her client, her broad torso shielding his face. On Lisa's earlier view, the queen bee had been kneeling and bound, but from this direction her mass swamped the man she sat upon. Only his legs, and his shaft invading her anal hole, showed his presence. Lisa admired a pretty butterfly crease, bulged out on a prominent mound, peeping from a glinting screen of brown hair. Marion's ponderous bulk arched as she vigorously bounced huge melons, alarming in weight, up and down. Threaded by thin blue veins, their pink aeriolae were the size of saucers with raw red paps. Her candid behaviour invited Lisa into the area. Queen bee allowed her kiss while Lisa's fingers trailed the ridges of belly fat and crept into her wreathed portal. Unsure of her own motive, Lisa drove into the cauldron, twisting and spreading the rippling tissues like a squirming octopus, giddy at playing with a woman for a second time that day. Withdrawing, Lisa unrolled the labia into a diamond flower as a bonus for their clients' keen appreciation. Her feathered caress followed the man's projecting iron-hard stub, a shocking comparison to the elastic tunnel she had just vacated, to investigate the scrotum's wrinkled texture. She cradled the balls, the root of his sex. At the junction, where the male length punctured the female aperture, she lingered, tracking the taut rim of a mysterious zone, Marion's sphincter, clenched on the girth. It seemed, quite suddenly, an intriguing method of penetration, perhaps an agreeable experiment. After thrusting once more into the cushioned furnace, she wiped the moisture on Marion's nipple during their last kiss. Lisa departed as briskly as she arrived but glanced back. The man had elevated the queen bee's legs and stretched vertically her ample pouch to a compact bulbous spear in the centre of her thighs.

In the main room Kim sat by her panting client, intently pumping his rigid glans, and holding a champagne glass poised at the lurid apex. Inspired by her skill, Lisa crossed the room and crouched in front, gripped by the extraordinary contrast of lewd actions with an innocent look. The man groaned, his emission flew in coiled strands, and pooled in the shallow bowl. Kim licked the daubed wilting tip, her eyes sparkling in triumph at collecting its seed. 'My favourite food,' she said, lifted the glass as if giving a toast, and tilted her chin for the clots to seep over the rim. As lazily as creeping molasses, a rivulet expanded and trickled down. Lisa reacted unconsciously with a sigh of envy.

Kim held out the glass. 'Join me.' In speaking the words, strings of ejaculate bridged her teeth. 'Don't swallow.' The viscous web elongated and ruptured.

Lisa raised the glass high, gathered a dense wad, and carefully harvested the last streaks. In her friend's kiss their lips slithered and smeared in oozing mushy film, their nostrils flooded with its strong aroma. When she consumed the elixir, Lisa could not distinguish the bounty from their own saliva.

'You clearly enjoy sharing things.' An elderly man had appeared. 'Why don't you do it together?'

Kim squealed in delight, 'Party time.' Dragging Lisa to her feet, she smiled at the man and said mischievously, 'My friend's wanted me for ages but she's too shy to ask. But it's so much better if we're bare, and she's wearing far too much. Do you want to help us out?'

Stirring with interest, a crowd assembled and Lisa watched anxiously, as if from the outside, rather than being a part of the moment. When her gown rustled to the floor she stepped away, trying to resist the numberless fleeting touches. One helper unfastened her stocking and another moulded her calf, lowering the stocking to her ankle. Someone else liberated the shoe from her foot and eased off the loose fabric. The same treatment was repeated but more fondling came gratuitously. She could not curb the intimacies and writhed and quivered, imagining herself in outdoor clothes coming in from the street. Her assistants would use this bewitching technique to strip her in gradual stages and all their familiarities, however incidental, would prolong her pleasure. The idea crumbled as one servant used her suspender belt's narrow band to rock back and forth in her crotch, creating an irrepressible stimulus. Melting, groped by so many, gave her a licence to be free, or even obscene, if that's how she chose to reward their attention. Lisa kissed her friend passionately, excited by acting wilfully – with a third woman that day – whose body, identical to her own in general form, had new and particular secrets to explore. Now she could indulge the lust she had felt in the shower.

'You're bigger than I am,' Kim murmured. 'You lie on the floor and I'll be the dom.'

Lisa gazed upwards as the men loomed above. Kneeling, Kim straddled her head and kissed her again, then shifted forward to nip Lisa's firming bud. Obeying the cue, Lisa took the hanging tip, a bright cherry or miniature penis, and gave it the gentle flicks that don't hurt but arouse quickly. Kim controlled their voluptuous progress and fed to Lisa the twin, seizing her own in return. Lisa tugged on the youthful springy pulp and Kim deferred her next move before kissing Lisa's fleecy abdomen. Lisa gladly reciprocated. The next advance placed the girl at Lisa's legs where she lay flat and forked Lisa's face in her spread thighs. Lisa absorbed from an inch away the ring decorating an alluring target, a drooping shield that curtained the desirable entrance. She petted the velvet surface of Kim's

118

derrière and inwards to the supple silk flesh of her succulent slit, and studied its glimmering furrows and colour modulations. They all matched her own yet were also dissimilar in so many beguiling ways. Using her thumbs, she separated and widened the yielding folds. Here waited a mouth, unlike her own, that she could actually kiss. In the slick vibrant funnel Lisa began a search for paradise. As Kim tapped her clitoris several times, accelerating her usually slow climb to orgasm, Lisa bucked and desperately buried her tongue in the sperm-lined sheath, a tropical cavern, her nose in the starred wrinkles of a dark hole.

Breathing her lover's bouquet she sucked in the warm pleats. Far away, Kim's wicked probes to her own passage floated her in delirious space. Both of them knew the acute spots and the time when tenderness should give way to force. Hunting in Kim's vagina, Lisa circled, plunged deeper, and stroked the stiffening horn. Trembling, Kim dispensed a dazzling froth of savoury liquor and Lisa rejoiced in the rich juice, exhilarated by her first contact with a woman's come. As Kim nibbled, her own climax burst in pulses of overlapping sensation.

Still shuddering, Lisa found a cold object pressed into her hand: a glass dildo resembling an icicle, spiralling to a blunted end. As the greased crown entered Kim's incision, a transparent lens refracted and magnified the inner walls. Lisa pushed inwards steadily and on the outward pull observed the curling pink reflections. Enthralled by the unexpected power, she carried on, oblivious to the muffled protests, until Kim's renewed juddering brought a wild satisfaction at what she had induced. Lisa hauled out the spike, transferred it into her own mouth, and appeased a yearning for her friend's taste.

Kim's hot gasps were soft penetrations inside her cunt but sporadic specks, raining down on the girl's butt, distracted Lisa from the lovely feeling. Spattered fat blobs of glistening cream insulted the purity of perfection and Lisa hastened to lick them off, ending with a patch in the anal hollow.

She rested, with sticky sap coating her lips and cheeks. Each inhalation gave more hints of tangy scent. Kim sprawled at her side, smelling the same. Had they done enough? They could go to Lisa's room and a mutual soak in a perfumed bath – and perhaps a more leisurely session.

Her answer came as two rampant red poles diminished the light. The weight of one of the men flattened her and the second covered Kim.

'You want some more?' Max transfixed her belly in a single, almost careless, glide.

Lisa could only lend herself lethargically to his use. Later his indifferent dominance affected her mood and she whispered feverishly, 'Yes, give me more.' She clamped his heaving pelvis between her legs, buckling his body into her own. His brute mastery served her nature as a primal female, coalesced with him, and she welcomed his twitches and spurts, shooting his spunk while still pumping hard, delivering the gift she truly craved.

Twelve

But it would never happen again.

Hazy from broken sleep, Lisa could not recollect any of the men, except Max, from the evening before. Just as she, to them, was an unknown woman available for use so they, to her, were anonymous clients, lacking names, personalities or distinctive features. Had she erased them as self-defence?

She heard a quiet instruction from the door, followed by Imogen promptly rolling out of her bed, and the creak of floorboards. Once the door had shut Lisa slid out of her own sheets and from the window saw two silhouettes walking away. Above the blackened greens of the forest the sky mottled, and bruised to purple.

Lisa finished her packing with time to spare and sat on the bed to review the sketches. These were one of the principal reasons for coming to Balmayne. A dozen were completed and more partially. Glowing with pride at her independence, free of an author, she flipped the pages and considered the development of this raw material to a final state. Her thoughts wandered to her favourite memories of the time here. Gradually she focused on a table, bent over and arms bound, her dress high to expose her derrière, and a cane poised to descend in a jarring, stinging flash.

There was still time to spare.

Idly inspecting the plain room, her gaze settled on Imogen's wardrobe at the far end. At the bottom a large drawer, swollen with damp, required strenuous tugs to inch it apart. Eventually Lisa withdrew a cardboard box and caught an elusive fragrance of perfume. The box contained a jumble of old photographs in smashed frames or crunched into pellets of nondescript paper. If photography had been forbidden here this stockpile called for analysis. Sitting on the bed, she examined them through cracked surfaces. Some were too scoured and indecipherable, as if they had been obliterated in rage.

One showed a close-up of a shaved vagina expanded to the sides. In the centre, held by subtle pressure, lay a faceted ruby, a magnificent glittering contrast, blood-red in the heart of the delicate pink pulp. Lisa visualised herself as the spread model, content to let coarse fiddling fingers adjust the stone; the random pricks of its spiky corners in soft tissues; the photographer peering at every detail. And afterwards, goaded to arousal, how could he resist taking her?

In the next, difficult to discern below shattered glass, a woman knelt with her rump to the camera. From within her small puckered knot fell a long rope of lustrous pearls, the same concept as the anal whip that Lisa had drawn. Someone else had beaten her to it. Slivers tinkled into the box as she plucked out another which showed a woman, walking in procession, wearing a mass of shimmering metal chains. From a shining neck band they looped to her nipples, from there to her wrists, her wrists to her labia, and from those tender membranes down to her ankles. Incredibly, even pierced and chained, she managed to smile! In a scratched and faded scene figures had sandwiched a woman, already plugged in two orifices, who reached greedily to fill the third. Lisa blinked and flushed. Without this evidence she would not have believed that multiple cocks could be so desired. A crumpled ball revealed a younger woman, white and slim and terribly vulnerable, lying across the broad lap of an old crone. A wall mirror repeated her firm haunches straining upwards. Grimly concentrated, the crone raised a bunch of spiky twigs. Scarcely able to breathe, Lisa imagined the needle-sharp barbs exploding and marking those gentle spheres.

Dropping the picture, she began rubbing her puffy vulva but then, among the glinting spines in the box she noticed more crushed prints. Fumbling to a halt she squinted beyond a maze of whitened creases at celebrations in ornate settings. In one, a group in bizarre costumes crowded a standing man supporting a woman impaled on his erection and levering herself. Spectators, also participants, groped the pair lasciviously. Lisa remembered the first evening and her own induction in a similar way. A second print displayed naked bodies dancing in frenzy, gleaming with sweat, near flames of fire. In a third, one woman, dressed in a fantasy of colours and shapes, towed a friend by the leather column sticking out from her groin. Lisa had felt the effects of that type of inflexible rod.

In the majority of photographs men were encouraging the women's flagrant excesses. 'But why are we so keen to respond?' *Are we easily influenced? Or vain – natural exhibitionists?* Lisa pondered the issue, then murmured: 'We're sensual creatures and men toy with our minds. They know our instinctive urges can betray our will.'

From the last damaged scrap she brushed away the jagged shards. Yet another woman, this time hunched forward by a male fist under her skirt. Judged by her screaming reaction, he must be penetrating ruthlessly. Lisa glanced at the man. With a wild dislocating shock she realised she knew him. Staring accusingly out of the past and straight at her, was Jon Bradley.

Impeded by her luggage, Lisa stumbled from the stairway into the hall where she found Imogen kneeling in front of Max. Her fan of hair drooped on her slender back and her blouse hung loosely at her waist. Watching keenly from the side was the same taxi driver who had brought Lisa to the house.

Ignoring him, Lisa paid careful attention to Imogen's skill. Spurning the use of her hand to masturbate, she relied solely on her agile mouth. With her jaws wide she advanced up her brother's stem until, achieving her maximum depth, her nose nudged its base. Retreating along the rigid length, her cheeks hollowed to provide the friction he needed. Her vibrating tits attracted the driver's interest and he stretched out to cup and fondle the compact flesh but Imogen expressed no surprise or alarm and continued her task, nostrils flared, eyes closed. Lisa studied her lips, clinging to the solid shaft with undisguised candour and full commitment contorting her face, plainly in love with the penis she served. Max grasped her head and loaded his sister's sobbing cavity with its teeming ejaculations, his creamy fruit. The driver chuckled in satisfaction and with a charged glance in Lisa's direction he picked up her cases and took them outside.

Imogen, wiping the spilt residue, said, 'We always reward him to keep him sweet. He does many favours and asks no questions so be sure to give him whatever he wants.'

'Me?' Lisa recalled his reference to generous tips: of sex, apparently, instead of money.

'Yes you,' Imogen insisted. 'You cannot refuse.'

'But you can say goodbye to this.'

Lisa replaced Imogen at the feet of Max, in front of the softening member which, only a few hours earlier, had invaded her own dear pussy. Gratified in some obscure way, as if departing from an old master now her friend, she planted sincere kisses in the warmth. Imogen demanded her own kiss and they shared an aroma from the same source.

As Lisa ran out of the building through rain, torn-off leaves hurtled by. At the waiting car she opened the rear door but the driver's curt gesture indicated the passenger seat. Resigning herself to the inevitable, she obeyed. The cab swung onto the main road and purred quietly, following the undulating route to the railway station.

'Lift your skirt, wee lassie, as you've been told to do.'

Lisa wrenched the material to her hips and squirmed down.

'You enjoy doing that.'

She tried to relax, though nervous speculations wore away her composure. The rain surged in hard irregular torrents and the wipers' drumming, sweeping the windscreen in briefly clear arcs, added a further distraction.

'Imogen told you about my perks?'

Lisa nodded, mute and tense.

The taxi swerved off the road onto a track, rocking and splashing in shallow water-filled ruts. The forest sealed them in to a narrow area of watery landscape, silver and green. A liquid horizon blended the sky into the summits of hills and a knee-high mist floated above the ground. No one would be about in this weather. With the engine switched off, uneven lashes of rain broke the silence and condensation quickly veiled the windows.

'Unzip me.'

Lisa complied and the rasp seemed abnormally loud. From the gap she extracted a limp organ.

'And you also enjoy holding that, wee lassie.' Afraid of admitting too much, she did not reply. 'So you can do the same as you did for Max.'

Giddily she humbled herself again to kiss the resilient tube, reminiscent of a friendly animal too shy to ask for stimulation.

'You can't get enough, can you?'

Lisa rejected shame. As the lax bar stirred to life she paused to mumble, 'Shall I bring you off?'

'Well, I appreciate an eager cocksucker. But if you're stuffed on the end you can't tell me what you've been up to.'

Abruptly Lisa sat upright.

'So get rid of your skirt and show me your fanny. Then start nice and slow.'

Bridging up, she unzipped and slid her skirt to the floor. Her pale skin glimmered in the curdled light and as she splayed her legs his eyes glittered with fascination and lust. At first her gentle ministrations were all the glans required but gradually she discovered pleasure in recounting events. With no pretence at modesty she explained frankly what she had done, including her own feelings at the time. Impetuously she mentioned the queen bee and indiscreetly dropped her name.

His raucous laugh interrupted. 'I dumped a good package in there, lassie. I had her on this very spot in the summer, over the bonnet. The sun polished her naked arse to giant hillocks of snow.'

Lisa pictured the huge blazing spheres. This hot stiff bayonet pointing up – the second she had held that had fucked Marion – looked even more desirable. It deserved serious respect.

'And did you strip to an audience?'

She concealed nothing and by the time she came to her finale he told her to stop. 'I don't want to come yet,' he groaned, and subdued his climax.

Lisa's ardour also receded but she remained in control. On resuming she spoke of Mary bound to the tree and her own impression of 'masculine' power. Describing its opposite, as a prostitute, she divulged the astonishing freedom, condoning any behaviour, conferred by the status. Despite her own ferment she noticed the penis ready to burst and moaned at a vanishing opportunity.

The driver gasped, 'OK, you can taste my balls.' He shoved back his seat, unfastened his belt and lowered his trousers. As Lisa fitted herself into the restricted space, his large hand separated her thighs and two thick digits pressed into her cunt. Nearby loomed his scrotum's corrugations, blanketed in thin curls. Her tongue bumped on the ridges and grooves of the crinkled sac. Seizing one of the oval plums she rolled her jaws over the prize, imagining its gruelly contents. The ponderous stem, ungainly in its rigid state, lurched above. Shifting deliriously to the second ball she sucked in the firm mass. A few inches away his fist pumped his shaft aggressively and twitched the pellet gripped in her mouth. He dragged her hair, compelling her to relinquish him and tilted her face. His sperm soared momentarily in silvery arcs and splattered down but she lost her view when a fat streak blotted her sight, and more fluid nestled into her hair. At the end of the spate he allowed her to claim the drool from his pouting slit. He pushed the clots and layers from her cheeks through her lips, and the male syrup slipped in her throat. Settling again onto his lap the weight of his flesh sagged, maintaining its rule on her temple. Only the beating rain on the roof disturbed the peace.

'Now I wish I'd given you a proper shag.' His fingers deepened within her channel. 'So that's a promise for the next time you come.'

There won't be a next time.

As the train gathered speed, Lisa rocked with its motions. In the washroom mirror she repaired her make-up and combed her hair, tugging painfully at crusts of dried semen. She now knew what it was like to be smothered in come. Since Pauline's instructions no longer applied she chose public modesty and fitted her panties, then, staggering drunkenly from side to side, she returned to her seat and collapsed with a sigh of relief.

After a short rest she pulled out her pad. In a rapid sketch, conveying the essentials, the compact globs flew towards her, increasing in size. No more than a bare, but sufficient, reminder it would be the last from Balmayne.

From her bag she lifted a crumpled paper and carefully levelled the creases. Beneath its cracks and blemishes the woman appeared to be enduring a harsh manipulation. Lisa grappled with her own mounting resentment. The visit to Balmayne was a part of her hidden life but this man, together with her children's illustration, belonged in a totally different compartment. This photograph brought the two on a threatening collision course. Why did he let himself be filmed? Previously she decided to keep away from him and Lisa renewed her resolve never to meet Jon Bradley again.

She gazed incuriously at the sodden country flowing past the rain-flecked windows. The effort that lay ahead would demand all her strength. In a few miles she fell asleep and there wandered in darkened streets, withdrawn and hollow, hugging the walls for shelter, arms wrapped to comfort her icy breasts.

Thirteen

In the studio she surrendered herself, and all her acquired experience, to the work.

Prowling among the pages laid on the floor she compared, classified and consolidated to avoid repetition. The first conclusion came quickly: that white paper had the wrong connotations of brightness and purity for this assignment. She rifled her stock of tinted papers for dusky browns and russets, ochre, dull greens and shades of grey. On impulse she paused to check the answering machine and discovered it packed with messages, half-pleading, cajoling, sometimes bantering, all from Jon or her nephew Ben. Underlying them all they both wanted her for the same thing but she required nothing from them and even vowed to forego her self-pleasure for the job's duration. Re-fixed on the task, she tested the condition of all her colours and brushes, inks and pens, crayons and charcoal.

The village shop delivered enough food to fill her fridge. She disconnected the telephone, covered the clock and shut the curtains. Only two small lamps penetrated the gloom as she began to tell her own story.

For ten days, wholly absorbed, she lived as a hermit in a cave. She did not leave the house, even to walk in the garden, ate odd scraps of food at random times, and stopped only if crushed by fatigue. Then she threw herself onto the bed and in a few hours rose again, haggard and unrefreshed. A shower was her only necessity, immersed in condensation and a white hiss, the water streaming from her hair as threads of glass, soaking heat into tired muscles. In her shrouded studio, preserving all her focus for what had begun to emerge, days transformed into nights with no difference between them.

Partially composed drawings scattered the floor and she developed several at the same time to add extra detail; more vigour perhaps, or build a shadow by cross-hatching, or duplicate an action from other positions to make it explicit, or less so, disguised in subtle obscurity. Scarcely conscious yet fully alert, haunted by incidents etched in memory, she recalled the moods and enhanced the effects of unrestrained sexuality. She refined each image to a crucial stage when it marked an episode with precise significance. At some hazy point, pale and drained, the recreated scenes stimulated her dulled spirit and she knew she had finished. Moreover, she needed no one else to confirm the quality. But she had almost burned herself out, like a raging forest fire that dwindles away. She had consumed everything lurking inside her; every thought and reaction had found expression on the page.

The sheets, divided by tissue paper, were stacked away. Finally she attached the telephone for a single call. In terse exchanges she agreed with Pauline a time and date, and wearily unplugged the 'phone.

With the aid of pills she slept for two days.

Lisa paid off the taxi and propped the portfolio on her leg while looking at the house. So many challenging events had occurred since her earlier visit, when she had glimpsed a few of the secrets within those walls. There might be more yet to be savoured. She climbed the steps and rapped loudly on the anonymous door, yearning to kiss her young friend. Instead a stranger, a blonde girl, confronted her. Bewildered, Lisa asked, 'Where's Kim?'

'Away on a confidential mission. You, however, are most welcome.'

Passing the line of mahogany doors, Lisa heard the same indistinct noises as she had before. Arriving at Pauline's office the girl placed her portfolio on the desk and retreated quietly.

A shiny grey dress accentuated Pauline's svelte form. The slinky material revealed her profiles and projected her nipples invitingly, framed by a jacket draped casually across her shoulders. But her eyes! They conveyed a predatory nature.

'Come here.' Pauline led her to the window for light to flood on Lisa's face. 'Balmayne has been good for you. You're transfigured. I'm sure you have no objection . . .'

Wrapped in her arms, a snaking tongue probed into Lisa's mouth. She consented with no reservations, drowned in their kiss, engulfed in wafts of exotic perfume.

At last Pauline said, 'Imogen has acquainted me with all your exploits. And then I heard of your session with Kim and suffered an unusual affliction, that of jealousy.'

'How did you hear about that? Imogen wasn't there.'

'Oh, that one he reported himself.'

Stunned, Lisa realised that 'he' could only refer to a man she had grown to hate. He had observed her with Ben, then her striptease, and now with a woman. He not only invaded her house but was also an arch voyeur! And Pauline was just as bad. 'That bastard Johansen,' Lisa complained bitterly.

'Don't be too critical of us. It would help if you learned detachment, rather than being so tense.' Pauline smiled and kissed her again. 'I can't contain my impatience. I'm dying to see if your results have also been influenced.' At her desk she unzipped the portfolio.

Lisa's anger reduced gradually. How much did Johansen actually matter? He existed in a past that would not be repeated. Only the outcome had real importance and Lisa had no concern about Pauline's verdict. She was vaguely aware of occasional mutters: 'These are fearless', or expulsions of air as if she was winded by a blow, but it all sounded far away.

'Wonderfully allusive,' Pauline said. 'Or perhaps dislocated is a better word . . . as if the true subject isn't here at all but just outside the picture's edge. Something is about to happen . . .'

'And the longer it takes the worse the suspense.'

'Exactly!' Later Pauline said, 'This is marvellous. Fluent and juicy. A centrifugal force that billows outwards, dispersing in wave upon wave.'

'A starburst.'

'Yes. Not the masculine shotgun blast, but the authentic rhythms of female orgasm.' She carried on, minutely inspecting the samples and after a pregnant pause, she concluded, 'The artist who made these knows the issues intimately. The substance is captured with genuine erotic power. I hope you feel proud of your achievement. I shall buy the complete set.'

Suddenly weak, Lisa plumped into a chair. Pauline's judgement clinched what she knew: that she had travelled great distances into her psyche. With the assignment accepted she could afford her dream, a month sailing in the Aegean: *That dark flying sea.*

Pauline sat opposite. 'When I asked you last time why you do this, you had nothing to say. But now I'm convinced you can give me an answer.'

'Well . . . the human body is probably the earliest artistic topic in the world. The most fundamental.'

'And sex?'

'A fundamental compulsion.'

'And is there a third?'

'Our brains – hard-wired to exaggerate significant elements.'

'So?'

'So . . . the bodies I draw must be virile, the act dynamic, and the situations emphatic and suggestive.'

'And why are those exaggerations necessary?'

'Because reality is a bore.'

'So boring! Welcome to the club.'

Spurning her own chair, Pauline knelt on the floor at Lisa's feet. 'To work at such an original level must have been a lonely slog. You must be ready for some company. A woman's essence is to be connected, isn't that so? It's time to relax.' Gliding both hands under Lisa's skirt she caressed gently.

Lisa settled contentedly. Pauline's delicate touch, combining feminine sensitivity with the assurance of a male, strayed upwards, giving time to adjust and to anticipate the coming stage. Lisa's arms hung by the chair for the loops of rope, first on one wrist and now the second, and both tugged severely behind her back. Held immovably, unable to breathe, she waited for the blindfold.

The slow progression reached the tops of her stockings and Pauline murmured, 'I'm glad you don't subscribe to disgusting tights.' As the seduction neared her pubes Lisa curved and stiffened in expectation. The ropes squeezed –

'What on earth are you imagining? Whatever it is, I'm certain you're willing.'

'Yes, I am.' Ardour quivered in Lisa's reply.

Fondling her thighs Pauline said, 'Your talent increases your attraction – you are defined by far more than the primitive urge of your cunt.' Lisa blinked in shock. 'Nevertheless, as I have been told, you like it pacified by regular exercise.' Pauline halted abruptly. 'But what is this?' Raising Lisa's skirt she added, 'Why are you wearing panties? That can't be allowed. Off they come immediately.'

Lisa hesitated but levered up on the chair's arms. Pauline promptly slid the wispy fabric down to her ankles and off her feet. Lisa shivered. It would be so easy to succumb to Pauline's appetite, and she challenged her shyly.

'Do you practise what you preach?'

Pauline stood, shuffled forward to straddle Lisa's knees, and gathered the hem of her dress. Lifting in small phases she extending the allure by holding each one before the next advance. Lisa followed its rise voraciously as, little by little, it divulged the glorious swell of Pauline's upper legs. The hem rose to the patterned tops of her stockings, distorted by an abundance of flesh and the cruel clamp of suspender studs. It arrived at an enticing glimpse of bareness above, and there it stopped.

Lisa stared at the exposed band, alarmed at her own arousal but confirmed by its strength. Sheer lust tempted her to brush away the provocative shield to the vital area. 'Higher,' she mumbled.

'Say please.'

'Please, higher.'

The hem climbed the taut lines of suspenders and in a swift lurch the skirt bunched at Pauline's waist. Lisa feasted hungrily on the view. The labia resembled a dank flower, protruding from a thin pubic veil with the assertion of a man's flagrant swag, and a similar voluptuous command. It looked as if it had fought many a strenuous bedroom battle.

'Not shaved,' Lisa noted. It seemed odd, almost a betrayal after Pauline's own demand.

'It comes and goes. While you're here you can do it for me.'

'I'd love to.'

Lisa scarcely noticed Pauline's foot on the arm of her chair until the knee restricted her, alongside her cheek. Only inches from her glazed eyes Pauline steadily and deliberately separated her pleats, inserted two fingers up to the knuckles, and rocked her hips. When she pulled out, her moisture gleamed in a thick coat.

Lisa relished the clean flavour smeared on her lips. It produced such an ache in her loins that she circled Pauline's spheres and hauled towards her the feathery mound. Inhaling the heady mixture of spicy perfume, alive with native scents, she wanted to drink more, much more.

Pauline wriggled her pelvis on Lisa's mouth and sighed, 'You have a strong urge to submission.'

Anxiously Lisa sat upright. 'What did you say?'

Remaining in position, her skirt hoisted, Pauline explained. 'It's normal for women to succumb to men. However, as they have gained independence, and now often rival men, some are prepared to explore the passive side of their nature with a woman.'

'And you think I'm one of those?'

'What do you believe?'

'That I need . . . unconventional things.'

'Of course. Ordinary things, as we agreed, can be so boring. In addition, as I told you for Balmayne, there is much to enjoy in obedience.'

'Hypothetically . . .' Lisa broke off, disconcerted by Pauline's knowing smile. 'What would I have to do?'

'Does it matter?'

Lisa recalled a slave tied to a tree whose acquiescence sanctioned her to play at being the master. In this reversal of status Lisa would have to take her place. *But that's what I did. I returned to the tree.* And a figure came across the clearing.

Lambent flames embraced her dear pussy and all she could manage was a husky whisper. 'When I saw you with Kim she mentioned whipping. Do you always whip?'

'Always.'

Unconditional, permitting no room for doubt nor hope to be spared. Lisa jolted at the assertive tone. What a huge rush of emotion coldness could bring! She remembered her experience of the cane. At the time she had thought of it idly as a special kind of satisfaction but now, with the promise, she wondered if she could actually bear it.

'You look dazed. You either trust me or you don't.' A flat ultimatum.

Trust. *The slave used that word.* Lisa croaked, 'How would I address you?'

'I am your mistress. You are my neophyte and now you will serve me.' Pauline pressed Lisa into her groin.

In contact with the pouting folds, Lisa ignored her fears. Grasping her mistress's buttocks she twisted awkwardly to different angles and moaned, frustrated. 'I can't get into you properly.'

'Let me sit.' In the chair, Pauline splayed her legs over the arms to present herself. With languorous passion she offered her ripe slit.

In contrast to Lisa's session with Kim, the absence of witnesses brought her a giddy wave of freedom. In privacy there were no limits and any whim could be indulged. She was hypnotised by the dusky oozing succulence. The air hushed and irrelevant objects melted away. A single blatant invitation filled her sight and it beckoned, dilated, monopolised all her attention.

'I'll soak you, so you'd better be ready.'

Lisa immersed her face in a bath of musky heat, and a heavy woman-smell from the mature furrow. From side to side in the wet trough she teased the elastic membranes, which rebounded in mutual floppy caresses. Her tongue, a lively penis, drove repeatedly in and out of the orifice, searching for greater depth and more extent on every plunge. Her own unbridled desire harmonised with her mistress's order and she yearned to take possession of the mystery. She coiled the pliant tissues and drifted up to the spot, the supreme spot, where she gently nipped the clit's hooded crest. A wicked idea planted a stubborn root in her mind. Blindly she thrust her index finger into the seeping cavity below her chin, withdrew and probed lower to the anal hole, pushing inwards. Her mistress writhed but Lisa persisted through the ring, gripping hard. Pauline slid down in the chair and widened her crotch. Lisa pursued the solicitation, sniffing the slightly opened sphincter, delirious at her mistress's fragrance. Investigating its texture of wrinkled silk, she felt its palpitations and forced into the secret recess, her nose buried in the soft layers above. Swooping again to the passage she craved she kept her digit's length firmly embedded in the dark aperture. Confused in eddies of swirling sensation she licked and sucked the stiffening wedge, and rapidly fucked her mistress to and fro. Pauline's thighs and hips trembled uncontrollably. Lisa swam blissfully in a complex liquid ambrosia before the shrill cries and violent spasms marked Pauline's prolonged release, drained by the power.

While they recovered silently Lisa rested on the smooth inner leg, her breath warming the vagina she had willingly succoured. 'You came like Niagara,' she mumbled.

'Then kiss me. Let me taste my honey.'

Lisa raised her head. Her drenched cheeks gleamed with the residue of flowing emissions.

Her mistress shut the third mahogany door and guided Lisa to the fourth, giving access to a starkly furnished room. The row of identical doors led into different spaces equipped to gratify a variety of preferences. The fifth

135

room, very much larger, contained a library with volumes on fine shelves lining the walls from floor to ceiling.

'This country's most comprehensive collection of erotica,' Pauline said. 'A few of our morsels are priceless – hundreds of years old. You can refer to it at any time.'

The young woman who had welcomed Lisa at the door approached eagerly.

'Janine is our librarian. For a small personal favour, applied to her rosy grotto, she'll find you anything. Sometimes I send her with Kim as a prostitute pair, a situation you have also enjoyed. Now, I'll have you in the next room.' To the disappointed librarian Pauline said, 'Your chance comes later.'

Behind the last mahogany door Lisa found an item of furniture, sinister in black and gold, resembling nothing she had ever seen.

'Now, perfectly still.'

Pauline unbuttoned Lisa's blouse, advancing slowly to delay the final result with light lingering touches to her neck and shoulders. Pampered, Lisa quivered luxuriantly. Pauline gathered the fabric and let it fall to admire Lisa's breasts bunched in a low-cut brassiere of filmy lace. 'Charming,' she murmured. Toying with the exposed flesh, she briefly fondled Lisa's nipples. Smiling, she unclipped the bra and lifted away the redundant garment. In a sudden change of mood she unzipped Lisa's skirt, dropped it to the floor, and roughly snatched off the stockings and suspender belt as if any layer of protection would be unpardonable. She paused, studying her first view of Lisa's form. 'As beautiful as all my reports claimed.' Cupping Lisa's bare pudenda she added, 'You have surrendered this exquisite thing to me. You understand that, don't you?'

Her mistress's demanding manner and the frank inspection of her nudity gave Lisa the same thrill as exhibiting herself to a man.

'But any pleasure you receive is incidental. I might almost say accidental. And now,' Pauline said ominously, 'it's time for The Chair, though it's actually a hybrid.' She turned Lisa towards it. 'A replica of an eighteenth-century French design with a few adaptations.'

Ebony wood glistened with polish. The piece blended a stool, a reclining chair, and a bed. At the front corners as high as a table were carved figures, kneeling men with massive jutting erections. Beneath their spread thighs lay naked women, their mouths blocked by testicles, and more women, masturbating in frenzy, buttressed the rear. Gold embroidery upholstered the inclined platform. At floor level two cushions cased in the same material ran from end to end.

'In this you can be used in different combinations.' Pauline held her neophyte's palm to a carved phallus and approved of the way she savoured the sleek column. 'On another occasion you will impale yourself on that but not now. Mount up. Put your feet on those plates on top of the men.'

Elaborate padding cushioned her spine as Lisa reposed in a position similar to a gynaecological chair but lacking high stirrups to support her legs. Pauline wrapped her ankles in Velcro bands, elevated her arms one at a time along carved projections, and used further Velcro to bind her wrists.

Secured, Lisa's thwarted efforts to move her limbs gave an extra frisson to rising lust. Abruptly Pauline disappeared and Lisa waited, panting apprehensively. Her mistress emerged, fitting a strange rubber glove which enclosed one finger as a penis, complete with a solid bulbous crown. As it came near Lisa blanched at a mass of excrescences – bobbles and short spikes – that deformed its surface.

'For me, this type of strap-on is extremely responsive compared to Imogen's crude bludgeon.'

At the first tantalising chafes Lisa curved in a bow. As the prongs bent and flicked, probing her labia from end to end, she twitched and shrieked. The stimulus deepened, the bobbles scouring her creamy walls and Lisa again shrieked and buckled. The unnerving massage consumed her entirely and by the end her beating sex ached for more.

'Squeeze.'

Lisa contracted onto the shaft, gasped explosively, loosened and tightened. When she relaxed the prongs scraped her channel haphazardly, as a giant itch that could never be scratched. Frantic, she twisted hopelessly as far as her bonds authorised. Her flesh moulded and bounced, and her pelvis tensed until the awful stimulation came to an end. The dildo remained, fully embedded.

'And this repays you for acting without my permission.'

A slimy blunt nose nudged Lisa's anal rim and a second dildo expanded her resistant sphincter. Pauline's impatient shove lodged a ball in the ring. Lisa protested but the force increased and a larger sphere burst through the clenched muscle. Despite the struggles, her mistress drove in a third and then a fourth ball fatter in size. Lisa's shrill cry recorded the dildo's oppression, invading and stretching unnaturally a private part of her body.

'Quiet, damn you! Get used to it.'

Leniently Pauline gave her time. Lisa gazed sightlessly, adjusting to a doubled violation between her legs, separated only by an internal membrane. Her mistress wrenched, then began a routine: a fierce jerk on the outward stroke and on the reverse a persistent thrust. The balls widened and shrank Lisa's anus at random, sending jolts of excitement to her clitoris, and her whimpering moans alternated with howls of objection.

Her vagina's sleeper sprang into life. Sometimes the two coincided but the prongs also varied in speed and depth. A compelled release ascended from where the two ran together. Wincing, Lisa attempted to store her impressions in memory but the irregular rhythm left her mute, at a glorious peak of ecstasy, in a flood too strong and confused to ever recall. Shuddering, sapped by the power of orgasm, she screaming silently and automatically gripped the chattels in both of her ravaged holes.

Later, from far away, she dimly perceived her mistress's sparkle.

'What a lovely defenceless picture you are. I shared with you all your contractions.'

How long ago since I became her novice?

Her mistress had proved to be a bolt of lightning: highly charged, unstable, and burning passionately. Once, she had spread Janine over a library table and instructed Lisa on using a dildo held in her teeth, her face compressed into the young woman's perfumed pleats. They yielded softly to every plunge which ended satisfactorily, in the final involuntary squirms and muffled cries.

And now this. Lisa groaned wretchedly, wondering if she would be able to bear it. But what choice did she have than to humbly obey? Her mistress had captured her, but so too had her own desire.

The air had cooled. Shivering, Lisa rearranged her posture, hoping to ease the fatigue in her shoulders or the implacable upward tug on her bound wrists. The rope, extending her arms high above her head, clamped them rigidly to her cheeks, restricting her sight to the front. To see anything on either side she had to spin clumsily as only her toes touched a glass plate in the floor. Her binding raised her rib-cage, emphasising their bars above her in-swept abdomen. Helplessness of this scale indicated a serious intent and Lisa crawled with greater dread of what could happen than prior to her caning. Suspended from all reality, insubstantial as a shadow, she thought of leaf-blades – razor-edged cuts – the slapping blades of a whip – whack! – and flinched, persecuted by her own imagination.

Alone in the empty windowless room, time had ceased and nothing existed beyond the present.

And the longer it takes the worse the suspense.

The modest illumination gently dwindled and Lisa watched the lamps anxiously, as if she could halt the encroaching gloom by a desperate exertion of will. When they died she expected her pupils to compensate and pick up the inevitable chinks of light, but only unrelieved black pressed on her eyelids. From behind, a chilling wave suggested an opening door and she pivoted hastily. 'Mistress?'

Below her feet the panel glimmered. A watery beam outlined her pale form in a shimmering subterranean vault. Her voice fractured uncertainly as she called out. She strained to penetrate the murk, caught an inky ghost and heard a faint whir, a peculiar whistle multiplied; too weird for interpretation. At the limit of vision thin strands flared in the ray of light and reappeared opposite as a narrow band. With a premonition, lurching erratically, Lisa tried to retreat from menacing flying filaments.

Airy as a breeze, threads unfurled in bewildering sequences. Under a few, concentrated across her thighs, she gasped and twisted violently. Switching attention too late, she had no preparation for the next harsh conflagration up her rib-cage, into her arm pits. Hot patterns overlaid and she could not catch their flight, slanting unpredictably from all directions. Abnormally loud snaps demolished her resolve as much as their stings and she writhed and buckled in the midst of a molten flow. 'Ah!'

Her affliction stopped. All sounds drained away except for Lisa's coarse breaths. Her tenderised flesh tingled from elbows to knees, and the pronounced thump of her heart shook her chest. The strikes had not been savage but the cumulative effect produced a suffused reddened glow. She had no clue whether Pauline, or someone else, delivered the torment and stared out of her trap but to no avail. During a vast silence, the promise of more to come weakened her self-control. Her tense anticipation mutated to fraught liquid yearning.

The ominous whirring, there on her right. From her left a ferocious series curled up and down, and both sides, raking the fronts of her upper legs followed immediately by her globes. Her mistress wanted to see them dance but Lisa started to panic, and cringed as a rippling fire ignited her belly. 'Ah!'

All movement ceased.

Lisa slumped heavily. Her thorax rose and fell like bellows convulsively, and consciousness zoomed far, then near. The beam revealed angry criss-crossed lines at all angles. As the sharp pangs diminished she gradually calmed, feeling obscurely changed. Her only awareness lodged in her raw nerve endings. The air felt colder, encouraging her nipples to stand erect, and there were disconcerting trickles below. At last she swivelled awkwardly to scan the room. Outside her cage lay only the impenetrable dark.

Her vulnerable stalks, snatched again, revived her to jagged frenzied life. Those snaking thongs, viper tails, were flickering tongues, a lover's bites. Of its own volition her torso leaned into the flames, coiling lazily as if, nurtured by each lash, it savoured the searing embrace. Lisa replied in a garbled mantra, her voice breaking in sobs. Her mistress generated a path through her skin that kindled a deep blaze in her sex, swollen with heat, and the strength of arousal made it easy to ignore the pain. Orgasm crept up from her loins until, with a soaring cry ending in a scream, she collapsed in climax; a rolling, devastating wave.

Shattered by the potency, subsiding in chaos, Lisa indistinctly sensed her body; its throbbing occurred elsewhere, somehow remote. Her captor, her mistress, stepped into the beam, naked but for long leather gloves. From the tips of her fingers and thumbs dangled two whips; ten lengths of toughened fabric. Clearing away the blisters of sweat, she kissed Lisa's slack mouth and faded from view.

A vague figure in slow motion, clothed in a mystifying aura, a hazy corona, examined the complex lattice of bright stripes. The soft pap of Pauline's silky breasts flattened into Lisa's own, provoked and sore. An arm looped her waist to hold her immobile and a foot rested on the slope of one agonised buttock. Lost in their kiss, Lisa scarcely noticed the compact stream of hot fluid splashing her mound, cascading down her thighs and calves to puddle around her toes.

Fourteen

Or perhaps that flow had been of her own making.

The recent incidents had been acute but there were no lingering doubts or regrets. Compared to a man, a woman's demands were reassuring, with giving and receiving in careful balance. Except for the whipping. That, surely, equalled a man's severity. *But I felt so alive!* In a few days she would no longer squirm as the shower's jets pricked the sensitive areas, and the marks she cherished would also recede. In regaining an unblemished state, she would lose the physical reminders but never the memory.

The answering machine contained no messages but Lisa was unconcerned about losing commissions for children's work. Her satisfaction in that field had declined, perhaps beyond revival. A note by the telephone, the award date of the Kate Greenaway medal, gave the only sign of those earlier ambitions.

And for now she needed time to lie fallow. Meandering through days in simple routines she patiently held herself ready for something to happen. She had no idea of what it might be or when it would come. Her instincts, trusted antennae, floated free.

Imperceptibly, over time, an issue emerged: how thin a line divided pleasure from pain, and the mysterious alchemy that converted one into the other. Sometime in the following week she finalised her approach to the subject. On one morning, as the frosty air of dawn pierced her thin robe and the birds competed frenetically for the food she had thrown, her thoughts crystallised and gave her a title. From her wardrobe she excavated a pellet of crumbled clothes. Fitting the sweater she inhaled its odour of mould, and the torn paint-spattered jeans were initially stiff and uncomfortable. These were her student clothes. Then, her sole ambition had been to succeed as a fine artist and it seemed appropriate to wear them now as she embarked on her new specialisation.

Loading a brush with black paint she painted the title on the studio wall: PAIN IS MORE MEMORABLE.

From the bottom of the letters surplus colour dribbled like tears. Emblazoned there, confronting her when she glanced up, the words goaded and spurred her on, inspiring a sequence of drawings and paintings. Spread-eagled in dense gloom she recalled feeling aloof, outside herself, looking at thongs descending eerily from quiet peace. As they landed unexpectedly – thwack! – misshapen animals, ugly birds, sprang from corners, claws unleashed. Pointed beaks snagged her areolae and pecked her teats. Her nerves flew up. They dragged across her boobs and fluid dripped in scorching lines. Impelled by a helpless jolt, a flash of white and a red band behind her eyes, an electric current shrivelled her down to the core. In the unsuspected power, the delirious exultation of that instant, grotesque bats perched on her shoulder.

'The whip's virility . . . it stings in my brain.' And there it stayed, transformed into her own desire.

Later she abandoned the attempt to evaluate. The pictures were so disturbing, their impact pounded her heart. She had lived within a voluptuous nightmare and achieved a new level of intensity; a giant leap into an exotic and erotically visualised world. But even these successes could not subdue her bubbling lasciviousness. Structure and discipline had vanished from her life and she burned continually for fresh exposure. *Am I addicted?*

Repeating an experiment from adolescence, she lay on the floor by her wardrobe mirror and studied her physique dispassionately, as if it belonged to a visitor. To investigate the nuance of curves, her hollows and gradients, she posed in a variety of positions to observe her limbs and their modulations from place to place. Her snowdrift globes re-arranged constantly into new patterns. In a fever dream a dim silhouette hovered above; a female with a luxuriant sable coat to her knees, whose features were her own.

I have a message for you.

As a man, Lisa watched herself widen the fur. An inverted tattooed orchid decorated her belly. It had snaking tendrils on both sides and the arrowed tip came to rest at the top of fleshy lips drooping below her crotch, doubling the invitation.

From the floor the man asked: *What is it?*

Lisa straddled his face, her hips bucking rhythmically. *Read for yourself.*

The man gazed upwards and reached into her, taking his time for a stealthy search in her pliable hole. He delved thoroughly, expanding her passage, and she quivered and gasped. His fingers touched a secret paper hidden there. He pulled it out, into the light. Unfolding a soaking wad, the man discovered ink streaked on the page. Whirling in scent, he deciphered the writing.

The message said –

The words –

Lisa writhed in familiar sweeping waves, jerking against her hand, consumed in the fury.

'Your imagination makes you too easy.'

Hunched over a steaming Colombian, Lisa sat in her kitchen, reflecting miserably that a fanciful vision had led her astray. She had squandered a large portion of Pauline's fee on new clothes but would she ever have an occasion to use them?

The postman's shadow obscured the glass panel of the door. Instead of the usual avalanche of circulars and bills, he summoned her with a loud rap. Outside, he balanced a substantial parcel and held out his pad for a signature.

At the table Lisa tore off the packaging and found the photograph she had admired in Jon Bradley's studio. She rapidly scanned the scrawled letter taped to the edge:

144

Where are you? I've been trying to contact you for weeks. When are you going to join the modern world – a computer, cell phone, e-mails, text messages – stuff like that? Even young kids have them, so why not you? Anyway, you were attracted to this piece so I'm giving it to you as an obvious bribe. Call me. Please!

On her first view of the picture Lisa had been fascinated but now the scene carried greater significance. She had entered that old-fashioned room with Angelique as a partner. The girl's flawless body recalled her adventurous spirit and this, at least, Lisa would have as a souvenir of their intimacy.

In the crush of affairs she had forgotten Jon Bradley, and even the photograph she uncovered at Balmayne. On rereading the note she wondered if she had exaggerated his danger. Twice in the past she resolved to avoid him but he expressed himself with the eagerness, or the naivety, of a boy. If he had sent her the picture he could not be all bad.

But his telephone rang endlessly. She had missed her chance. He would be travelling, gone for months or years –

'Hello.'

'Jon!' Breathless with relief, she resembled an infatuated girl. 'It's Lisa.'

'You're kidding me! I was convinced you'd buried yourself in a convent. One of those Orders that never comes out.'

'Thanks for the photo. I love it. It's going to hang in my bedroom.'

'There's no accounting for taste.'

'Some time ago you promised me a slap-up meal. How about it?'

'Good!' he said. 'What about this evening? I'll send a taxi.' He paused, adding, 'I'll even pre-pay it. See how keen I am?'

That's all it needed to restore her mood, the idea of a good meal in company. The day passed placidly and as the time approached she relished the evening to come. With another artist she could discuss their favourites in technical terms. Who would he support, Picasso or Matisse? 'A non-question,' she murmured. 'He's a male, so it's Mr P.'

The shower's heat lifted her nubs and she smiled at their sensitivity, always willing to respond to any stimulation. At last, perfumed, her make-up complete, she laid on the bed a new scarlet dress and a string brassiere which would allow her nipples to poke through the gaps. The brevity of the dress would show the tops of stockings, advertising a tart. Hardly appropriate for a public restaurant. But tights were too hot and the only solution to remain cool would be bare legs. The toughest decision took a long time. Wear panties or leave them off? Regretfully she concluded they were essential, or her dear pussy would be in peril of display; again inappropriate. As a compensation Lisa chose her finest pair, almost transparent blood-red lace. The mirror confirmed that the bra and panties blended well as fragile barriers, combining adequate function – just – with a hint of transience.

Falling from her shoulders, the shaped bodice of the dress cut low across her bosom to flaunt her globes. The material over her hips and bottom moulded the outline of tempting curves and its hem scarcely screened her panties. As she leaned forward to the glass the skirt rose and a naughty rim of lace peeked out.

The door-bell clanged, announcing the taxi's arrival but the same moment, from the studio, came the telephone's urgent summons. The answering machine picked up Pauline's low tones and Lisa interrupted. 'I'm here,' she said, a throb in her voice.

'I've been missing you.'

'Do you want me?'

'Soon . . . no one takes the whip as well as you. But it must be deferred for now. You're going away for a time, provided you agree.'

'Agree to what?'

'I have a proposal that I believe is feasible, so listen carefully. There is an elusive society with no name, no base, and no formal organisation. Rumours about what goes on have been rife for years. The members come together once a year for an exclusive event – their recent meeting was in Cambodia but they move to a new location annually. Details are controlled by direct verbal communication between the members. It's a true secret society. There have been many attempts to unearth and infiltrate their annual event and I have been one of the most active. This year I've had good luck and may shortly find out when and where it's happening – and you are the perfect choice to be there.'

'Why?'

'To record what they do.'

'Why not send a photographer?'

'Any type of normal recording is strictly forbidden. It's one of the ways they protect themselves.'

'If I can't draw how am I suitable?'

'You have the eyes! Allied to a photographic memory. During the event you must observe all you can and produce the goods on your return.' Pauline hesitated. 'I must be honest with you. For a man it would be impossible to gain entry. But as a woman you can . . . well, merge in.'

That slight uncertainty, something unsaid. 'You mean, join in, don't you?'

'To maintain your credibility you would have to do whatever is necessary.'

In a sudden flare of suspicion Lisa demanded, 'Is this why you sent me to Balmayne?'

'You had to be . . . prepared.'

'Trained!'

'Yes.'

'And you gave me some extra training.'

'Which you enjoyed. Anyway, I thought we shared the opinion that reality is boring. You should not cease to explore.' After a silence Pauline continued, 'There is a further reason why you're ideal. Your imagination is so vivid that, for you, it constitutes actual evidence. Your life fuses with dreams and fantasies, all in one.'

'You may be right, but why is that an advantage?'

'Because it powers your work.'

Wait till you see the latest stuff.

'I can offer you a great deal. First, guaranteed publication. Second, a single volume, all to yourself, of the highest quality. A very large fee. And the opportunity for fame in this specialism, ranked with Bellmer, Beardsley, and others of that select group. Your style is distinctive enough and you have the inestimable asset of female sensibility. I told you how highly we value that.'

Still resentful at being manipulated Lisa weighed up the risks, basically unknown, and set them against these assurances. 'Guaranteed?'

'I have a sponsor with sufficient funds. A long-time collector. I have even invented an apt title – "Exposé".'

All so simple: a 'very large' fee, a publication of high quality, a guarantee. Lisa discarded her doubts. 'OK, I'll do it.'

'I am so relieved! You are the only one with the entire package of skills. We'll discuss the arrangements as soon as I have them.'

'And who is the benevolent sponsor?'

'Mr Johannes.'

The line cut dead. Simultaneously the bell rang out, shredding her nerves. At the door Lisa gestured feebly to the driver, imploring his patience, and slumped onto a chair, fighting for calm. First Johansen, a sneak, whom she had grown to hate. And now Johannes, 'a long-time collector' of erotica, apparently, as well as of children's illustration! Was it he who bound and clamped her before the cane? The two names haunted her equally. 'Why do they keep interfering?' she cried aloud.

Her speculations ended, as always, inconclusively. She had to get away from their influence. The prospect of Pauline's job subdued her anger, at last replaced by vague excitement. In the meantime a good meal in a pleasant environment would provide a useful remedy. She checked the basic items in her tiny bag, no bigger than her palm, and decided to include the photograph to watch as Jon squirmed with embarrassment.

At the end of its brief journey the taxi swung through wrought-iron gates and up the gravelled drive. Lisa had never approached from this direction and the building seemed more imposing than ever. At the main door she stepped out and the car swept away inexplicably. She had assumed it would take them on to the restaurant.

Around her, like a warm cloak, descended the peace of evening dissolving to night.

The instant she rang the bell Jon opened the door and lurched back. 'Wow! You've changed.'

'It's only a new dress.'

'Sure, that's superb. But it's your whole bearing. You're a different person.' He added slyly, 'What have you been up to?'

'Oh, this and that.' Lisa tried an inscrutable smile.

'Here and there?'

'Exactly.'

'Mysterious lady, you may enter.'

In the hall she asked, 'Which restaurant are you taking me to?'

'Well, rather than go out I suggest we eat in.' He glanced anxiously at her stony expression. 'I can see you've made yourself gorgeous but there's no need to look so threatening.'

'A slap-up meal you said, not a snack in the kitchen!'

'Your cynicism is misapplied,' he said primly. 'We'll go to my restaurant.'

'Your what? You own a restaurant? Where is it?'

'In a wing of the house. It's available only to my friends – there are some here now. Despite your scepticism, it operates to the highest standards.'

'Your friends? They must be the visitors the village gossips about.'

'Yes, that could be so.'

'If you swear it's as good as you say, I might be persuaded.'

He grinned. 'Hand on heart.'

Their route led past his studio but it went unnoticed by Lisa, preoccupied by the latest indulgence for wealthy folk to spend money. Each time they met she discovered further facets to Jon Bradley, the successful artist. A short corridor ended at double doors and he stood aside, allowing her to pass.

After a few paces Lisa halted, stunned. In a finely proportioned space the size of a ballroom, glass chandeliers cast patterns onto a painted ceiling. Opposite a wall of French windows a row of huge ornate mirrors bounced the light, supplementing the golden glow of a luxurious carpet. Across the floor a number of dining tables had been widely separated and Jon led the way towards one placed by a window. Outside, in darkness, shimmered the trunks of a cluster of trees, silvered by hidden spotlights in the grass. Awed in spite of her initial reservations, Lisa settled onto a stylish chair cushioned in satin. Three waitresses moved efficiently about their tasks. They were dressed in black skirts with a split up one leg and white blouses of thin material, permitting a view of their breasts' voluptuous sway. A fourth, serving at a table, endured the exploration of a male guest under her skirt though the woman sitting beside him appeared unconcerned. At several tables the women were topless and at one, a man sat with two partners who had both discarded their skirts to sit bare-legged; one pair pale and slim, the second stocky and tawny-skinned. Their stockings rested on the floor and redundant suspender straps hung limply. Lisa felt as if she had slipped, without any warning, into a sensuous world in which no type of behaviour would be condemned, and therefore anything was possible. Again she revised her opinion of Jon who clearly accepted these rules, or even encouraged them.

'Have you ever sat in that way?' He indicated a woman with her skirt bunched at her waist who revealed long thighs and elegant haunches. Her flesh gleamed in the same gold as the room.

'Definitely not!' Lisa emphasised her indignation.

'I've been told it's a great feeling. Can I tempt you to try it?'

'No. Thank you.'

'There is, however, a major consideration . . .'

'Yes?'

'It only works if you're wearing no panties. Are you?'

'Of course!' She sounded decisive but could not help saying mischievously, 'I'm amazed the seats aren't stained.'

'Oh, some of them are. We think of them as souvenirs.'

'Like the panties you stole from me.'

'Yes.'

A waitress, with scraped-back blonde hair, came to their table carrying a bottle and corkscrew. Visible beneath her thin blouse were the bronze discs of her areolae. Holding out the bottle to Jon she said to Lisa, 'He prefers to uncork the wine himself.'

'I enjoy the phallic symbolism of the screw.'

'And the cork's gradual insertion,' the waitress continued.

'Slightly resisting. And that faint squeak at being pierced.'

'Plus the grateful pop as the cork emerges from its tight little hole.'

They both smiled affectionately. Jon returned the uncorked bottle and the waitress filled their glasses, took their orders, and withdrew.

Jon proposed a toast: 'To ravishing Lisa.'

She adopted diversionary tactics. 'Tell me about your recent stuff.'

'The last time we met, you were an ordinarily beautiful woman. But now . . . you have an aura about you. You're radiant.' Lisa remained quiet and tense. 'And I'm certain why.'

'You are?' If he could guess accurately at some profound change in her it might signify that two sides of her nature, normally strictly apart, had started to blend. Worse, that the alteration had begun to show. Discomforted, she gulped her wine.

'My theory is that you've been doing a special commission. So what could it be . . . It's obviously salacious.' Jon paused to reflect. 'A Kama Sutra for teenagers? Or an edition of the Marquis de Sade?'

Lisa put on a sad tone. 'If only. It might pay the bills.'

'At the very least it must be an instruction manual. "Tips for Kids". Am I right?'

This time she laughed out loud. 'Way off.'

'And you're still admitting nothing.' Jon reclined in his chair and sipped his wine, appraising her closely. 'Come on, Lisa.'

He had used that same coaxing technique in the modelling session but Lisa refused to answer. To confess her secret contradicted every inclination as well as the ingrained habit of years. She remembered Pauline's assignment and the title she had given it: and that's what Jon wanted from her now. *Do I dare to expose my true self?* Lisa breathed deeply to steel herself. 'Well ... against my better judgement. It might be classified as ... well, as a series of fantasies.'

Jon's interest suddenly sharpened. 'What sort? Science fiction? Gothic horror?'

Surprised, she mumbled, 'No. They're – um – sexual.'

'I knew it!' he declared triumphantly. 'What a pity you haven't brought a sample, I'd love to see one.'

Lisa sought refuge in the wine. At a nearby table a woman had surrendered her clothes, leaving a cascade of jewellery as the sole adornment between her ripe globes. She had unveiled herself to her escort who examined her with a fixed expression. Lisa wondered how long it would be before he pounced but where would he do it? Not in here surely?

The waitress delivered their meals and Lisa realised that, whatever else Jon might or might not be, his recommendation for the quality of his restaurant and delicious food was justified. She had never eaten better, or in such sumptuous surroundings, in the whole of her life.

'In the absence of a specimen you could describe one.'

Perhaps the accumulation of wine and the room's intimacy seduced her. With only a fleeting trace of regret, Lisa broke the barrier dividing her private and outward lives. She selected an uncomplicated scene that allowed her to wander in reverie, and when he prompted another she improvised freely with additional incidents and lurid depiction. By the time she muddled to a halt, Lisa was struggling to conceal her fervour. Jon sat transfixed, equally inflamed. 'That's very good,' he said. 'Your inventiveness is a marvel.'

She swallowed the contents of her glass. Beyond the window, in the tree's illumination, she caught a pale glimmer: a running woman pursued by a naked man. On the edge of darkness they stumbled to the ground, the man in the fork of her legs. It seemed as illusory as a silent movie but the waitress distracted her. As she bent over the table to top up their drinks, Lisa stared openly at her teats.

'Do you wish to suck them?' At Jon's question the waitress straightened expectantly. Her hand touched the buttons of her blouse, apparently ready to comply.

Lisa could feel how much her own desired that treatment. She blinked and shook her head, attempting to clear her confused thoughts.

'On the first visit you shouldn't rush her,' the waitress said to Jon, and sauntered to her position at the end of the room.

'She's right,' Jon agreed ruefully. 'To compensate for my disappointment, you could explain one more.'

Licentiousness and indulgence on all sides, permitted uncritically, tempted her further. Lisa's example had such vivid suggestiveness that it lured her into the action, and an elaborate graphic account. Abruptly she stopped. Somewhere along the line she had inadvertently blundered from the prudent disguise of 'her' or 'she' into 'I'.

'If I saw you doing that I'd salivate,' Jon said fervently.

'What?' Lisa gave him a look of offended astonishment. 'Acting like the girl in the scene? I'm outraged! It's only a fantasy.'

'So is your outrage,' he replied calmly. 'Come on, Lisa, don't pretend. We both know better.'

Her ploy collapsed. Nursing resentment, she bolted the dregs of wine.

'Let's have our coffee in the conservatory.' As Jon clambered to his feet he collected the bottle. 'And we might as well take this to finish off.'

Lisa passed the waitress who grinned sympathetically, as if she predicted what would happen next. In the glass-panelled comfortable space groups sat in scattered chairs and many of the women were undressed. The situation recalled the photographs at Balmayne, and the one in her purse. Jon led her to a vacant corner where they sat facing each other across a low table.

A different waitress came towards them. She wore the same blouse as those in the restaurant but had chosen to accompany it with a startling skirt and no panties. At the rear the skirt trailed to a respectable length but the front had been cut away and soared to her hips, framing a large triangle of magnificent and lustrous curls. Lisa gave in to a surge of envy. In contrast to her own decision, the woman retained her proud bush and quite correctly favoured a daring costume to display it. As the waitress stooped to pour their coffee her pendulous bosom swooped forward, trembling in small alluring upheavals. *Do I dare?* On the point of accepting the offer Lisa heard a strand of music with a characteristic driving beat, and the reminder of her own striptease swamped the notion of a risky experiment.

A woman with eyes of liquid crystal strolled through the room. Sleek and poised, she glided to a central table and rested onto her elbows, entirely relaxed as the focus of all attention. *Susan – a suitably posh name.* The man who followed her raised her dress high on her back and tugged her panties which fell in a froth of white lace to her ankles. Susan shuffled them off and parted her legs. As the man unfastened his trousers, a livid bloated tool slumped from his fly. Lisa spotted the exact moment it slid into her slippery channel, as wet as her own, in Susan's breathless smile.

At last Lisa recognised the operating principle governing the conduct around her. The guests, without inhibition, shared their own pleasures generously for everyone else to enjoy.

'You're hiding it well.'

'Hiding what?'

'You appear unshocked. You really have changed.' Jon surveyed her coolly. 'I suspect you've only told me some of the story. You have more goodies to tell.'

From her bag Lisa pulled a scrap of paper. She laid the photograph on the table and kept him guessing, ostentatiously pressing it flat. 'You've been to Balmayne of course.' She spoke casually but glanced up quickly to catch the instinctive reflex betraying the truth.

'What's that?' Jon's blank features revealed nothing.

'I found this at Balmayne.' Lisa revolved the image and searched him again for a sign of guilt.

Jon peered among the maze of creases. 'Must have been taken a long time ago.' She could see him testing versions of a cover-up story. 'What did you think?'

'You don't deny that it's you?'

'Oh it's certainly me. And this is Betty – a great girl, up for anything! We staged this little tableau at an art college dinner. Its theme, if I remember accurately, was sadomasochism.'

Liar. 'How did it get to Balmayne?'

'Whatever that is. Perhaps Betty was responsible.'

Liar. 'That picture you sent me – that was also shot at Balmayne. You said Venice.'

Jon shrugged negligently. 'A friend gave it to me.' *Liar.* 'It's such a bizarre thing that I never cared for it. But I'm glad you do.'

During a barbed silence Lisa drained the last of her coffee and for a while drew into herself. Ecstatic sighs attracted her to Susan who had lost her demure composure and strained on the verge of her come. Lisa observed her with the tolerance, evident here too, that she had valued at Balmayne. In the same spirit she gave up her intention to hound Jon for an answer. Let him have his secrets; she still had a few of her own.

'Let me show you the house.' Jon picked up the bottle to lead the way and Lisa abandoned the photograph on the table. As they passed, he patted Susan familiarly, making Lisa absurdly jealous. In the adjacent room they discovered not one, but a pair of strippers, dancing fluently to a circle of men. Lisa noticed immediately the advantage they had over the single practitioner. Writhing their tits and bellies together, they exchanged the oil on their skins,

155

enticing each other to a jittery state. And when the time came they would need no inducement from the men to go all the way. Lisa flushed, unsure if she preferred watching them or being watched herself. She had the confidence and ability to rouse them all with her power. If only she had the chance!

Jon led her to doors on the far wall and into a hallway at the foot of a broad staircase. 'Up we go.'

Lisa started, aware that he would study the swaying hem of her flimsy skirt. It lightly fondled her cheeks and disclosed her panties, as she knew it would. The pear-shapes of her sweet derrière swivelled sinuously from side to side. An elderly couple descended, the woman silver-haired and unclothed, holding the man's drooping organ. Unconcerned by her slack flesh – *Silver-haired Sylvia* – gave a friendly nod. Distracted, Lisa did not at first heed the touch on her waist and resumed her climb. As the contact shifted onto her mound she tensed and grasped the banister, floundering with shorter steps. Under her skirt a commanding grip on her pudenda's bulge brought her to a stop, hunched on the rail. She remained trapped, tremors rippling her spine as Jon, mumbling incoherently, kissed the nape of her neck. Her own hand rotated strenuously, using his fingers to excite herself and ease the ache, forced onto a rigid bar within her buttock cleft. The two pressures partially quelled her burning desire but at the inescapable thought of sexual control, seeping moisture tingled her loins. Struggling to oppose him, she staggered up the final stairs to a landing.

Jon placed the bottle on the floor and inclined comfort-ably onto the banister. The obvious lump in his groin emphasised a demand that required no explanation.

Confronted by his authority, Lisa melted. So many examples on this curious evening, when she had crossed her own inviolable boundaries, had prepared her for this invitation. It seemed irresistible and so right that she could now contribute to the hedonistic mood. She knelt and rested on his erection: *Stone-hard.* Above her, he loosened his belt. Teasing herself, she gently nipped through the fabric shield, then unzipped his fly and dropped his trousers. Dizzily, in the odour of musk, she examined the stiff root emerging out of a straggly mass of pubic hair. She would possess this sight constantly, in her memory, and loved the foreskin's docile acquiescence, creeping away, pliable as the folds of her own dear pussy. She noted the contours of veins mottling the shaft; the firm ridge extending to his balls; the compact velvet plum and its flanged rim; the narrow incision that would deliver his gushing cream. Experimentally she flicked the undulations of the curves beneath and drove onto the mushroom cap that fitted her cavity perfectly. Emulating Imogen, she glided inwards, jaws wide, striving to gobble every fraction, and on the reverse she tightened to provide suction. Sometimes she adhered like a limpet but only to the slope of the crown and occasionally she tantalised the rod by slapping it onto her tongue, or pumped vigorously to jerk his testicles. Hungry again for the dark fruit, she guzzled on its fat knob, and disregarded comments from passers-by to concentrate on the task. At any moment the eager flood of emissions would –

A man's voice crawled in her ear. 'Your boobs should be out.'

Of course, just as it should be.

He prised Lisa's fist from the stem and straightened her arms to the side but she denied any further attempt to give up her prize. Her zip rasped and the dress pushed off her shoulders onto her hips. He tweaked her nipples which clenched spontaneously, projecting like studs through the gaps in her bra, until the clasp unsnapped and her breasts spilled in a swift lurch, a heavy thump. The dominating wedge nudged the rear of her throat but she maintained her posture, arms lowered and lewdly gratified at performing well; patient, even when fully plugged.

The voice rumbled, 'We're all impressed by your dedication in serving a strict cock.'

It's made for my penetration.

Motionless in a pose she relished, she heard the approving babble of guests. Used by the two men – the immobile bulk of one and the second's roaming caresses lifting, moulding and pinching her teats – she reconstructed the man as the taxi driver who had pawed Imogen. The penis muffled Lisa's panting as she did her best to polish the bulbous apex clogging her mouth.

'Now continue.'

Rapturously she resumed, avid to receive her reward. Easing to and fro she glanced up at Jon's taut features. Stifled by his girth, her low moans registered yearning for the rich food. It arrived suddenly in explosions of hot sperm and some of the abundant globs of viscous fluid trickled out but she held on tenaciously. Seasoned with his taste, she lapped the crown shining with her saliva, while the glans abated gradually to a well-mannered condition.

Hoisting his trousers, Jon said, 'You're very good.'

As Lisa stood up, her dress slid to the floor and she kissed him passionately, appreciating the soft resilience of his lips compared to his iron pole. Separating, she raised her arms for the sheer thrill of allowing her panties to outline her pouch.

'Drape yourself on the rail.'

Gazing down on foreshortened people, she wondered what he would do. She associated the position with spanking but surely not here, in public? He read her mind and muttered, 'It's worthy of a smacking.' On the left, and on the right, Jon's teeth dragged off her panties little by little as far as her knees. A wicked urge prompted her to stick out her rump provocatively, presenting the whole expanse which deserved his admiration.

'Shaving suits you.' His words warmed the area. 'You're completely erotic.'

Lisa visualised her genitals as resembling his drawing, a lurid exotic flower with her syrupy labia peeled open, dilated to huge proportions.

His stimulation, electrically charged, explored her crevice. Roused frantically, she squirmed against him to encourage his access. Wet licks on her bare pleats drifted up to her anus and the tip, boring into the orifice, infected her brain with a scandalous thought she had always rejected – how would it feel? – but despite her own quaking lust the muscle tightened instinctively. He pulled away and she turned to face him.

Jon devoured the view of her nude pudenda. 'I only wish you'd asked me to shave it off,' he said wistfully.

'I didn't think of asking you at the time.' But she did understand him, recalling her own delight at her mistress's order.

'I could have kept a piece as a souvenir.'

He's obsessed with souvenirs. But this one Lisa accepted. 'Next time, perhaps?'

'Let it grow out – I enjoy hacking at a big bush. And there's something else my eagle eye's spotted. You're relaxed when naked, more than you were in the modelling session. Also –' he paused to weigh up a new accusation '– you had no objection to a stranger handling your tits. What have you actually been up to? It must be way beyond extra work.'

She lost her shoes as Jon towed her up a new flight of stairs and she noticed her clothes strewn on the landing, discarded as carelessly as her own secrets. At the frank inspection of a strolling couple she preened her nudity, tumescent and proud. Mounting to the top of the stairs, they passed an open door and Lisa hung back, enthralled by a hushed scene. A standing woman leaned over a seated man. She gripped his shoulders and groaned steadily as he screwed a long dildo up into her belly. The man continued, ignoring the silent observation framed in the doorway. At a quiet command, the woman straightened and walked in a dazed wavering line towards Lisa. Fascinated, Lisa absorbed the tube flapping and swaying. The woman's thighs bowed awkwardly to accommodate its size and she tried to prevent it from falling out by clenching her muscles. She appeared as a lovely vision who –'Come on!'

Lisa responded to Jon's impatient tug on her arm. She had been intoxicated to see a display similar to her own experience at Balmayne. So that's how she looked to her audience!

Jon steered her into a room with a massive double bed. Lisa adored its lavish brocade and the glittering brass bars at its head, but then she did an involuntary double-take: velvet wristbands dangled at the sides. Into her mind flashed Jon's drawing showing her clad in striped stockings. These flagrant ties confirmed the belief that he wanted to bind her, but the idea no longer worried her as it once had.

After swigs of the wine, Jon offered a drink to Lisa. She declined and he placed the bottle in the centre of the floor. Sitting on the bed some distance away he murmured casually, 'Squat on that.'

Stupefied, she stared at him. 'You mean . . .?'

'Yes, that's what I mean.'

The slim taper glinted seductively. Totally dormant, but utterly poised, it almost beckoned. She dithered breathlessly, finely balanced between the enticement and flat refusal.

'Would it help if I mentioned that it's a private game, solely for us?'

A private game?

As Lisa considered the notion a telltale twitch betrayed her body's decision. She obeyed the impulse and straddled the bottle, and deliberately confronted Jon. Gazing down on the neck, a colossal dildo pointed suggestively up at her crotch. Below the hole, rippling amber clinched her fate. Inflamed, she began to lower herself.

Triumphantly Jon sprang from the bed and located a stool behind her. 'You can hold onto that,' he said. From the bed he watched intently.

The narrow vertical neck and the ruffled wine; his fixed fervent attention. Lisa grasped the stool for essential support and the first touch of the damp rim chilled her outer membranes. A bold shape nestled inside and she rotated delicately, expanding her folds, descending cautiously. The neck settled deeper and Lisa panted. She had never done anything so perfectly crude and the fact excited her. As she levered high her spine arched and she emitted a loud gasp at the subsequent plunge. At the lowest extremity, when the slope precluded more depth, her vagina disclosed its full elastic stretch.

'That's a sight I won't forget,' Jon purred.

Her movements quickened, floating and slumping her breasts in natural waves. She gabbled in the midst of a potent compound of humiliation and rapture. One heave lifted the bottle clear of the floor and for an instant it hung suspended in space until her next lunge drove the rigid cone to the hilt. Crazed, she carried on relentlessly but during the pumping her own fluid burst out in unstoppable streams. She froze and whimpered pathetically, mortified by the gurgles and raucous splashes into the wine, leaking around the brink.

'Yes!' Jon blazed ecstatically as he leapt off the bed and pushed Lisa onto the floor. She lay supine as the bottle tilted and the stinging contents surged in and out again. In rapidly changing sensations she struggled with shame as the mixture bubbled and tickled her anus, and ran underneath to drench the carpet.

Jon hoisted her ankles and raised the bottle, cascaded wine internally, and tugged out for the last spurts to flavour her pubes. His lips pressed her labia, feverishly hot and already parted. Her drizzle breached the opening and spilled out to his avid mouth. An expert tongue reamed her passage, persisting over her erect and tingling bud, extracting one orgasm after another while she quivered and moaned, defenceless against him.

In the shower, her sex swollen from furious sucking, Lisa snuggled gratefully to the man who had licked her clean and rewarded him by smearing his chest with the clinging soap on her paps. Detaching the spray, he washed her as she twisted lazily, glistening like a seal. He instructed her to lean on the wall, held one of her legs high, and played the jets on her sensitive perineum, subtly caressing the bridge of her two apertures. 'That's wonderful,' she whispered, writhing luxuriantly on the upward force. The consoling warmth converted to needles of ice, and she bucked and yelled, contorting in the biting glacial flow. At last, when the water stabilised, she collapsed, laughing but shaken. 'For that you should dry me. I need to be pampered.'

Later, on the bed, she asked, 'What will you do about that stain on the carpet?'

'Maybe nothing,' Jon said. 'I may keep it as a souvenir of the time you revealed how far you'll go. You constantly surprise me.'

'And you surprise me. You must have tasted my . . .'

'Your piss. An extra flavour.'

'Have you done that often?' she asked, shuddering at a sharp image of repeating the whole subversive act.

Jon hoisted onto one elbow and peered at her closely, judging her reaction. 'I might, from now on. We're going to meet regularly.'

'Is that what these are for?' She gestured to the fabric loops, bonds of confinement, which recalled a collection of implements laid on a table.

'For you? Not really. They require a lot of trust and you don't trust me enough – not yet. But that will alter, in time.'

'*You either trust me or you don't.*'

Who did trust Jon? One, or perhaps many, of the women in the restaurant? Lisa could see the elderly woman who had passed on the stairs – Sylvia – naked and available, tied by the wrists. At the sides of her rib-cage heavy nipple clamps dragged her bulbs abnormally low. In the fork of her legs drooped a dull red fig with a rich smell of mature wine. Lisa manoeuvred the fat vibrator and felt the soft tissues give way, unable to resist –

'What's the matter?' Jon asked curiously.

Lisa's guilt burned on her face and she blurted hastily, 'We can't meet at all, just yet.'

'Why? Don't tell me you're going away. You've only just returned! For how long?'

'I don't know.'

'Where are you going?'

'I don't know that either.'

'What do you know?'

'It's a special commission. It could be important to me.'

'A children's story? Or one of the naughty kinds?'

Lisa wriggled uncomfortably. 'I don't want to talk about it.' To distract him from more questions she fitted her lips to his flaccid glans – her cock, the one she would own – to start the delectable process again.

'Wait.' Jon rolled away, retrieved the bottle from the floor, and held it to the light. Through the shaded glass the last liquid shivered at the bottom. Upending the bottle, he slopped the contents onto his groin. 'Now carry on.'

Taking the limp tube, Lisa's nose immersed in a complex aroma rising up from the saturated hair. She savoured the scent for what it might contain and delayed the task for her own contentment, satisfied only when she could wait no more for the stiffened penis, rampant and ready.

'You're very persuasive. Turn over.'

Her bosom crushed into the counterpane and she cradled her head in her arms, vaguely aware of her own mounting desire. He demanded further spread and she waited obediently, shifting position to clutch the bars. As he began to stroke her butt and into the cleft Lisa stirred, breathing silently, her flesh yielding but searching too for his confident palm. He moved decisively to the target they both coveted but the muscle shrank involuntarily, protecting itself from violation.

'No one's had you here,' Jon muttered approvingly. 'Relax. You're going to enjoy it.' He inserted patiently and rotated gently to and fro.

In a wave of consternation, Lisa recollected Marion's yawning orifice. Would she have to pay the same price for surrendering her last virginity? As the finger reached its full extent she quivered, excited despite her anxiety. The obstruction circled, prodded, fluctuated, gripping her entire consciousness. Gel smothered her sphincter before it stretched at opposite sides. Paired digits pierced her sex just as a straight thumb enlarged her more reluctant hole and worked in both places at the same time. Capitulating to his appetite Lisa answered each thrust with a muffled groan.

Increasing the lubrication, rigorous rods drilled her again, in and out of their rightful homes. Their opposed, uneven rhythm generated a seething furnace. Sick with apprehension, she thought she might faint at any second even though she pushed back. By the time his preparation came to an end, demented by her own lust, she needed a thick shaft plundering that vital canal.

The weight of his body settled along her spine. Exactly centred, a blunt cap with no mercy shoved her hard into the bed. The pressure did not ease away, or even cease momentarily, and would never retreat. The insistent girth distended her gradually, coercing her into a different world. Above, he grunted, and she grabbed the bars, rocking in wild-eyed desperation until a final rending lunge. Impossibly strained by inflexible bulk, Lisa cried out wretchedly: *I'm splitting in two!*

Penetrated by a mass of rigid heat, familiar motions were bizarre sensations. Her taut ring precisely matched the circular pole and its rim of pain contrasted with the stimulation further within. Her loud staccato yells registered every emphatic plunge as his testicles smacked her labia and thrilling jolts shot to her clit. Her tender horn chafed unbearably onto the bed and propelled her into a vast space. The tight vigorous member, shunting in and out, fused them together far more powerfully than in her vagina. This was a unique deviation in quality, a truly profound manipulation. Wonderful friction and potency compensated for the loss of her climax. Keening and whining, she craved the first male gifts deep in her rectum and the pulsing organ gratified her carnally, shooting its semen in long spurts, making her whole.

Fifteen

It used to be called the fundament. *And fundamental is the only word to describe it*. The ravishing Lisa endured had lingered for days.

At the end Jon told her to squat in front of a mirror, knees apart, studying her battered pussy which revealed the inner membranes raw as a gaping wound. Globs and bubbles of spunk nestled in the folds and clogged her entrances. At the time she had been appalled at the sight and now wished she could erase the memory. And not only the sight, but erase his words too.

As the taxi arrived at the door he murmured, 'You took it well.'

'Took what?'

'You like it – being fucked in the arse.'

Incensed by his coarseness, her cheeks flaming, she fled from the house. At the end of this assignment, if they did meet again, she would have to find ways to guide his hunger.

From the window Lisa watched miniature boats scattered on the silvery lagoon far below but the distant islands of Burano and Torcello were lost in a haze of blue. As the aircraft banked for its descent into Marco Polo Airport she checked her bag for the extra items: the map, a black card with an intricate embossed logo in gold and royal-blue bearing her name – Yvonne von Guilliem – and a cell-phone that Pauline had insisted she carry. 'The event is happening in Venice but that's all I have,' she reported.

'You must get there immediately. And stay in contact as long you can, so keep the phone charged and switched on at all times.'

Tiresome airport formalities ran their course and at last Lisa, in a straggle of passengers, stepped onto the water bus. After crossing the northern fringes of the lagoon it entered the serpentine waterway of the Grand Canal and shortly came to the 'classic' section where, as in a fantasy film set, palaces emerged on both sides. Lisa remembered them from the time when, as an impoverished art student, she had come here, sleeping rough, to visit the Biennale. The boat chugged noisily, and zig-zagged from one bank of the canal to the other, avoiding gaggles of boats from all directions. Once, in a cluster of gondolas, the boatmen serenaded their customers with an impromptu aria. Smiling, she gazed eagerly at past glories in the faded bones of the Ca' d'Oro, House of Gold; the painted façade of Contorini Dal Zaffo; the Foscari palace – a compact jewel – and on to the central square of the city, Piazza San Marco. Beyond the exotic tapestry, the wide expanse and air of the lagoon came as a relief from the confined canal, and her journey finished at the far end of the city, at the Arsenale landing.

In a small pine wood, a park at the water's edge, she relished the sun's heat tempered by a cool breeze from the sea. Using Pauline's map, she navigated the route to a rented apartment, twisting through old streets with high strings of flapping linen in the gap between tall buildings. After a difficult hunt of unmarked doors Lisa eventually found the apartment of three rooms with discreet modern furnishings. There, in a garden of grass and spindly shrubs, she sat, in quiet dying light, for her evening meal.

If she received no phone call she had the freedom to do what she wanted, so she spent the next day in the city pursuing a few of the tourist trails. On the regular boat she travelled up the canal to the Rialto bridge and dawdled the length of the Merceria, drained by humidity in the midday sun and held in a winding human river. They all spilled out into San Marco where she stopped for coffee and cake at the Caffe Florian. To hell with the expense – her 'very large' fee would pay for indulgence. From the tall elegant Campanile she looked across the myriad rooftops of the city, spread over its hundred islands; and the pink and white confection of the Doge's Palace with, below, a bank of gondolas rocking at distinctive mooring poles, striped in red and white. That evening, glutted visually, she sampled the seafood at an outdoor restaurant in her local area.

Lisa hoped the phone's continued silence meant that Pauline's best efforts had, once again, been thwarted. Substituting the incredible opportunity for her forfeited holiday, she returned to the city on the second day to draw the famous views. The patterns and colours seduced her: the burned reds of some buildings and the delicate beige tracery of Gothic stonework. Sitting for hours, shaded from unrelenting sun, she filled so many pages with meticulous sketches that she had to buy a fresh pad bound in marbled covers.

On the morning of the third day she conscientiously tested the phone. From London Kim answered to say that news could be expected at any time and advised her to remain close. Lisa strolled to the wooded park where shadows of tree trunks etched the gravelled paths in bands of blue-grey. Standing on the lagoon's brim she could see, two miles away on her right, the arrowed Campanile. To her left the low hump of the Lido formed the horizon. A group of mothers were talking while their children romped, and Lisa spotted a book with a familiar illustration on the front – *L'Avventura de Tommaso* – her very own Thomas Tadpole. The character recalled a different and more innocent life now abandoned, perhaps forever.

Later that day, wearied by too much meddling with drawings, she wandered into the garden and casually examined a sparse assortment of half-dead plants. Through the tall leafage of scrawny shrubs she noticed a bright gleam from reflective glass and behind them discovered a bawdy phallus, two feet tall, balanced on a pair of enormous balls and curving upwards to a spade-shaped head. Transparent at the tip, emerald green swirled along the stem and darkened to a bloody red in the bulbous sac with black at the base: the lurid, typical style of Murano production. Lisa fondled the silky-smooth crown and her hand traced its slit, a narrow indentation. During a cheerful masturbation her fingers barely touched around the shaft until, shuddering in hot prickly tension, she imagined the sculpture as a giant dildo, cold and hard, dilating her warm pleats.

Her mind whirled. What else might be here? She left the inert object to explore the apartment. In the main room she halted and focused, whittling down into herself, rotating slowly. Ornaments. Paperback books of no merit. Framed pictures from which nothing of interest could be gleaned. A pile of tourist leaflets. Her gaze lifted to an upper shelf – and the border of a thin card poking from a book. The angle, a tantalising lack of placement in the neat and tidy room, attracted her magnetically. Reaching up, she tugged out a postcard showing a photograph of industrial buildings. The inscription read: *Witwatersrand Gold Mine, Transvaal Province.* This must be a joke. Deflated, and feeling vaguely cheated, Lisa wondered who would send such a boring card. She flipped to the reverse, hoping it might contain a clue, but the space for a message was blank. At the bottom, a single line of print: GREETINGS FROM JOHANNESBURG S. A.

S. A. – South Africa. Miss Gibbs said Johannes came from there.

The air dimmed and hushed. 'My name does begin with a J' echoed in Lisa's brain. As she began to forge a link a strange weight burdened her shoulders. 'Johannesburg – Johannes – Johansen –'

Beside her the cell phone shrieked, causing her to jump in shock and fumble to kill it.

'Tonight!' Pauline shouted. 'It starts tonight.'

The news shattered Lisa's peaceful interlude. Now her promise compelled her to accept whatever consequences might come.

'Here's the address.'

In a daze of uncertainty tinged by fear Lisa wrote the details. 'What is it, a house?'

168

Pauline laughed. 'It's a genuine sixteenth-century palace. I only hope for your sake it has modern plumbing. Now, listen. Without your entry card you have no chance. Apparently each one is numbered but it's only revealed by infra-red.'

'Don't worry, it's safe.'

'You must get there between ten and ten-thirty. After that no one gets in or out. Give them your card for analysis. If you get in they will search you.'

'Why?'

'For a bug, a miniature camera, anything that might be remotely operated.' Pauline's hectic excitement changed to concern. 'Are you OK?'

'I'm fine.'

'Will you be safe?'

'Why wouldn't I? If they find that I'm an impostor the worst they can do is to throw me out.' A sense of unease disturbed Lisa's blithe confidence. '*Stay in contact as long as you can.*'

'I'm sure that's true,' Pauline agreed.

'Have you told me everything? Is there any danger?'

'They're so secretive. How determined are they to protect themselves? Just be careful, and call me as soon as you're out. Oh, by the way, you'll be pleased to hear that I'm buying the latest drawings, the ones that came from your whipping. The effect it had on you – I'm still shaken. Did you enjoy our recent session?'

'Very much.'

'So did Janine and Kim.' Pauline stopped for a moment. 'I envy you, being so near to them.'

Lisa smothered the intervening hours in a mute routine, bathing scrupulously and shaving her entire body to present herself as perfectly as nature permitted. She applied perfume and make-up, and wore her usual clothes. Studying the map, she found the address in the Dorsoduro district, five stages up the Grand Canal, where a series of winding streets led on from the Accademia station. Inspecting her vital identification, the logo's interlocked lines and sombre hues conveyed an authority that affected her with stabs of anxiety alternating with giddiness. She put the map and card with some money into her bag but left out the phone.

At last, sitting quietly, she resumed her speculations about the events that had occurred since, in her agent's office, the first communication arrived. That lure to the Cross Street cinema seemed so long ago. Lisa had believed that Pauline must be responsible because she had made herself known and given instructions. Actually, a more nebulous person lurked in the background. Lisa's heart thumped as she repeated the broken chain. 'Johannesburg – Johannes – Johansen –' and concluded '– Jon!'

It all fitted. Jon: an arch voyeur and a master of manipulation. And he had gloated about Cambodia – its fabulous landscapes etcetera – where, according to Pauline, the group last met.

She remembered his words: 'You've always been a rebel pretending to be a conformist.' He had uncovered her hidden life and played an elaborate game. The sequence of episodes – notes, dares she could not refuse, and the false information – had kept her arousal high, influencing her consciousness. *He understands the art of timing surprises.* She had glimpsed a new side to him in the photograph from Balmayne but, by then, he had already decided to open it up, with the visit to his house. He had also shown himself to be a consummate actor, asking about her affairs yet acquainted with all the details – including those she had not mentioned. But why, having supervised her development, did he now want her to realise his central role? It must be a liberation, allowing her to float free and make her own unhindered choices.

She settled onto the approaching task: observe and memorise. *Exposé.* A good title. She would draw them, quite literally, out of the shadows. And as for her own challenge –

Lisa glanced at the clock. Time to go.

During the journey, isolated from all activity, she sat within a transparent dome, only faintly aware of the boat's jarring vibrations and heavy impacts at landing platforms; or the crew, securing and casting-off with practised fluency; or the tides of chattering couples going to a theatre, restaurant, or home; ordinary incidents on an ordinary day. She, in stark contrast, voyaged in the other direction, into unfamiliar territory.

At the Accademia station she disembarked, moving like an automaton. The boat pulled into the Canal, dulling the raucous power of its engine. Lisa's fellow passengers hurried away until she stood alone in the final rinsed colours of the day. A rusting chipped sign on a crumbling wall confirmed the route and for a while she took comfort from the blossoms in window boxes, or the peeling paint on a wrought-iron grill. These simple conventional things anchored her to reality. The light modulated. Sounds faded to whispers, emphasised by the clatter of her shoes. Blank stone façades closed around her. Her loud strides carried her into an older vicinity, disconnected from tourist Venice, and back in time to an earlier age. This had always been a city of secrets that sealed its inhabitants in seclusion and mystery, giving no hint of what lay disguised by the outer doors. The occasional smell of laurel leaves drifted from concealed gardens. Turning a corner, she immediately lost herself and checked the map by a street lamp, its missing glass pane shedding a yellow glow. A tinny bell chimed steadily as if summoning her to Angelus. On the walls of a narrow alley her distorted profile sidled over flaking brick and a solitary star blazed in the blue-black rectangle of the sky. The air chilled.

Halfway along the alley she passed a plain unvarnished door with no outer handle and a panel barred by an iron grill. Treading cautiously, her skin prickled. A projecting buttress offered sanctuary and she hid behind it, paralysed at going into a situation with no idea of what to expect. *For every experience there's a price to pay*. What would she do if things went wrong?

She heard footsteps, much quieter than her own, and squinted beyond the obstruction at a muffled figure who knocked at the door. The bars of the grill brightened, an object was transferred and the light snapped off, plunging the figure to invisibility. There came a period of empty suspense followed by a dull thud and harsh scrape, and a spilling yellow band. A silhouette squeezed through the gap and the door shut instantly, evoking a victim trapped and swallowed. In the restored darkness, more dense after the brief illumination, Lisa struggled to view her watch. Five minutes to the deadline. She tried to think clearly about this venture as a great opportunity that many might covet, regardless of risk. Surely, the chance to learn many things and establish her credentials in a new field of specialist work, was sufficient inducement? *OK – so what is my plan?*

Two minutes.

Clasping her courage, Lisa murmured, 'My plan is . . . whatever happens.' Urgently she strode to the door and rapped hard. The clamour died away but the grill stayed shut and she began to panic; her watch must be wrong and she had left it too late. She failed to notice the spreading rays but then fumbled her card into the grill, trembling, a flush burning her cheeks. The beam cut out and she waited, frozen, in limbo. They would be testing her card but the delay caused her heart to drum, and she could not suppress her turbulent waves of emotion.

Thudding and scraping, the door parted, scarcely wide enough. Absurdly grateful, she wriggled past but before she had time to see anything the light switched off.

'Your name is Yvonne von Guilliem?'

'Yes.'

'Are you here of your own free will?'

Perplexed by the question, Lisa floundered. What? Ridiculous! That could not be true.

'Answer! Are you here of your own free will?'

'Yes.' The word ejected spontaneously, a speeding bullet destroying pretence. With the startling revelation her fear, kept at bay all afternoon, drained away. Her ribs unlocked and she breathed easily, the air infused by a jasmine scent.

People, mere shapes, surrounded her. One snatched her bag and a second removed her coat. With no words of explanation alien hands ranged her body, detaching her clothing piece by piece. Unresisting, she recalled a fantasy, of being stripped by a gang of helpers but this, an efficient and impersonal search, contained no eroticism. They pawed at her flesh for gratuitous pleasure. Nevertheless, it had an extraordinary effect and Lisa adjusted innocently to each forfeited garment, even to endure the coarse probing between her legs. She knew their purpose but her moisture leaked as if rewarding them. When the examination – *Initiation?* – came to an end someone fitted a pair of ornate Turkish slippers, of baby-soft leather.

'There.' An outline pointed across a courtyard, to a carved stone entrance.

Released from clothing, calm in her mind, Lisa passed a splashing fountain – a boy riding a leaping dolphin – into a blackened building pervaded with the smell of perfumed dust and dried flowers. She paused uncertainly, inhaling the sweet and agreeable fragrance. Noiselessly a ribbon of tiny lamps on the floor lit up to clarify a dim path stretching far ahead into obsidian dark. On either side, glittering red and silver objects conveyed an atmosphere, a lascivious aura. Only the faint scuff of her slippers broke the stillness as she progressed further, ever deeper into her natural place. It was here. She could sense, though not conceive what 'it' might be, on the tingling surface of her skin.

She arrived at doors standing ajar. Within, a beam from above enclosed a passive tableau of naked women sitting in a curve on spindly gilt chairs. As Lisa crossed the space silent interrogations measured all her proportions but did not disturb her tranquil mood. Nearby were two unoccupied chairs, somehow ominous. Why were they –

A bell chimed once, decisively, signalling an end or something about to begin.

Lisa sat on a plush brocade cushion and surreptitiously returned the inspections. Opposite sat a pure African with a broad flat nose and flaring lips: a magnificent Amazonian warrior. Her hair had been straightened and smoothed. Huge flamboyant earrings touched her densely tattooed shoulders and matched the rings on her fingers and thumbs. To her right sat a glossy coffee-coloured Arab, with lustrous brown areolae. The intensity of her gaze transmitted a shrewd intelligence. Next, a Slav with chiselled features, a voluptuous mouth and hooded eyes, all framed by cropped strawberry-blonde hair. Below, slumbered her ruby-tipped breasts. Another woman, whose appearance suggested a Mexican or a Cuban, poised and inaccessibly remote, had long raven hair. Beside her the next olive face showed no trace of imperfection. Her oval eyes had a sullen hint of Asia and a sleek feline quality revealed itself in languorous grace. Her mouth puckered in a strange half-smile as if she had begun to consider tempting behaviour. Then came a Spanish or Italian woman. Statuesque and proud, she had an insolent beauty, burgundy lipstick, and a dangerous glinting expression. Her pubic thatch had almost the same copper hue as her skin. In contrast, a Japanese girl had jet-black hair, short-cropped, and eyelids and lips painted in silver. Demure and reticent, she gave no clue of what she could be thinking about. Lisa passed on to a Caribbean mulatto with immense black pupils, enviably self-assured. Her striking figure, robust as a man's, was so taut and sinewy-muscled that she could have been carved from a block of wood. Her large arrogant nipples were turgid; stiff and erect with excitement. Last came an extremely white, freckled girl, perhaps Irish. She had a delicate glamour, eyes green as glass, and a mane of thick red hair scooped in a ponytail. With a small firm bust, her pubic hair glowed reddish blond, abundantly curled on her mound but trimmed neatly to edge her slit.

Why had they come here and for what did they hope? Were they all, in a similar way to Lisa, living an alternative life?

Despite her buoyant spirits she wondered why the organisers, whoever they were, wanted everything to be on display. None of the women collected here could pretend to charms they did not possess. Perhaps the men did not care for the refined skills of seduction. If so that would be disappointing, as a loss to the women of their feminine

174

wiles, and also a distinct creative failure. Lisa began to speculate. How would she, if given the task, construct a session like this? Perhaps –

'Welcome to you all.'

A low voice reverberated out of nowhere; from no discernible spot.

'We shall conduct ourselves by simple rules. Whoever you happen to meet at mealtimes is a friend, equal in status. At night we sleep alone unless you ask for company. Third, ignore events in which you have no part – they are nothing to do with you. Finally, remember that you have two currencies. The first is your body, already given to our stewards, and the second is your imagination.' The voice paused, giving them time to digest the instructions. 'Banish all inhibitions. Accept the opportunities of this special occasion. Our time together will, perhaps, prove to be unique in your lives. So, when you are required to present yourselves for auction, do not hesitate.

'The member of our community who outbids the rest is the one who, among us all, treasures you most. He becomes your mentor and has the authority to regulate your actions day by day. He may take you at any time and in any way he chooses, or give you away. If you disobey our rules you may compel him, regretfully, to change his role – from mentor to master.'

Lisa stirred with interest. They were being introduced to a theatre of enticements coupled with prohibitions. The two combined to ignite her senses.

'Forget your past. All you need you will find here . . . Now, walk around your chairs in a circle.'

By unspoken agreement the women started anti-clock-wise, moving sedately. But in this manner they emulated polite schoolgirls which gave no relief to slow-burning adrenaline, a furred static of sex. The peace shattered suddenly with a high-pitched keening wail; the Arab's ululations. More women followed her lead, clapping and swaying, and a few spun in lithe dances. Lisa heard musical laughter and low debauched tones, and realised what they were doing; she had made these same declarations of individuality in her own bedroom. Regardless of differences, the women were affirming their own belief in themselves as quasi-magical temptresses. Lisa joined the elation but preserved her independence confidently. Smiling, she glided serenely, absorbed in the artful deportment of her supple form. At the height of her powers, brimful of sexual energy, vapour, rather than blood, drifted through her limbs.

'Return to your seats.'

The women settled, buzzing with animation and engaged with allies, recognised intuitively. They had convened from various regions of the world but Lisa perceived the sympathetic signs, the instinctive passwords flashing subconsciously, and an undercurrent of insight and trust. Why not? They were all in the same boat. But there might also be something else going on. Perhaps the women shared a particular ability to channel carnal lust into enigmatic art. Perhaps they had all been selected for that precise talent. Lisa hoped the organisers would appreciate the gift or, even better, be able to duplicate it themselves.

'Your mentors are coming to claim you.'

An air of anticipation inflamed the group but Lisa had no concern about who might have bought her. Whoever it was she would act the same. From the shadows at one end of the room a line of shrouded figures emerged and assembled gradually at the back of chairs. Gilded masks and trailing ornate robes, including gloves, concealed all identity. Lisa could see the mentors opposite but not her own, though his robe nestled her cranium in a wordless command. Some of the women shifted apprehensively, indicating an ancient fear; not only of the inscrutable masks but of the evasions behind such disguise. Lisa experienced no dread at all. Comfortable, from children's stories, with dressing-up and make-believe, the mounting tension caused her to ache deliriously.

'Stand.'

The women pivoted for a first view of their own mentor and tried fruitlessly to interpret the nothingness of their men. They were not even effigies. Lisa's own mentor, taller than she, wore a ram's head and a crimson robe embroidered vividly in silver scrolls. All the men proffered an arm in an old-fashioned gesture of courteous invitation. As the pairs dispersed quietly on several routes Lisa felt intoxicated by the stately ritual. It seemed so right that she should be naked while her unknown, perhaps unknowable mentor, maintained a remote presence. He escorted her along gloomy corridors and up a flight of dully-gleaming marble stairs, whose cold infiltrated her thin slippers. They arrived at a dimly lit room draped with maroon satin hangings.

Lisa prepared herself without anxiety for a storm of emotion, perhaps sustained, driven by a devastating consuming desire. In her resilient depths, and in her mind, she would soak up the tempest's force.

Instead, his relaxation surprised her. His calm survey encompassed the top of her head to her shoulders and neck, lingered on her nipples, then her belly, and the prominent lips of her cunt. He turned her round to admire her haunches' sweet hemispheres. He must have perused all these features during the parade but now subjected to minute inspection what he had bought. Lisa remained passive, surrendering each nuance to his judgement, imprinted by every ardent pressure, yearning for his kiss. But the ram's mask prevented direct contact and so did his velvet gloves, most gently tactile of all materials. They roamed her breasts, lifting and soothing, and over her buttocks. As an expert lover he clearly respected female sensibilities and knew how to play on them, rousing and fine-tuning her response, leading her deviously but steadily to one certain end. Submerged, Lisa widened her legs to allow his access. He stroked her labia and when he thrust inside she arched in marvellous distress, wrenching against him. In the velvet-clad finger-fuck, entirely different to the stewards' coarse treatment shortly before, she gasped tremulously and lubricated. The sleek fabric tightened on her bud and her knees buckled. Clumsily she repaid him by fondling the bulging pack of his genitals.

'Do it properly.' A rumbling mellow baritone came from the mask.

Lisa knelt, fumbling for a gap in the robe, opening it from the waist. She reacted with a sharp intake of breath at a ponderous tube of dark flesh, indistinguishable from the adjacent area. Her mentor was black! For a moment she struggled, assimilating the multiple dusky shades across his groin and massive muscled thighs. His foreskin's mottled folds shaped the crown of his penis but the bald base had been as thoroughly shaved as her own dear pussy.

Inhaling the vital male aroma she murmured ecstatically, 'I want to . . . I can't resist . . .' Her palm enclosed the tube and rolled its slack envelope to nurture it passionately. As the member quickly came to life she panted and moaned, and her free hand reached up and flattened on the slabs of his abdomen above her head. She glimpsed the shaft sticking out of her mouth – ferocious ebony piercing her ivory – and continued the regular motions to and fro. Expelling the tumescent stem she examined all its surfaces, glimmering and ridged as a rock wall, and again pursued its luscious taste. Teasing herself, she barely held the slope in her lips and simply warmed the compact knob. Sliding forward, just a little, she touched the helmet on her cavity's roof and lapped beneath the sculptured flange. Hoisting the jet sac of his testicles she wondered if its heaviness signified the quantity of sperm he would soon supply. Lured beyond endurance, she attempted to cram the whole length in her throat but could manage only a few inches. Immersed in a musky bouquet she fed on his balls, and visualised the inexorable advance of his sap from its secret root to the swarming lava overflow, filling her richly. Feverishly she came home to the flared cap where her tongue dragged a thin creamy thread from its tip.

'Lie on the bed.'

Scrambling to obey, Lisa reclined on inky satin sheets. At the bed's foot her mentor discarded his gloves, dropped his robe and finally took off his mask. In deafening silence his commanding aura swept the room. He devoured her with an appetite so palpable she could feel the effect of his gaze on her skin. To her he appeared a vision of potent beauty, a glossy sensual map to explore, and she studied the planes of his chest, the sucked-in control of his gut, and his narrow loins; loins of steel. On one strong pectoral a tattooed bird of paradise climbed to his shoulder but, descending his biceps, its wings coalesced with fronds of foliage. Most dominant of all, confronting her as a stern challenge, even a threat, his engorged glans glistening and curved as if unable to support its weight.

'Show yourself.'

Slipping, Lisa drowned in honey. Spreading her knees to their maximum, she prised her pleats apart to offer her gaping hole, a thrilling obscenity, to the daunting erection. In a single glance her mentor's voracious eyes enticed her into a magical world she could only vaguely imagine.

Swooping down he rubbed his thick girth through her cleavage. She bunched her arms to the sides to push up her globes, using them as a sexual organ, and relished the amazing silky glide between. A bulging monster slithered out from its hiding place and snaked temptingly towards her face as a taut scrotum nudged the underside. The monster withdrew to lurk within her pulpy mass, but as it pressed out, Lisa's amorous heat lifted progressively.

His swift smooth entry, unusually long and broad in her moist passage, stuffed her so full she could scarcely stir. He pumped in a steady rhythm, tossing her breasts eccentrically. Her slimy walls grasped his rod in a liquid fusion and each insertion punched out an exhalation of joy. With no warning he slapped her left boob and then its twin, and Lisa cried out as the jolts transmitted their power straight into her impaled vagina, creating sparks as he moved. Trapped in his arms, she revolved and swirled as if he had waited too long, storing his vigour solely for her. Briefly he stopped and turned her over, deeply embedded, to fuck her rigorously from the rear, then swivelled her again and she stared up at his sweat, mingling with hers and running into the sheets. In serene currents her rise mounted but he began to drive with greater speed to satisfy his own relief.

'Give me more time,' she whimpered.

He pulled out and rapped her sensitive stalk with a solid club. Lisa choked and jerked in exquisite agony; a startling rebuke that launched her onto the upward path. And when he resumed his tool captured her, reducing her to a simmering essence. Heaved by his forceful lunges, crying out in perfect pleasure, she replied to the passion he gave to her. Folded into a sweeping rush, sobbing and laughing at the same time, she begged him to carry on, loving the way he manipulated her clitoris, bucking wildly, dissolving away. She lost count of the times he compelled her to come, contracting by reflex to clasp the invader in a velvet vice. At last, in a flood of rapture, she gladly received the series of bursts exploding his seed.

Later the avalanche of tremors dwindled, subsiding gradually. In the comfort of post-orgasmic lassitude Lisa watched the ceiling, rippled by the moon's reflection on water. She followed its flickering lines, well defined near to the window, fading further away to indistinct shadows. 'What is your name?' she whispered.

'Mentor is good enough.'

His refusal to name himself, familiar from Balmayne, made no difference. Why should it, when she had her own disguise? She assessed a number of possibilities, hunting for something dignified: Eugene, Daniel, Leo, Gabriel, Guy, David. Which of these suited him best? *Daniel. To me you're Daniel.* 'I'm glad you chose me.' After a pause she added, 'Why did you?'

The slumbering form shifted lazily. 'I can't believe that female self-awareness hasn't already supplied the answer. Every pore of your body oozes sexuality.' From the canal, weak indecipherable sounds drifted in. 'And that's sufficient to feed your vanity.'

It was. Lisa rested, cocooned in peace, content to lie beside the most skilled lover she had ever known. Twice more in the night, roused by touch and his breath, she held him in the hot clench of her muscles as tight as she could; he, shooting hard and groaning aloud; she, taking possession of all his spunk.

Sixteen

She awoke reluctantly from a drugged sleep to brisk shaking. Past her mentor's silhouette the window showed no glimmer of dawn lightening the sky. 'What time is it?' she enquired hazily.

'Time to prepare. Don't bother with make-up.'

Swinging to the floor, Lisa put on her slippers and lurched to the old-fashioned bathroom with antiquated plumbing. After dabbing glacial water on numbed cheeks, she tugged a comb through her tangled hair, and tried to close the door.

'Leave it open.'

'I need to be alone,' she pleaded.

'Leave it open.'

Lisa hesitated resentfully until a memory of Jon, calling this a private game, helped her to squat flagrantly on the toilet's cold rim in view of the man. While the bowl echoed and amplified her splashes, Daniel's humiliating inspection missed nothing of the stream pouring out of her pouting lips. As the flow died to a trickle she restored a semblance of pride by wiping flamboyantly.

Ignoring the protest, her mentor gave her a gilt mask; a glossy boy with an amiable smile. From the shell she picked up an odour of sickly corrupt perfume and, in the mirror, contemplated the peculiar sight of a boy's bright and frozen face on a woman's mobile form. In the alternative identity she also discovered a surprising sense of freedom.

'No costume,' Daniel said.

He led her along corridors resembling a maze. Lisa clutched the arm of his robe as she had before, surging with pride at the man who had selected and paid for her. Black and sleek as a tide-polished stone, he walked in a field of energy, a charged space pulsing with masculine strength. They arrived at a marble staircase with gold-leaf statues on the balustrades and she climbed in front of immense tapestries perished by age, and confusions of painted cherubs on the ceiling above. The maze of corridors ended eventually at a room with tall mullioned windows, now faintly pink in the first trace of dawn. It contained a gigantic bed, isolated on a dais, as if arranged for performances. Daniel sat Lisa on the edge but returned to the window, detached from her by distance and separate thoughts.

Silently, a naked white man appeared in the doorway. He wore the mask of a stag and Lisa named him spontaneously. Stag-man must be the reason she had been brought here. Like her, a nude woman with the features of a friendly boy, his static head contrasted with a normal body. Bewildered, Lisa attempted to comprehend the situation: a stag-man with a woman-boy? A startling level of unreality. Watching his rapid approach, she forgot her speculations, fascinated by his swaying jiggling penis conveying assurance arrogantly. Stag-man settled on the bed at her left, Daniel on her right, and they both widened her legs so far apart she had to lean back on her hands for balance. Playing with her labia, they exchanged murmured comments about its attributes as if they were aiming to sabotage her self-esteem. From opposite sides they gathered her pleats and their fingers, a pair of probes in her succulent fruit, loosened her warm secretions. Losing control and quaking visibly, Lisa understood from their seriousness that, for them, her dear pussy was the most important stage of an introduction. They acknowledged her sex as if it represented the whole of her! And her mentor seemed to be persuading stag-man, or even selling to him, the merits of this intimate spot, already sampled by him.

'Kneel on the bed,' stag-man commanded. Submitting to their pleasure, Lisa obeyed. 'Now, bend right back. Rest your head on the cover.' She arched as required, her calves tucked under her thighs, stretching her torso, her pudenda thrust high as her summit. 'Spread yourself.' Lisa followed the instruction. 'Look at that fine curve on her narrow mound.' Stag-man cupped and moulded her pouch, penetrated her channel and circled his thumb on her firming nugget. Lisa trembled and gasped. He abruptly released her and ordered, 'You do it.' Tentatively she reached forward to fondle herself and her middle digit slid into her sheath. 'Better than that! I want three, going in hard.'

Lisa broadened her vagina unnaturally and glided into her juice. Dazed by her self-manipulation she distrusted the evidence of what she saw: a black fist nurturing a white erection. Shocked, her emotions strained, she moaned, 'Take me.'

'Lie down.'

Lisa promptly complied. Stag-man placed her feet on his shoulders and drove his shaft as far as it would go in her sloppy heat. Beyond the slits in his mask his eyes gripped her in a steel trap while he ploughed relentlessly to the hilt. She bathed his ferocious cock in copious fluid but even that did little to ease the brutality of its domination. Her mentor sat behind her and Lisa twisted towards him, begging for his protection. Resisting her plea he raised her sagging weight and the two men cramped her into a compact V between their bodies. Stag-man seized her right nipple and screwed outwards, extending the delicate tip to a thin point. 'Ah!' Lisa's sharp screech resonated within the mask. Her tormentor plunged heavily as if, concerned for his own gratification, he had not even heard her cry. She drooped weakly, supported by Daniel's chest, but stag-man wrenched her left bud out from her breast. 'Ah!' The twin pressures, fused with his forceful penetrations, juddered her frame. His groin thrusting into her crotch made blows like a hammer and Lisa struggled hopelessly against a power too savage to fight. With a wounded roar from deep in his gut he spewed a torrent and at the same moment her mentor let her fall to the bed. As she bounced, stars vibrated across her vision. Stag-man's curt gesture dismissed her, as expendable.

'You may go. Wait for me in our room.'

Alarmed by Daniel's unwillingness to defend her, or even to provide minimal comfort, and then by his blunt rejection, Lisa tottered stiffly to the door. She wondered why he wished to ruin her approval of him but could not concentrate. Her teats throbbed dreadfully, competing with her abused orifice subjected to the rule of an iron bar.

The corridor felt unfamiliar and she cast about for clues but remembered little of the route. At the first opportunity she branched off only to find that all the corridors were the same. She turned into a new section, probably wrong, but she had no choice. Where were those stairs? She delayed her slow progress to clumsily wipe away the seeping sperm. Now, more than ever, she needed her mentor's reassuring arm but, as she drifted uncertainly, the flow of cool air helped her to calm.

I thought, by now, I knew all about intercourse. The merciless copulation had been a cruel awakening. Worse than that, far worse as her spirits revived, came a gradual realisation that the experience could be added to other, special kinds, of occasional satisfaction. The appalling idea of latent masochism distracted her and twice tricked her into blind ends. Retracing her steps she searched diligently for a new direction, but in dim light the building resembled an impossible labyrinth.

Unusually, one door stood ajar. Lisa's instinctive glance recorded ancient windows with red and blue glass stained by the sun. In the next instant, wistful as a child, she cringed into the shadows to absorb the scene. Set between two veined columns of pink marble a woman, beautifully tanned and with blonde hair, sat precariously on the edge of a stool. Her wrists had been bound above her head and a bulky ball-gag hollowed her cheeks. Briefly, Lisa registered a fact of difference; she had not been among them on the first evening.

The woman's ankles, shackled to the ends of a bar, were held wide above in a pronounced V. Rubber stockings compressed her thighs and finished near to her labia. From bands in the rubber, metal clips with fierce jaws dragged apart the soft lips. Lisa winced at the elongated diamond, a vivid entrance to the woman's womb, and recalled the crush of clamps on her own paps. But how does it feel in those tender membranes? And for treatment of this sort where would she get her reward? Perhaps from new awareness, which her brooding eyes seemed to confirm. They gleamed, welcoming the man who positioned himself in the fork of her V. His pumping hips disguised the action from Lisa's view.

Puzzled, she took the chance to run past the door. If that woman had not been present in the original group, were there more people here than she had supposed? Again Lisa tried to discover her way but in the palazzo, as fugitive as a faulty memory, things that should go together refused to fit. Huge mirrors doubled and tripled the area, repeating aspects that were not even there, and one splintered her mask into multiple fragments. At vertiginous stairwells she stared up at skylights caked in dust and also encountered an odd illusion: instead of looking up it was into a well, or into space. Fearing she might never succeed, she arrived at a stairway and recognised the tapestries and a painted ceiling. She ran down, her heart thumping in relief. The lower corridor, lined by shut doors leading to countless rooms, carried on into the distance. As she hurried, the doors, each one a barrier, started to intrigue her. Like the doors in Pauline's house they concealed secrets but these, vital for her assignment, had to be opened up. Reducing her fevered pace, Lisa chose a door at random and knelt to peer through the keyhole. Her mask prevented her from getting close. Impetuously she snatched it off and threw it to the floor.

On a bed the Japanese girl sat with her knees bunched to one side. Loops of pearls glimmered beneath the small cones of her tits. Squeezed by her thighs threads of black pubic hair, untamed as wild blossoms, unfurled on her pale flesh. Poised, unblinking, the girl gazed at a multi-thonged whip. The boy beside her murmured and offered it. Lisa, watching attentively, imagined the conflicts surging in her brain.

Seduced by his words, the Japanese inclined little by little. She gently lifted the whip and the strands spilled from her palm as she kissed them respectfully. The boy accepted her subservience with a strangely contemptuous, terrifying smile. Lisa's sympathy went out to a neophyte who would shortly undergo a trial she would not be able to forget.

A shape suddenly blocked the keyhole and Lisa reared away, unnerved by someone approaching her hiding place. Hastily, hands shaking, she put on her mask and scurried away. Sooty velvets and flashes of silver emerged on all sides, and gusts of illumination blazed from windows and doors. Breaking into a run she hurtled around a corner straight into her mentor who grabbed her arm to check her flight. 'Lost,' Lisa gabbled, clearly distraught.

'Complete your make-up,' he said. 'It's time for a meal.'

That happened – how long ago? Incidents, occurring too fast, had blurred her mind.

'Your first public exhibition!' Her mentor's voice rang with pride.

'What shall I have to do?' Lisa asked anxiously.

'Whatever the arbiter tells you.'

'Who?'

'The arbiter plans and conducts the session. He may also permit a sequel.'

'Why can't you do it?

'We are rarely allowed to perform that role if our own women are involved.'

'A pity. How many will be there?'

'That's difficult to say. Members select from a range of events.' Daniel saw her discomfort. 'Don't worry. Your legs are magnificent.'

Lisa's costume consisted of a green satin top and a similar mini-skirt. 'Only them?' she asked mischievously.

'And your reputation is already growing.'

'Reputation for what?'

186

'That you are a natural voluptuary.' He laughed at her disbelieving expression. 'Surely you know what you most desire.'

Stunned by the comments, and by their implications, Lisa noticed little during their walk until they entered a room where a crowd had gathered – many more than the number of mentors she had seen. *Who are these extra men?* On the edge of a circle Daniel freed her grasp, urged Lisa forward, and behind her the gap sealed. On the far side stood the Spanish, or Italian, woman whose smouldering manner suggested an unpredictable, incendiary character. Raven hair fell onto one bared breast. *I'll call you Bella Donna because that's what you are.*

A robed arbiter appeared. 'Introduce yourselves to the audience.'

The women paraded the perimeter, stalking warily as if they were rivals. But when a spark ignited, Lisa replied to the unspoken challenge by strolling across, and Donna responded to her kiss with the intensity of a passionate man. Again taking the initiative, Lisa located her friend's fingers on her own sex and whispered an invitation, buckling slightly at the unexpectedly greedy possession.

Applause rang out.

'Naked.' The women complied with the order promptly. In contrast to Lisa's smooth shave, revealing her slit, Donna's dusky belly had a compact screen of gilded curls at the base.

'Sit on the floor, facing.'

Demonstrating a shared lust, they attempted various combinations to achieve their best fit. Finally Lisa, her knees raised and spread, straddled Donna's waist and sucked her dark nipple. Donna leaned away, her face to the ceiling, groaning at Lisa's flickering tongue.

'Lie down.'

This time the women obeyed reluctantly. Supine, legs stretched to their full span, the tendons of their inner thighs jutted out, taut as cables. They squinted along their own length at the vista of the other's shielded aperture. Spectators enclosed them, examining their artlessly splayed bodies in every detail. Above loomed the arbiter holding a fat tube of shiny material which flexed alarmingly as if eager to infiltrate. Dismayed by its size, Lisa shuddered and caught her breath.

The arbiter pushed one end into Donna's vagina. As it travelled slowly into her depths her brows furrowed, her eyes screwed tight. A few seconds later the opposite end sank into Lisa's passage, and she too grimaced as the girth distended her walls. The women lay still, resigned to their passive congestion.

'Begin.'

Donna's lunge drove the crown so hard into Lisa that it seemed to nudge the door of her womb. She gasped explosively and tried to combat the pressure by forcing back, partly in vengeance. Her senses fogged in cross-currents of swirling stress, assisting and fighting her friend in a glorious mutual fuck. Exclaiming and moaning, choking and uttering small cries, they revelled in the command that both delivered yet neither controlled, thrusting their hips alternately and rocked to and fro by their partner's power. Lisa's arms extended outward and as she arched she lost the rhythm –

'Stop!'

On the brink of release her emotions screeched in protest.

'Kneel,' the arbiter said, 'but keep it inside. I want your arses together.'

Lisa blundered to match Donna, awkwardly half-rising and swivelling. Eventually, on elbows and knees in reversed directions, they waited for the next instruction. Lisa visualised what the men could see: a thick rod projecting from one orifice into its consort, linking them. Maybe it was nice for them but she hated the pose, far more humiliating than the previous one.

'Continue.'

Lisa again mirrored Donna. Mounting tension swamped her shame as their buttocks thumped and distorted, vibrating with each impact. She flinched as the dildo rammed into her cavity but, however remorselessly she returned the stroke, she only shoved the column further into herself. Trembling, her loins melted.

'Halt.'

Whimpering pathetically, Lisa drooped to the floor.

The arbiter refused to let them unshackle. He synchronised the complex moves until Lisa rested on her shoulders, folded in two. Her legs sprawled past her head and her toes touched the floor at the sides of her face. She gazed upwards. Donna hunched over her groin as a male with the most enormous appendage, and began to pierce vertically –

'Ah!'

Inert, unable either to resist or retaliate, Lisa struggled to contain her reaction. In the midst of profound penetration, a true coercion, her juices flowed and she resumed her inexorable climb to a peak. At this stage, treating them mercifully, the arbiter let them go the whole way so the men could witness their transient smiles and panting laughs, their ripples and screams of exultation.

Her channel emptied, leaving it throbbing, abused to its limits. Her tormentor collapsed beside her, the dildo still gripped and swaying in her pussy. A sequel followed with no respite as one spectator flattened Donna to the floor, snatched out the dildo, and proceeded to use her immediately. And before Lisa had time to unwind she glimpsed a penis swooping to capture her gaping split although, dilated by the gross tool, she was scarcely aware of any dimensions. She clenched her muscles to gratify the live vivacity, trying to bear its ceaseless drives. Timing his exit, he spunked in a stream, flooding her anus in a teeming pool with random pearls spattering down her neck and cheeks. He knelt, and the smeared mulberry cap insisted that she drink the residue, and the remaining beads he scooped into her mouth.

The plumbing gurgled fitfully and the water, supposedly warm, ran cold. Lisa emerged shivering but refreshed, combed her hair and pinned it on top, then finished her make-up carefully. It pleased her to wear a thin robe, a gentle buttercup yellow, Empire in style, as a change from her nude state and she spent a few delighted minutes inspecting herself in the mirror. A firm knock on the door interrupted. Outside stood a steward, one she had noticed earlier, sturdy in build and dressed as normal, bare to the waist. A dense mat of silver strands on his barrel chest, his massive arms with clubs for hands, suggested mature years combined with youthful strength. Against him her proportions were those of a delicate girl. Acutely conscious of his stare roaming her body beneath the gown, she wondered if he had been one of them on her arrival, groping her.

'You come,' he said speaking in English, heavily accented.

'Where? To my mentor?'

'No ask. Come.'

She did so, along endless aisles of shut doors, hiding secrets she yearned to uncover. Deprived of so many opportunities! A severe loss to her assignment. At last the steward opened one of the doors and beckoned her to enter a library stacked to the ceiling. It had a strong musty smell and minimum light. She paused for her pupils to adjust and saw her mentor's profile, revealed by a lamp. Huddled over a desk, he conferred with a second man who appeared to be an Italian. *So you are . . . Gianni.* The carpet silenced Lisa's steps as she glided towards them curiously.

Daniel glanced up. 'Charming,' he said. 'I've called you in for a female opinion of this specialist field of art. It's probably unfamiliar to you so be prepared for a shock.'

Her mentor's colleague shifted to one side. Wedged into the space between them, she peered at a sheaf of erotic images.

'This one has an amorphous quality,' Gianni explained, 'that allows many interpretations.'

Already absorbed in the scene, Lisa agreed absently. 'Yes, many.' Some of her own experiments had explored similar effects.

Attempting to concentrate, she leaned further, despite Gianni's possession of her right buttock. From out of the scratchy ambiguous drawing materialised the luminous

190

figure of a young girl, dancing, naked. Brilliant white and gold rays spilled out from her as if she was lit from within. Vibrant black-browns and bloody reds conveyed her dark confines. A radiant patch of vermilion glowed as a warning, and in the upper corner dazzled a scrap of chrome yellow.

Her mentor fondled Lisa's crevice and nudged her sphincter.

A brooding man in the gloom watched the girl. The atmosphere – so malign! She danced innocently, ignoring her danger.

On Lisa's rump the distractions altered frequently, adding to the picture's weird passion.

'By Gustave Moreau,' Gianni murmured.

'Yes,' Lisa confirmed, jerking as he probed her labia.

Daniel's vigour jammed her onto the edge of the desk and she gave in to his will by widening her legs. His fingertip, wrapped in her gown's fabric, investigated her stubborn hole. At the same instant he flipped the page to disclose the next picture. Like a flash of burning sun on a pane of glass it scorched her eyes. Disturbed hopelessly by the twin pressures, Lisa fought to conceal her instinctive reaction. How had one of her own come to be in this collection?

'Here is a new, a supreme, artist,' Gianni said, 'with a highly distinctive style. We particularly admire him because he doesn't merely describe, but evokes sex. He goes beyond illustration to actually inhabit sex.'

And Pauline's fastidious attention to detail had ensured a beautiful reproduction. But no one else in the world knows a piece of work as intimately as the person who made it. Every line, shaded area, or emphasis in the action – all of them had, disguised in the version here, a history of development that only Lisa could understand. As usual, inflamed by her own results, she wriggled on the anal obstruction. Incautiously she began to trace a section which –

'That's enough.'

Remarkably the men set her free. That, coupled with her mentor's severity, upset her badly and she tried to placate

191

him. 'I was enjoying that. They're so stimulating. Can't I see them all?'

'Enough,' he repeated harshly.

Dejected, Lisa wandered away from the desk and hovered indecisively. At one moment she was desired by both and in the next cut off, and dismissed. Across the room they muttered as they packed away the examples and snapped off the lamp, reducing the room to a dim illumination. Daniel approached, took her in his arms, and kissed her ardently. Bewildered by the sudden change in his mood, she responded with no reservation, striving to make amends for an offence she had unwittingly caused. He broke off and revolved her to confront Gianni who took her as amorously as her mentor had done. Suffocated in his kiss, her belly felt his stirring arousal. She rotated to her mentor and the touches she craved restored her shaken confidence. He passed her back to his friend. Laughing breathlessly, Lisa wondered which of them intended to use her. The flimsy gown fell to her ankles, yielding her torso to roaming caresses wherever she turned. As their robes joined hers on the floor, she knelt and politely offered her mouth to the guest. Plugged by the aromatic lump of flesh, she sucked avidly, in love with her duty, while nurturing the weight of the resilient black cock in her palm. Swivelling from one penis to the other she switched from masturbation – dragging the foreskin hard to leave the sculptured crown starkly outlined – to her warm seductive cavity, and exchanged again, back and forth. The men spoke to her quietly, feeding words and phrases that seized her mind with thoughts of continuing service to both. She received her initial reward as two stiff rods sandwiched her cheeks.

Instructed to rest on all fours, she chose to slump lower, hollowing her spine and extending her arms far forward to show humility or perfect submission. Spreading her knees, she presented the alluring mysteries contained in her cleft and waited deliriously, hoping a tongue would lap the slow trickle on her inner thigh. They would be studying her frank display and pumping their erections – her erections – prepared assiduously for her own penetration.

192

When her mentor's dusky form lay by her side Lisa straddled his waist, allowing the broad helmet of his wet stem to split her fragile lips. At its maximum depth, she gasped at the girth's distension but gradually slid up and down, savouring her own massage until he held her steady, levering up from the floor. She pitched in accordance to his rhythm, content to be mastered.

He stopped and encouraged her to remain still, hunched over his face. Gianni's thumbs plunged into her anus, stretching rigorously. Trying to adapt, Lisa grimaced and squirmed but groaned aloud as his shaft expanded the reluctant muscle, progressing relentlessly. Enduring the invasion of two penises, separated only by a thin membrane, the doubled strokes were like nothing she had ever experienced. Her pelvis fired and the impetus revolved her boobs in circles. As they crashed together in soft collisions, she ebbed away into her body's enforced sensations.

The men rearranged to engage her differently with Daniel behind, fast in her cunt, and Gianni demanding her oral skills. Lisa resisted, then accepted the nauseous taste glutting her throat, her forehead crammed into his abdomen by her mentor's thrusts. Crazed, she screwed her nipple frantically, increasing her own distress.

Briefly the chaos ceased. Slack-jawed, she gazed helplessly along a piercing black pole bringing the welcome sweeter flavour of her own cream. The stranger slipped smoothly, deeply, into her rectum. To them she performed as a simple vessel, her apertures useful for their intemperate needs. But her own needs were paramount. Balanced precariously on one hand, she pushed bunched digits into her neglected orifice, goading the mobile wedge in her rear.

Unsatisfied, they repositioned once more. Whirled about, Lisa resumed her first pose with Gianni lying beneath and rocked to Daniel's regular beat. He had applied lubrication but even so his member had far greater authority than the one in her elastic pussy. Her mentor emphasised his command by pulling out several times, and left her gaping, before his bulk speared again. Yelling triumphantly, he spunked and immediately quit. His emissions bubbled out to seethe onto the organ below and Lisa visualised the Italian's motions returning the fluid home, in her vagina. But now she yearned for the vacancy to be filled and stuffed two consoling fingers into her sphincter. Gianni unloaded his seed in long spurts and Lisa sagged to the floor. Reeking of semen she sank dizzily, recovered, and declined, vaguely aware of Daniel scooping the deposit out of her sex and smearing a layer onto her perineum.

She glided effortlessly from end to end of the pool, cold at the bottom but cool at the surface. Exhilarated by quiet freedom, and the contrast of the sun's heat with refrigerated skin, Lisa completed extra lengths. Absurdly proud of her strength, she finished and clambered out to sprawl on the grass, her arm shading her eyes. These peaceful intervals, granted unpredictably, were cherished by all the women and a few of them were scattered now, lying naked on the lawn in the enclosed courtyard. When they talked, the relaxed scene reminded Lisa of one of her favourite paintings, Ingres's languid and sensuous harem, and she marvelled at her own residence in such a sheltered environment. Occasionally a mentor would invade the calm by fucking his woman in full view, or giving her to someone else he invited. Daniel had never subjected her to a public insult of any description.

'Come.'

Squinting lazily Lisa saw the steward looming above, unmistakable with his glinting silver hair and animal power. He stared down, inspecting her features candidly. *How long's he been watching me?* She sat up and said, 'I must take a shower.'

'No. Order.'

Fitting her slippers, Lisa rose to her feet. Order? What could that mean? Apprehensively she followed the steward into the building, initially blinded after the sun's glare. Her sight restored only as they arrived at her room.

She found her mentor smouldering with uncharacteristic rage.

'What's wrong?' she asked.

'Stand still.'

'What have I done?'

He crouched to fit padded cuffs, linked with a short chain, to her ankles and wrenched her wrists behind to tie them with rope. In altered circumstances, or if he conveyed excitement, the bindings would have been thrilling. Instead, his icy manner impelled her to instant alarm. He jostled her roughly out of the room although, hobbled by the chain, she could only shuffle awkwardly.

Lisa whimpered and attempted supplication. 'Master –'

A curt gesture cut off her plea. Hustled in total confusion, she could not understand what was happening. Some kind of game, of fluctuating and contradictory moods? At her side he appeared implacable, not the person she thought she knew, and his grip hurt. Halting at a door, he thrust Lisa across the threshold.

At the far end a slim nude female lay on a red velvet cloth surrounded by enormous white candles. Smaller versions lined her abdomen. Was she posing for something? Asleep? Drugged? Melted wax trailed sluggishly, coagulating on the pale figure. A sickly scent of faded flowers pervaded the air. Flames jumped and blazed erratically and the wavering light hollowed an agitated space from shadow. The nightmare claustrophobia had no reasonable interpretation. Lisa choked, trying to subdue her panic.

'Why are you showing me . . .'

Silently, her mentor dragged her away. She lurched clumsily, her hobble-chain scraping and rasping on steps. They descended two staircases into a subterranean tunnel where Daniel opened a low door of plain wood.

He led her into a huge vault with a freezing stone floor and arches curving up into the gloom. They approached a number of columns resembling penises with accurate bulbous tops and Lisa's blood chilled at the harrowing vision of two women strapped to them. Facing, their expressions were stunned masks as each witnessed the punishment inflicted on the other. But Lisa flinched at the crisp slaps of leather and the weak reflex of begging cries. 'What have I done? Master, tell me what have I done?'

He forced her, cringing, onto the frigid surface of a vacant column and tied her arms around the fat circumference. Freeing one ankle he secured them both in the same way, wide apart. At last he explained her offence. 'You were recognised spying at a keyhole and that breaks one of our cardinal rules. You were specifically warned about that.'

On the far wall a distorted profile recast him as a leering monster. Lisa, absolutely immobilised, felt suddenly drained, not solid at all. She began to shiver, gabbling, 'I'm sorry, I'm sorry.'

Impassively he picked up a gag and stifled her with a rubber ball stretching her mouth. Her glazed eyes tracked him to the wall and a collection of instruments that she had studied at Balmayne. Unhurriedly, allowing her stress to rise, he tested several to judge their balance. All the air sucked out of the room. As he pivoted, she tensed and shrivelled, poised on the edge of a swift drop to oblivion. Without hesitation and no apparent regret he made the first burning slash to her belly. The stroke fanned out, narrowly concentrated on her left and broadly dispersed on the right. Lisa buckled and a loud muffled cry leaked from the gag until the next, a careless backhand, scoured her sensitive breasts. She twisted frantically in her bonds, her cries the only deliverance from strikes that seared like a furnace at full blast. Compared to Pauline's arousing session this punishment, truly severe, could not be construed as satisfaction of any sort. For a moment Daniel paused to monitor her sheen of sweat and her general state. His third lash singed her inner thighs, scorched the tender tissues of her dear pussy, and fringed her entire body in flame. Unable to bear it, she screamed and writhed hopelessly.

He lifted her chin to find a trickle of tears lining her cheeks and spoke from a few inches away. She could scarcely hear the words. 'That's all I'll give you – this time. You are much too good to put out of action. But if you spy again the next will be much worse.'

Daniel reversed the whip. In slow stages he pushed the blunt end into her moist aperture and paused to jiggle the tool. Lisa's muscles gripped the corrugations though each advance caused her a shudder of shame.

'I'll leave it in there to soak,' he said and walked away.

Deserted, Lisa hung in her bonds. Her torso, striped by sets of coarse red fans, throbbed with unearthly fire, increased by the humiliating plug within her passage. There were no sounds in the room. Her companions were also slumped motionless, and corked in the same manner with the tails of their whips pooled on the floor. Through a long interval of solitude Lisa moaned quietly but on Daniel's return she stirred, gratified by his presence and the hope of renewing their union. He extracted her gag, permitting her to ease her strained jaws and slipped out the whip, releasing the awful pressure. He held it up to show the handle impregnated with her secretions and she acquiesced to the demand to taste her juice. The others did the same, the stubs of their whips projecting from their mouths.

When he untied her bonds she collapsed to the floor. He stooped, gathered her limbs and carried her to her room limply draped across his arms. During succeeding hours he nursed her, soothing ointments into portions of purged flesh, particularly her swollen labia. She could not have been more cosseted, defenceless as a baby to all his frank touches. Deeply contrite, she accepted him as her sole comfort. He alone protected her, and beyond the immediacy of his warmth and concern lay only the palazzo, infinite and threatening.

Dimly she grasped that Daniel's physical games, and the abrupt transitions from role to role, were intended to keep her constantly alert. But this treatment had taught her a stark lesson. Her contract with Pauline would have to be broken in order to survive her time here. She dared not take any further risks and would have to ignore the events around her.

Seventeen

But it proved to be difficult. How could an ingrained instinct be disregarded, or trained eyes avoid catching clues?

Her marks had faded to faint patterns. Sometimes, naked at mealtimes, she flaunted them as tattoos; a result, not of disobedience, but the independent cast of her nature. Fortunately Daniel indulged her trivial pretence. Nevertheless she nurtured a secret, a memory of ecstatic fragments, of darkness inside the glare.

He finished tying the hood. A lattice of pure white silk constructed a mesh and Lisa peered out from a taut cage.

'This conceals your personality,' her mentor said. 'It transforms you into an object – that is, an occasion for fantasy. Nudity, as always, makes you instantly available. Do you know what you are?'

'A mysterious . . . anonymous . . .'

'A mysterious and anonymous fuck. Does the notion appeal to you?'

'I'm not sure.' Lisa recalled her caning at Balmayne, a dress hiding her face in a similar fashion. 'It's happened to me in the past,' she said, adding boldly, 'No one can use my mouth.'

Admitting her courage, possibly another charade, Daniel smiled and offered his arm. As they walked, only slight soreness on her inner legs disturbed her. They entered a room which floated in the watery yellowed light of aromatic candles, to the grunts and gasps of a strenuous copulation. The candles were mounted on the branches of leafing trees at both ends of the room, but in the middle Lisa could barely discern a man's haunches flexing rhythmically. His mask, that of a small beaked bird, contrasted peculiarly with a much larger lion mask, worn by a woman hunched on her knees and pumped vigorously from the rear. A lion controlled by a bird! Involuntarily Lisa observed the points of her spine pricking out of her skin and her blonde hair, darkened to antique gold by the illumination. Her tongue protruded between her lips as if she needed a cock in there at the same time.

Daniel guided Lisa into a more opulent room with an elegant chequered floor of red and black tiles. From a vividly coloured tapestry woven figures laughed at the scene of four women suspended in a row, shackled by wrists and ankles to chains from the ceiling. The women vibrated and swung at every thrust and could only respond with garbled shrieks. But their legs, like pincers, trapped the men who laboured powerfully; they were actually preying on the men to extract their sperm. Closer, Lisa became convinced. *She's devouring him to absorb his seed.*

'Look to the front.' Her mentor hissed a clear warning.

A short corridor led to their destination, a drab area walled in smoky grey glass, and they halted at two leather bands hung from above. Daniel fitted moulded cuffs to Lisa's wrists and told her to raise her arms, as if surrendering to robbery. He carefully adjusted the cuffs in the high position, kissed her lips through the silk veil, and departed.

Alone in the desolate room, shrinking menacingly, she calmed herself. Where had her mentor gone; the man, supposedly, who treasured her most? A smooth upward tug stretched her arms to their full distance and then her feet lifted from the floor. Dangling in space she rotated a little, but due to the moulded cuffs felt no distress except for the twist in her shoulders. A dense hush settled again and she waited passively, as she must, for whatever would come.

The glass walls began to shine. Elaborate engravings in the grey panels bounced eerie shapes in all directions and her own body, in the exact centre of the room's design, formed an important piece: the only dynamic element. Wondering how long she could take her weight before it grew intolerable, she emptied her mind.

Time elapsed, silent as death, monotonous and meaningless.

A group of men arrived, relaxed and unmasked, chatting idly. Lisa stirred, giddy with gratitude for company. She recognised none of the men but there were too many to have been the mentors on the first evening. Who were they? Several considered her with appreciation but no distinct interest. Perhaps they were all sated by previous sessions. With a sudden thump of her heart Lisa remembered a woman tied to a tree and realised that Daniel had deserted her deliberately. He had left her as a tempting commodity for anyone who might, on a whim, fancy her. But that woman, a slave, had a blindfold as solace and Lisa had no such immunity, she could see them all.

'Well, whoever-you-are. You've obviously been a bad girl.'

Lisa focused on a man inspecting her fanned marks.

'Lovely,' he murmured. He wore a cobra as a silver ring. 'Do they still hurt?'

'Not now. But my shoulders are killing me. Can you lift me up for a minute?'

His forearms under her knees bore her weight and his breath warmed her crotch. The probing of a wet tongue swerved in the sleek creases of her mound and started to lick out her groove. Lisa quivered, relishing the attention, and some of the men turned to stare at how she was being affected.

'I'll have you,' the man said and dropped her abruptly. Lisa moaned at the restored tension, steeling herself to bear it.

'Who is she?'

'No idea, but she's a beauty. Even racked, her boobs aren't flattened.'

They caressed her contours randomly, fondling her globes to test their supple resilience, and possessing her narrow pudenda pouch. A finger crammed her vagina and a nail scraped the perimeter of one pebbled halo.

Lisa groaned and arched, reacting wretchedly to cold treatment, worse than she had expected. No one had learned her name or cared who she was. In lacking identity she had no individual value and her presentation, as Daniel had said, gave her the status of a mere object. A palm kneaded her butt, squeezed and slapped hard as a paddle, and her shrill cries answered the strikes. She could do nothing to protect herself or influence their conduct in any way.

'Put the caps on those fantastic tits.'

The men clustered in a circle. One isolated her teat and pinched, projecting it forward. Another positioned a clear plastic cup over it. A tube led to a rubber ball which created a suction, sealing the cup onto her delicate flesh. Lisa gazed down as the vacuum firmed, drawing the whole tip of her breast into the cavity. On her opposite side came a second cap and the same force elongated the crest until both nipples and their areolae were bloated and tightly restricted within their rigid confines. Lisa's fleeting smiles, blending pleasure with grimaces and squirms, exposed her extreme stimulation. 'She's loving it.' The scrutiny of so many men increased the strain of the invisible clamps.

From behind, a tough grip elevated and widened her legs so she appeared to be sitting in mid-air. Combined with her prominent medallions, the pose lurched her into an agony of self-consciousness. A splayed exhibit for examination! With the next awed comment she fluctuated again, towards pride.

'She's felt the whip on her cunt.'

A slimy blunt crown nudged her anus. Lisa tossed and grunted at each short thrust, as a harsh tumescence dilated her channel. Fully penetrated, she automatically stood on his thighs, balanced there between her feet and wrists.

The man muttered in her ear, 'Move on me.'

Lisa climbed the callous shaft and on her descent it drove to the hilt. She rose and fell, her rhythm ragged, panting hoarsely.

'It must feel like sitting on a spike . . .'

'Rammed up her arse.'

Crude language, that once had aroused her, now seemed abhorrent. The group – birds of prey – male raptors – watched her subjugation with glittering eyes. Their intensity amplified her self-reproach. They were studying a whore savouring her own manipulation. One of them produced an instrument, an implied threat, and Lisa knew she was truly lost; her vacant throbbing cunny could not withstand the insistence of any vibrator. The audience demanded more than to see her fucked and wanted orgasm with no disguise. Apprehension mingled with unfulfilled desire and her hair-trigger lubrication flooded at once.

The man in her rear slowed his actions and held Lisa, taut as a bow, her sex gaping and ready. The tool separated her pleats and traced her receptive slit. A thick girth burrowed inside. Erratic oscillations swept her passage and prodded the lurking penis which resumed humping powerfully. As the unrelenting head rotated her clit, the air rent with Lisa's cries, locked in a maelstrom governed by others. They induced heaving waves up her belly and back again mercilessly, to both her abused orifices. The men's voracious appetites went unappeased until she had juddered in one, then a succession of helpless climaxes.

Unaware of the fierce surge in her rectum, the bulk slid out and her muscular ring shrank, at least closer to its normal size. The compression on her chest dwindled and the cups released their clench with a pop, leaving her reddened peaks sticking out grotesquely, hypersensitive.

Later, exhausted, she needed support when lowered to the floor.

'Return to your room.'

No word of comfort or congratulation from any source. What else could she hope for, from a set of raptor males? Sore and weak, she guided herself by clutching the walls. In an empty corridor she leaned on the stone wall to claw at the knot of her hood and tore it off, throwing the hated mask to the floor. Never, in future, would she welcome anonymity. She craved consolation, a word addressed solely to her, a distinct individual dignified by her own name.

Glancing in both directions, she hesitated, uncertain of the route. On all sides the building lay silent except for stray out-of-place echoing sounds. Groping her way carefully, she continued, passing an open door and there, in black space, a number of thin beams flicked to and fro; torches, combing the dark. Hastily, no more than a phantom, Lisa slipped through. The spokes of light converged some distance away, on a pale girl tied to a chair. During the time it took to unleash her bonds, Lisa scarcely breathed. Led away, the girl's ankle bands permitted only a leaden shuffle to the far end where a door, revealed by a brief glimmer, shut out the figures. Lisa cursed her incessant observation that stored these uninvited images. If only she could look at things vaguely, without properly noticing, and avoid absorbing them so deeply into her mind.

On the point of departure she heard a smear, or a babble of noise, succeeded by swiftly running steps. Reverberations confused their course and Lisa pressed into the panelled wall, fearful of someone else hidden here. In a momentary flash, the merest pulse, she registered a new door and glided, as warily as the most cautious of all creatures, poised for instant flight. She entered a tiny room with a wall picture obscured by a layer of dust. Brushing the glass curiously, she uncovered the lines of an old engraving. Intrigued, she extended the arc and out from the wall leapt the bitter frown of an elderly man – a judge, a tyrant? His mouth formed a thin bar and a mass of cross-hatching hollowed his cheeks. From dense shadow his nose stabbed out, vicious as an axe. His cruel magnetic glare, focused entirely on Lisa, sent an electric current sizzling from her brain to her feet, and she made herself whirl away. *I must stop!*

A window began to glow. Unwillingly she glimpsed a billowing, eerily lit drapery and a motion, fluid as mercury, melting in soft halo. A nude girl floated with supple and fluent grace, the embodiment of young flesh, dissolving in fragments. Her golden mask reproduced the bland features of innocence. In a drifting luminous mist her legs scissored the window's blaze. As she rippled out of streaming light, advancing on a group of men, Lisa saw a deviant object below her waist: a pubic wig trailing low on her thigh. Luxuriant curling strands of hair stroked back and forth, its lurches resembling a ponderous cock, but the slim female added the enticement of teasing gestures. Lisa could see yet hear none of the weird tableau and told herself she imagined it all, but a vision so real had to be true.

One of the man swivelled. Had she accidentally scraped the glass? Wheeling, Lisa ran crazily in a black trench, and caught a looming shape at the edge of her sight. At the double doors she crashed out, into a draughty endless corridor. Completely unnerved by all that had happened, she slithered to the icy floor. Bending her legs to her chest, she wrapped her shins in her arms and her head sank onto her knees. As her strength drained away she wept.

It was there, at some unknown time, that Daniel discovered her after a frantic search, crumpled at the foot of a wall in a remote area that no one visited. He scooped her up and she rested against him, inert as he carried her, a featherweight. 'Yvonne' he murmured, 'you're freezing.'

In her room he showered her, soothing every part of her body. The water's unexpected turbulent heat filtered her bones and gradually lifted, out of her ashen colour, a rosy pink. He dried her in warm towels, rubbing vigorously, as she watched the commanding spread of his black fingers over her skin. He held her buttocks and pushed his face into her belly, almost an act of supplication. Struck to the heart, she inhaled the fragrance of wet masculinity; his musk, his texture was his alone, his substance unique. In their narrow world his voice submerged in her pussy's fever, raised to his lips. His tongue, flattened onto her clitoris, flowed her away into peace. Recalling the desolation of anonymity, she volunteered banal words for the first time. 'I love you,' she whispered.

Eighteen

He soon tested the rash declaration, roughly shaking her shoulder.

'Get up and prepare. No time for make-up. Quickly.'

Fogged by sleep, Lisa staggered from the bed and into the bathroom. The arctic water brought a coarse radiance to her cheeks. She put on her slippers, tidied her hair, and picked up her gown.

'No clothes,' he ordered sharply.

'What's wrong?' Refusing to answer, he subjected her to the humiliation of a pitiless impatient inspection while she used the toilet.

He jostled her along the corridors with unreasonable urgency and a painful grip on her arm. Something must be badly wrong. Unable to keep his pace, Lisa desperately tried to consider what might have happened. Had she been observed on the preceding day and reported? Would Daniel repeat his accusation of spying? Now acutely alert, Lisa's heart beat the air wildly in front of her chest. 'Master . . .' she gabbled but a tough jerk rattled her teeth. In panic she recognised their route; these were stairs the hobble chain had grated upon. 'Master!'

He stopped abruptly. 'Don't worry,' he growled and dragged her again.

How could she be unworried? This time there would be no reprieve. His flogging would go on endlessly.

'Inside.'

The same door, low and plain. Lisa cringed onto the cold wall.

'Go on!'

The same vaults curving into the gloom. Further away were the same penis-topped columns. Tears of remorse impeded Lisa's view. A naked woman had been pinned to the stone like a specimen, her arms and feet splayed outwards, above the floor and slumped forward, supported only by the restriction of her bonds. Expecting to be tied to the opposite pillar, Lisa's thoughts dwindled down to their solidarity. To witness their punishments would be to share them and thus help the other to endure. *But how can I bear it?* The woman smiled faintly as if giving a welcome and Lisa saw that it was the Japanese, the one she had spied on, and assumed was a novice. Robed and masked, the woman's mentor hovered in the shadows.

'It's you she's chosen,' Daniel said quietly.

Chosen for what? Tiny currents prickled Lisa's spine.

'She requires you to whip her.'

Shocked, Lisa stared at him with no understanding. How could she possibly do such a thing, knowing the extent of all its effects from those of stimulation to those that seared? And how could a person who had received the torment be ruthless enough to use such a potent device?

'You cannot deny her.'

Dazed, Lisa noted her glossy tan glinting with fine blonde hair – and a lattice of blushing marks. 'She's already been whipped.'

'We have discovered she has uncommon tastes. For her it's sexual. It brings her to a climax.'

'I've never done it before.'

'My hunch is that you'll take to it naturally.'

The surge of adrenaline caused by his bewildering haste now vented itself and Lisa spun, blazing in anger.

He defused it by thrusting a whip into her fist. 'Try it.'

A corded handle. Regular and comfortable, it fitted her palm. Well balanced for easy control. Through the air its thongs whoomed with the resonance of authority and Lisa expanded their range by flicking her wrist. A more vigorous sweep exploded against a column and her mouth dried. A secret seduction had spoken aloud. The whip started to respond, not as a simple adjunct to her arm, or even her will, but as if independently alive with its own terrible inborn desire. From her it needed only one thing: to give it flight, liberating and amplifying its latent power. She had not sought the opportunity but it presented her with a tantalising, an irresistible, invitation.

Limp and mellow, voluptuous leather trailed on the woman's lightly blemished surfaces, waiting for the muscles to clench involuntarily. At that moment its thongs unfurled, travelled, and landed to a hungry bite. The woman jolted with a quivering cry and her brown pupils dilated in surprise. An instant later she subsided, locked in profound emotions. The reaction affected Lisa strangely and she broke off to stalk the room, her torso and arm bending as one for additional force. At last, she turned.

Distantly the whip's flickering motions – forehand, reversed – nipped and snatched the writhing form. Its varied notes, the authentic voice, accompanied cries and moans of tortured ecstasy. Flaring fingers reached out to the buckling flesh, to scorch and magically burst apart the glittering patterns. In their true element they swung tirelessly, fixed on the task, and dim cracks left behind their traces of lust.

Wrenched out of Lisa's grasp, the whip clattered to the floor. She halted, her breathing stertorous, fighting for calm. When the mist cleared she gazed blankly at stripes, and weals where lines had crossed. The whip's dreadful appetite had transformed the women to a sculpture of fire.

'Look at her face,' Daniel advised.

But Lisa could not make out if the woman felt absolute pleasure or absolute pain; they seemed identical. She had, however, a resolute gaze conveying something ineffable, a mystical joy beyond Lisa's comprehension. With the whip as an intermediary, they had together entered a dangerous place, far from any kind of normal encounter. Was it really sexual for her? Is that what the opalescent drops trickling down her leg confirmed? Lisa marvelled at a strength so resolute and the depth of courage hidden by that demure exterior.

'You know how it should be finished.'

Automatically she picked up the whip, its handle upright. The cords settled into the supple lips and glided easily in lubrication. Unable to check a wicked temptation, Lisa pushed in and out, vibrating the vaginal walls, ensuring a long shuddering flow until a blocked dam suddenly collapsed and the woman convulsed. Sympathetically, Lisa also began to shake as if freezing water had soaked her bones. Jagged, elated, leaving the whip in position dangling to the floor, she met Daniel's scrutiny.

'I could swear you've had an orgasm too,' he said.

Her mentor's silhouette loomed at her side. But how had she come to be here, rapturously?

Two figures, caught in a wavering beam. The woman knelt, knees spread. Her arms, bound behind to the elbows, were joined as one. In the same thin white rope meticulous bindings cut into her breasts, distorting them to shapeless lumps. From the mesh her nipples stuck out in odd directions.

The man's pedantic attention to detail showed the delight of a fetishist. Concerned with the tidy appearance of intricate lacing, he laid one strand neatly beside the next, trussing her carefully into a web. Lisa knew that, to him, she gained beauty with each tie.

'He intends to honour you.' She floated on tides of euphoria.

The man attached a third rope linking wrists to ankles.

The shortening cord dragged her backwards into a curved bow, immovable. Her head pointed upwards, her eyes filled with the light, her cunt opened and raised.

That pose must be a strain yet she utters no sound.

A fourth length threaded the woman's crotch and deepened into her rear crevice, separating her puffy tissues.

Ah! Soothing velvet, not coarse.

Swelling flesh on both sides disguised the band. It emerged from the top of her slit in a gleaming line – an alien, or a chastity belt. Vertically the rope fastened onto her neck-band. At the pressure on her tender spot, she jerked silently. Lisa stifled her cry. She must be – could feel it – liquid below the waist.

'You are incomplete without penetration.'

A blunt crown widened her anus. It stretched gradually and her own falling weight drove the obstruction tightly inside.

He abandoned her there. Compactly bound and stuffed full with only sensations for company.

An object of beauty, isolated in the encroaching dark.

A scene she observed – or her own experience stored in memory – haunted her still, colouring her mood.

'Oh!'

'Don't squirm!'

Lisa's mentor lifted and squeezed her globes to paint her teats in the same brilliant red lacquer that coated her labia. 'I'm sure you realise the importance of erotic elaborations.'

The wet brush licked and tickled unbearably.

'Yes I do, but I've never been treated to this one before.'

'You must have led a sheltered life,' he grumbled. 'Now the shoes.' He gave her a flimsy pair of sandals with narrow straps for support.

Lisa balanced tentatively on thin heels. 'Am I to be naked?'

'Under this gown.' Daniel fitted the delicate fabric over her shoulders. As it fell to her ankles Lisa revelled in its purity, so translucent the material almost vanished. It declared its presence by ornate clusters of flowers and birds, in gold and black, which clung to her skin. Combined with the earlier adornments – a single row of pearls circling her forehead and hair clamped in a bun – she resembled a sixteenth-century courtesan who might, in her day, have been prepared similarly for the same kind of assignation. To help her she would of course have had a maid, not a man, and Lisa grimaced at his firm tweaks, extending her nubs for emphasis.

The feeling persisted as they walked, she holding his arm in the required way. A courtesan might have travelled these same corridors. The alliance, or perhaps that lingering image of bondage, might explain her vivid consciousness of what she carried between her legs: Jon had called them a woman's jewels. Once Lisa had loved only her boobs and neglected the rest of her features but now she treasured all the aspects that many valued so highly, and whose own insatiable cravings led her on. They recalled Kim who had said, 'I come easily.' Lisa's own struggles to orgasm were also in the past. The structure of these events and – essentially – their unpredictable traits, had conspired to loosen her up. Now she, too, came easily.

Her mentor halted by a door indistinguishable from any other in the complex building. Lisa paused with no anxiety. 'This will be a solo session?'

'No rivals and no collaborators. You alone. Your selection reflects our esteem for your quality.'

Hairs prickled on the nape of her neck. Within the room they waited only for her. 'And you are the arbiter. I'm glad. What have you planned for me?'

'Something special, so follow my instructions. But also, as a voluptuary, listen to your own instincts.'

The spacious room had floor-to-ceiling windows at one end. Lisa advanced serenely into a large central area defined by two facing couches undisturbed by the oppressive, even ominous, smell of sperm. On each couch sat three unmasked men wearing martial cloaks with embroidered silver designs. Many more men were bunched in corners of the room. Lisa remained proud, remote from them all, but alive to the charged climate of lust. The moment – her celebratory moment – had now arrived.

When Daniel located himself she anticipated the initial order. 'Model the gown.'

Excellent. He gave her the freedom to influence and mould the perceptions of those around her. But as she obeyed, in broad circuits of the room, a previous exhibition distracted her – the first time she had watched Kim. That young woman had taught her that eroticism resulted from acting slowly and theatrically, with a formality close to ritual. And later, at Balmayne, Kim had taught a further lesson, that of performing fearlessly. With these examples Lisa employed her body for deliberate affect.

She glided, upright and gravely aloof, the sheer gown revealing every nuance of her figure. How satisfying to be covered, yet able to display its splendour decorated by flowers and birds. Her steps rearranged them like slippery tattoos. The creases of her sex would undoubtedly focus the men's thoughts, as would her bobbing tips, and so too her sweet derrière. They would all be studying her pale spheres, their seductive swaying and quivering, and the shadowed cleft hiding her secrets. In the atmosphere of brooding intensity she floated among ingots of sunlight scattering the floor and flung her challenge to the whole audience who marked her flamboyance with approving low murmurs. It pleased her to volunteer her curves to their gaze for no one else had her distinction as the sole target of their attention. As magnetic as an actress strolling on stage, she embraced it all as her natural right and re-entered the central area wholly relaxed.

Familiar rumbling tones announced the next phase. 'Strip.'

Another subtle and leisurely rite. Her gestures and all her potency were now directed onto the couches, blotting out the men elsewhere. But she wore so little her difficulty was to prolong the process and create the significance it richly deserved. Swivelling from couch to couch, she swept the gown enticingly to enhance her limbs. Hesitating, as if shy of revelation, she slackened one of her straps and let the material sag gradually to expose one glorious tit. Turning to the opposite couch she brushed aside the second and the gown rucked to her waist. The window's illumination glossed her surfaces as she began gyrating sinuously, her arms weaving the air as a writhing, hip-waving seraglio dancer with a painted pussy. The gown sank to her rippling abdomen, to her smooth pouch and then to her thighs. As it sighed to her ankles she kicked off her shoes and kept up the dance, rotating, sharing her favours to both, fondling her coloured crests, delighting in supple swelling flesh. She could see the men's agitation and feel her own beginning to stir breathlessly.

Daniel held up his hand. 'Good. Sit there.' He indicated one of the couches and two men who had shifted to leave a gap.

A nice sequence: a parade in her gown, her nudity, and now passed to assistants to complete her debut. Her face and smile, even her figure's taunting allure, were less important than their finale.

Reclining on the couch, her arms spread casually along the top, she offered her lower half unprotected in any way. Both men raised her legs onto their laps, her knees widened to full span. Sliding outwards but settled comfortably, the position allowed two fingers, a brown and a white, to gather the soft outer lips, split her apart, and present her gaping entrance to all the observers. They held the pose to give the assembly a period of time for examination, accentuating the opened portal as her vital introduction. Lisa fluttered luxuriantly. Yes, this is how it should be. An intimate, and perfect, precondition.

'Ready.'

In the centre of the space lay a man and her aides led her towards him. Squatting, she fed his stiff cock into her wet pit and sat erect to drive it deep for a few thrusts. From behind, a kneeling man demanded her anus and straining, panting, she took in the whole of his length. With her passages occupied from different angles, Lisa could only heave passively but her pelvic area tightened and fired. A third stem searched for her mouth, reaching so far in her gullet she choked and retched. She tried to be conscious of the separate penetrations but competing blurs of movement and pressure fogged her mind. For whatever duration they chose to dictate she would merely absorb their sensuous power. The massed effect transfixed and ruled her, sheened her in perspiration, and the iron-hard gag gave a laboured urgency to her cries of need. She belonged entirely to these shafts which finally coerced the shuddering peak. As she jerked in the force of her cunt's convulsions they carried on obliviously. Hot emissions flooded her throat, followed by the respite of unstifled breath, and succeeding spurts spewed into both her stretched apertures.

Rolled to the side, drained of her strength, she gasped like a stranded fish on the shore. During this hushed interval, empty and desolate, Lisa remembered Pauline's opinion of her aptitude for submission. And Pauline was right. It ensured that all Lisa wanted could be obtained here, ending in the havoc of animal copulation, unpretentiously justified; and consummation, a devastating joy.

But the changes around her happened too fast. From the floor, lifted to a couch, she found herself unprepared, her legs straddling a sitting man, her back to his face. His glans nudged her rear hole and in one fall she pierced herself to the hilt – 'Ahh!' A second man, standing in front, seized her labia. He distorted the yielding flaps into a flagrant funnel and she burned in shame. With stunning virility his brutal club plunged inside and she wailed, again reduced by unrelenting appetites. Through her internal membrane the mobile organ stroked the stationary one in her anal channel, a screwing action more disorientating than she had felt before. A third man knelt on the seat at her side and dragged her to him. Skewed awkwardly, she could not centre his shining bulk and its solid head bulged her cheek. Crushed to his belly, incapable of participation, she rocked dizzily, controlled by imperious bayonets unremitting for their own relief. In her vagina came the pulses, then the spouts of fluid onto her tongue. She swallowed a portion but some flowed out and the next inhalation drew a wad into her nostril. The man behind retained possession, clasping her hips as she hunched forward, abandoned to his use. In the midst of his vigour her orgasm did not build but suddenly burst. She screamed, tossing frantically as he erupted within her profound heat.

Unfolded, laid on the couch, they permitted her time to recover. Her breathing quietened. Awareness of the muted and motionless air slowly returned. Rising at last, Lisa pivoted and slumped with no artifice; a mere shell bearing her sanctioned loads of semen. Hazily she looked at the opposite couch where her mentor stood among the spectators who were all assessing her state. But why? Had he planned a sequel? Why didn't he take off his robe and let her feast on his gleaming form?

'Continue.'

What did that mean? Continue what? Lisa's gaze locked on Daniel. His silence gave her no clue but his eyes gripped cruelly, willing her to do something. Gradually, clumsy, she slithered to the carpet, supported by the seat's edge and balanced on the balls of her feet. Concentrating, she recorded an imperceptible nod but struggled, unable to pick up his next cue. By a strange intuition he prompted a memory of a pose that Jon had required, reflected by a mirror; a position she had wished to forget. But this, Daniel convinced her, she would have to repeat. Lisa spread her knees to their greatest extent in a frank exhibition of her flushed and abused genitals. He rewarded her progress with another slight nod but she knew he intended her to go further. She tested the belief by lowering one hand, palm upwards, beneath her crotch. His eyelids flickered and she whirled with love. Despite appearances, male dominance and female surrender did not operate in this place. Equal roles had, after all, linked them together in collaboration.

Projecting her pelvis forward, all her mental abilities converged onto one spot. Clenching her abdomen, she relaxed briefly and squeezed again, her thoughts precisely focused onto the task. From her pouting lips emerged a creamy deposit and she held it there for all to see. Renewing the compression, thick come gushed out, pooled in the hollow, and dripped between her fingers in dangling swaying clots. She raised a lengthening streak and relished the saved sperm leisurely, a delicious treat, an extra helping of the men's seed now enriched with her own flavour.

Her audience approved but her mentor seemed to be encouraging more. Disconcerted, Lisa recalled her first sight of Marion who produced –

Is it possible?

Reinstating her hand at her crotch, she opened and then contracted her sphincter several times. It released a supply and she harvested that too, recognising the zest of wild transgression both as a gift to her mentor and to the crowd. Sinking two digits up to the knuckles in her steamy slimy orifice, she milked herself, retrieving sticky packets and rivulets, and devoured them all gratefully.

The room resounded to applause. Nourished and sated, she glanced up at Daniel's broad smile. Even though he remained at a distance his presence sustained her, and a well-earned shower would efface the lingering traces and odours of spunk. But her mentor walked away and Lisa's anxiety began to mount. She had never gone so far or been so bold. Where would it end? She rested onto her knees, waiting and still watched vigilantly. Perhaps her stress actually developed from growing discomfort.

Daniel returned escorting the Caribbean mulatto, one of the original group. Naked, a polished sculpture of flesh, her sinewy muscles rippled with a coating of oil. Her eagerness to join Lisa conveyed a perverse desire, and when Daniel stopped and gave her a signal she did not hesitate to lie on the floor, her head near to Lisa's fork.

'Get on top of me,' the mulatto murmured.

Mystified, Lisa shuffled above the wide brown face.

'I'm looking straight into your fanny. So just let it go.'

'What?'

'You need it, don't you?'

The arbiter interrupted. 'Give satisfaction to a piss-whore.'

'It's my thing, honey – it's what I do. Go ahead and gild me.'

Lisa's heart thumped. Her mentor's alert scrutiny affected and influenced her. Of course! He had trained her for this. Realising that each individual in the room expected her to obey, she tensed and prepared herself. A few disappointing drops spattered down onto the glossy contours below. Then Lisa delivered a dense narrow stream splashing onto the scarlet rim. Dazzling white teeth parted to reveal a cavity, ample as a cave, receiving the spate. A bubbling mass accrued before the woman erupted like a venting whale, pouring the acrid fluid over her cheeks. The gurgling deluge filled her eye sockets and soaked her hair, and she opened again to sample the taste. Lisa had no experience of such power combined with fascination. She visualised herself – there – twisting from side to side, bathing deliriously in a hot cascade. Her relief as the pressure dwindled shaded to regret, but as loose whorls fell erratically, the mulatto rose to lick away the final shreds. Gasping and saturated by Lisa's emission she lay back, its full strength wafting up.

Applause erupted.

Yes, it had been a collaboration with Daniel as her perfect partner. 'But I'm afraid.' Lisa whispered. 'Do you think I'm debauched?'

'Magnificently debauched.'

'Vile?'

'Wonderfully vile. And these are accolades to prize.'

'It's amazing to do what I did.'

'And you enjoyed the performance?'

'Thanks to your training.'

'You mean you're exempted from guilt?'

'Yes!'

But during the night she stared into the dark, haunted by insidious words pounding in rhythm to the beat of her blood: debauched, vile, accolades.

The irresistible allure of eroticism de-stabilised her personality. She became someone else. Was that an outcome of any type of transgression? *Where is my limit? How far do I dare to go?*

Pastel tones of dawn coloured the sky before her troubled sleep resumed.

Nineteen

But these private conditions, unconstrained by reality, required transgression. And how could she fear being changed by passion when she agreed so readily?

Lisa drifted in uncharted time, her normally lucid gaze obscured by illusions and spectral fantasies at every turn. On the brink of hallucination she could no longer detach substantial events from those of delirium. Recurring fragmented memories, receding, persisting, wavered as if in the haze of a sun.

Here, in an ancient chapel washed in pure white, glittered a wall of mirrored glass. In front of the mirror a woman had been strapped by the wrists to a slim bar cantilevered at waist height. Her ankles were separated, her spine hollowed and parallel to the floor, head drooped.

The solid shaft glided into its rightful home. At the pleasurable flow, in and out, she glanced up at the man reflected behind her and caught sight of her own features inches away. After a few strokes he pulled out and the blunt crown, smoothed with creamy lubrication, nudged her anus. The girth stretched her restricted orifice and she squirmed to accommodate the new sensation. The penis again withdrew, plunged into her sheath, and she writhed at another need to adapt. Regular thrusts followed steadily and then it returned to her anal channel. Lisa watched the exposure of all her emotions: brows furrowed; blushes and grimaces; weak smiles and gabbling cries. The insatiable organ switched repeatedly from one aperture into the alternative she offered willingly and the woman revelled in feeling its total command while, at the same time, recording her face as a shining vision of ecstasy. Torrential sperm flooded her rounded hole and further spume filled her liquid vagina.

The woman clenched to retain her gifts, leaking none.

Her mentor, who appeared to resent sharing Lisa with anyone else, kept her close and used her jealously. In thrall to his constant lust, he could always make her want more, ever-deeper explorations. His possessive attitude comforted her. If they had met in different circumstances she would freely have given herself to him alone.

Blue, throbbing eerily, illuminates a kneeling woman sandwiched between bulky black thighs. A fat glans, even though flaccid, spreads her jaws. The African sat by his side, kissing him, one pendulous bulb grasped in his hand, a fat purple bud stuck out from his fingers. Clutching the tumescent length, the servant shifts and devours a view of crinkled raven hair, stiff as wire, and outer tissues, splitting apart to reveal the inner membranes. A brilliant pink pearl, compulsively sexual, shimmers at the heart of an ebony sheen. She sucks in the enticing folds, immersed giddily in a musty tang and strong flavour, investigating the velvety walls. Her fingers replace her tongue in a cunt of ripe honey, at the same time aiding the rod as she must. The soft cavity, so resilient compared to the hard male.

An incident observed distantly. A faint dream.

Yet affirmed by vivid touch and acute impression.

In lapping the gaping pearl, the servant resembles a bitch on heat, tracing the clit's stalk, circling and teasing its crest, gorging the fluid. Returning to the rigid stem her actions quicken, moaning quietly, urgent and serious for the sap she craves. From the tip she takes the spouting ejaculate, thick and savoury, and fits her mouth carefully to the pink pearl. Engulfed in wet flesh she blows out her masculine bounty, feeding stars into the inky fathomless depths.

* * *

The atmosphere had modified in a subtle way as Daniel prepared Lisa with greater elaboration than for any previous session.

'You know, of course, that you're beautiful,' he said. 'But what is the purpose of your beauty?'

'I regard talent as far more important,' she replied casually.

'Talent for what?' His sudden burst of vehemence shook her, but then it subsided and he shrugged. 'The purpose of your beauty is to provoke obsession.'

Spontaneously Lisa recalled her striptease at Balmayne. *Is that what I was doing there?* 'I hate that idea. It could spell danger.'

'Occasionally,' her mentor admitted.

'Why are telling me this?'

'That's your next task.' He led her forward to a cheval mirror. 'It begins here.'

He had pinned up her hair in a style to support a tall curving headdress, black as a cockerel's glossy comb, and rimmed her eyes in khol. From her neck draped a heavy beaded choker of jet. Her shoulders and chest were uncovered and the antique bustier of white lace lay below her breasts, their supple bowls dramatically emphasised by areolae painted in purple. The bustier shielded her belly but not her pudenda. He had also painted her pubes purple but larger and bolder than her pubic hair had once been. Black stay-up stockings finished near to her crotch and matching lace gloves sagged above her elbows.

Disturbed by an image she did not recognise, Lisa whispered, 'It's bizarre. You've made me into a degenerate showgirl.'

'Not so. An exotic. An aristocrat.' As if regretfully, her mentor lingered in their kiss. 'You are a supreme woman who combines carnality and mystery. That's why you wear no mask – your face, like your body, should be visible.'

She held his arm as they walked, her shoes ringing confidently on the stone floors in contrast to the usual shuffling of slippers. As they travelled the corridors and descended flights of stairs she almost, but not quite, spotted a familiar mural here, a tapestry there, or a mirrored corner. But one aspect could be in no doubt: Daniel's uncommonly grave manner verged on sadness. His stately decorum suggested an approaching climax and Lisa's grip tightened to seek his reassurance.

They entered a stunning room of huge scale and rich decoration. She gazed, awed by sparkling ornate chandeliers, brilliant stalactites. Across the ceiling, a vast barrel vault, and halfway down the walls frescoes, painted into the plaster, vibrated with colour. She had no time to study their themes and focused instead on a crowd of men and scattered women who lined the room on both flanks. Some wore surreal masks: a cat argued with a clown, a lion conversed with a moonbeam.

At so many frank inspections of her splendid form she tingled electrically and wondered if she could actually be, as Daniel had said, provoking obsessions. Serene, undistracted by the thought, she moved with consummate naturalness and simplicity, head high, her feathers swaying gracefully. Her steps jiggled her bosom, accentuating her areolae's stark display.

At the far end they joined a waiting group, the nine robed mentors and their women, all unmasked. This, the only time they had convened since the start, was clearly intended to be a special event.

Like somnambulists the women were engrossed in their own trance as if, in the intervening period, the world had been reordered with each of them, individually, at the centre. All were presented bare-breasted, a few hoisted prominently in harnesses. The Irish girl had florid tassels dangling from her teats and bright blue pubic hair, the Japanese similarly in scarlet, and the African had been dyed green; colours chosen to compliment the hues of their skin. As Lisa herself, other women with shaved mounds had their labias rouged though she, alone, wore purple. In a variety of ways they all shared one feature, with their genital areas identified significantly.

The room fell silent. Nervous expectation hung in the air. A voice reverberated, 'Take your women for the last time.'

Chilled, and pleading, Lisa glanced at Daniel but he gave her no hint of response. Impassively, with no haste, the mentors separated and her own brought Lisa to a halt in an open space, away from anyone else. 'A statue,' he murmured. She obeyed, perfectly poised as he took off her headdress. He slowly unhooked her bustier and she managed to control herself while he fondled her boobs, even when he roused her to incandescent desire. 'Good.' Only then did he grant her an avid kiss and she repaid his caress through the gap in his robe. As he shrugged off the garment she pulsed her groin into his, dragged her nipples over the burly pectorals and licked his tattoo, his bird of paradise. She had never had sex with her mentor in public and the proximity of an audience affected her powerfully. A hunger for exhibitionism caused her to swiftly rise, increasingly feverish. Already moist, she sank to her knees. She had known the dark penis in every mood, more completely than any in the past, and long ago had memorised it from all angles. One day she would draw its entire detail, many times. But despite her eyes' accumulated experience, its tactile sensation inside her mouth still felt marvellously intimate. In its firm and softer curves, the hardening projecting veins, and the crowning glory nakedly exposed, she rediscovered the essence of carnal delight.

A moment came when it lurched up, independent and proud. Lisa followed the instruction to lie with her calves under her thighs, head and shoulders pressed to the floor. As Daniel knelt to spread her apart she briefly noted her comrades, some positioned on all fours to permit their mentors a choice of entrances, as she would herself, promptly, if obliged. But her arched torso and churning loins pointed to the glittering shaft, imploring to be stuffed here and now, without delay. The advancing organ, hot as a poker, teased her yearning pussy and explored her compliant passage deliciously. Easing back it gradually deepened, to and fro. His leisurely thrusts seemed to imply respect and calmed her own anxious tempo; he valued her enough to prolong their mutual pleasure to the maximum. Speared on his member and fired by the watching company, Lisa extended her arms at both sides to indicate her total acceptance. He pulled out and rapped her clitoris several times, his pole as tough as a baton of wood. She gasped and craned upwards, acutely sensitised. The renewed penetration took away her breath as if the stifling girth crammed her jaw instead of her belly. Absorbed in the imperceptible shifts in seamless strokes, dominated utterly, she had no concern for achieving release. It was enough to have him moving within her, in front of many attentive witnesses. The most beautiful fuck she had ever received ended with him rooted above her and fused together, fully sheathed as one. His treasured sperm poured into her furthest depths and she contracted to squeeze him dry, milking him to possess every drop.

His motions diminished and the assertive instrument, having done its vital work, declined. She could still feel its power and she always would. Clutching the dwindling time desperately she stared into his face, again locking the planes and shadows in memory.

The dreaded announcement came: 'Surrender your women.'

Daniel lifted her, still embedded as she wished him to be, and she snuggled to his chest in a search for protection. He raised her chin for their final kiss.

'Don't leave me,' she whispered tearfully.

'We are all bound by the rules.' He withdrew and gently disengaged her arms. Standing, he looked down at her – surely with love? – swivelled, and walked away.

Lisa sat on the floor, desolate. She had begun the session as a mystery, a remote seductive vision, but could pretend no longer to anything so grand. With him gone nothing but emptiness remained. A slumped inconsolable woman tried to divert her misery by gazing up at the ceiling fresco. She noticed its subject for the first time: a vigorous orgy with a chaos of strewn bodies like the aftermath of a war. In the same split second her mind ripped in fright at a looming climate of raw lust. She glimpsed her sisters surrounded by figures and froze, horrified by what was about to happen.

Impatient gestures kneaded her globes cursorily. Pushed forward onto her hands, probing fingers from her rear located her mentor's precious deposit and smeared a layer over her buttocks. Reeling at lewd suggestions murmured in her ear, she could not tell how many there were. A warm touch declared its target and, as her sphincter eased its panicky clench, his weight propelled a rigid length inside. In front appeared a purpled glans which allowed her to play with its luscious texture before its bulk drove into her throat. With a groan the man discharged in her rectum just as the penis's broad slit spat repeatedly onto her lips and wiped her in drooling residue.

A wicked force grabbed her between the legs and revulsion conflicted with involuntary appetite. Her body had its own imperative, its physical needs reigned supreme, but competing demands from all directions required access in different ways. The combined effects drained her will and she abandoned herself to servile whoring, assisting their wanton greed with vagina and anus and mouth gorged. Though she was degraded to a dumb unknown object, an orgasm rippled through her, passing unheeded by men who cared only for their own relief. A strict olive-coloured erection held her solidly, spewing a lavish amount of savoury semen. As one tool replaced another, the ordeal persisted relentlessly and from this sealed chamber of ravishment there could no escape. At the squirming centre of all attention, Lisa swam feverishly in heat and movement and spraying spunk. Close to a second delirious climax, she begged them to stay and let her shoot to her own salvation but callously they pulled away and constantly broke the tenuous edge. Plastered in sweat, a hefty aromatic rod bathed her cheeks in spouts of hot ejaculate and she altered her pose, accommodating to whatever they wanted, soliciting any stimulation to send her crashing.

Inexplicably the mass of pulsing energies languished. She struggled to retain them but they continued to fade – they failed – their contacts were lost. They eliminated their dominance and with it removed the all-consuming flame of their burning passion.

Bewildered by the desertion, Lisa stumbled to her feet. The barrelled ceiling echoed a muffled uproar. Her sheen mingled blisters of perspiration with male sap splashed in globs and whorls. A strand swayed from her chin and more dribbled from one teat. Slopping the streaks from her arms and thighs, the viscous fluid elongated as she flicked the clinging threads to the floor. Her dazed condition cleared gradually and she started to observe her companions dispersed all over the room. Nearby, a smooth-skulled woman had wrenched her lips to an animal snarl, her brow lined with creases and furrows. Might she have been a spectator, reluctant to participate? Or one who had volunteered to join her sisters? Another, with perfect submissiveness, displayed her genitals. Her blue pubic hair, stiffened by emissions and her own lubrication, resembled barbed wire. Lisa pictured her own apertures, swollen and blushed, imprinted by all the rampaging shafts she had endured.

Her freedom ended abruptly as the ravenous beasts, with the power to subjugate women, seized her again. But now she decided to take the initiative; voraciously she would have them all. Her cunt, a boiling swamp, commanded hungry organs of any shape and size or perfunctory haste. Booming resonated in her ears as one sank into the gaping crater she had once feared. She writhed, as if in her element, immersed in liquid cascades, salty flavours and musky smells, fighting to survive. These masters were, at the same time, her unwitting servants. In a dark vortex of flesh she had no choices and desired none, except to be thoroughly, gleefully defiled although, in one small corner of her brain she recognised these incessant cocks would change her forever. Unable to retreat from their strength – or from her own pleasure that exposed an impure part of her nature – she realised an awful, depraved truth; that she loved the impersonality that dealt with her as orifices to be loaded with seed. Her automatic responses swirled in dream and as one master-servant ejected she urged a fresh brute to soothe her ache, to heal the wound. Dissolving in waves, each breath emerged as a hoarse grunt. A justified paddle flashed, razor sharp, on her left haunch and then on the right. She jerked and choked on a tumescent gag and bore down on twin penetrations to bottle her tension. At last, coerced to blessed oblivion by too many insatiable demands, she began to float in a soundless void punctuated by quivering lights – decreasing steadily to faint glimmers – vanishing – drowned in black.

The fucking tore her to fragments, scattered the pieces, unravelled her mind. Vanquished, she lay on the floor inhaling the pungent coats of slimy fluid. Later, a feeble whimpering shell, she crawled slowly, easing her soreness, hunting vaguely but obstinately, among the discarded forms of immobile dolls with all their limbs askew.

Twenty

But her search yielded no sign of him anywhere.

She floundered, lost and confused, until someone came to her rescue and lifted her from the floor. Carried on brawny arms, a matt of silver hair smothered her face. In her room the steward showered her, washed and cleaned her scrupulously. She submitted meekly, conceding without protest to each quiet instruction, even the most intimate. Grateful, yet baffled by his new authority, she tried to bear his bunched fingers deep in her pussy accompanied by his thumb in her anal ring. Perhaps he did it to ease the muscles, or perhaps he seized the occasion gratuitously as his own reward.

Having dressed her in her normal clothes, he escorted her to the door of the palazzo. There he kissed her and she responded ardently. Outside, in the cool crisp air of early morning, she managed to pick up enough clues to totter through the streets, her heels dragging wearily on the cobblestones. At the landing stage a noisy boat – reminder of a real world beyond the palazzo's seductive confines – arrived in a few minutes. Out in the crystal light of the open lagoon a strong cold wind tugged at her hair but did little to revive her spirits. She appeared blank as a cipher, stripped of all knowledge of her previous self. From the Arsenale landing she wandered drunkenly towards her apartment. Pausing only to tear off her clothes, she collapsed on the bed, retrieved the mobile phone, and punched the keys. After a short delay she murmured, 'It's me. I'm out.'

'Are you OK?' Pauline enquired anxiously. 'Safe?'

'Exhausted. Safe, yes.'

'How was it?'

'Too soon . . . can't talk.'

'When are you coming home?'

'Maybe . . . three days. I must be alone . . . sleep.'

'I understand. Oh, I mustn't forget – congratulations.'

'For what?'

'You have just been announced as the winner of the Kate Greenaway Medal. The media's full of it – they say *Misfit Toys* opens up new territory in children's illustration. I've even bought a copy myself.'

'Oh, god! I'll hate the publicity.'

Lisa snapped off the phone and fell into sleep. Incidents whirled endlessly and disturbing sequences overlapped. As the remnants faded, she rose from the bed and stretched sluggishly.

Her watch confirmed that noon had come and gone. Now she could relish her solitude and the resumed control of her own body. And she also had the leisure to reflect and summarise, beginning the process of development from ideas to images. Her vivid experiences would ensure their power. She washed, tidied her hair, and hauled on her clothes. Still barely conscious, she prepared the essential requirement, coffee, and had the time to gulp half a cup before a firm knock rattled the street door. Puzzled, she did not answer and the knock came again, hard, insistent. The interruption was unexpected – it should not be happening – and she moved resentfully.

But there was no shock, nothing so sudden. She looked up at the inquisitive gaze of a tall black man, neatly dressed in town clothes. Projecting from his cuff glittered a gold Rolex. 'How did you find my address?' she asked dully.

'Our agents discovered it some time ago. May I come in? We must talk.'

Numb, Lisa turned away into the room where they sat on opposite couches. She remembered the texture of their relationship and even at a distance could feel the pulse of charisma. Abruptly, disjointedly, she began to plead, 'This is so unfair! I can't cope . . . I haven't revived. I don't know . . . me . . . myself. I can't decide . . . who I am . . .'

'I know precisely who you are. What fooled our security checks is that Yvonne von Guilliem actually exists.'

'How? She's a fiction.'

'On the contrary. She's an Anglo-German translator based in Brussels.'

'And what gave me away?'

'The response to your own drawing. It was impossible to disguise and your familiarity was obvious. Many of us have a copy and admire your work. You were told so at the time. And from there it was easy to trace you to Pauline.' Momentarily he lapsed into silence. 'Clever of her. We had failed to consider a trained observer who needs no equipment – just the chance to see, and from that to recall everything. We found that you live in the same village as a member of our organisation – it was he who obtained your entry card. And why is Jon Bradley not here, as he usually is? Because he didn't want to complicate things for you, on a covert assignment. So – he betrayed us. He's out of the loop permanently.'

'And me? Am I in danger?'

'Of physical harm?' The man showed his contempt. 'Of course not. We don't operate that way.'

'But you're going to ask me to stop.'

'Are you willing?'

'No.'

The blunt rejection deflated and saddened him as if she had punctured his dearest wish. For an interval they appeared to be in separate rooms until he roused himself with a sigh of resignation. 'OK. Here's the scenario. Pauline sends details of her forthcoming publications to connoisseurs all over the world. We comprise a substantial portion of her clientele and we can also influence the others. Given the extremely high cost of production, when she receives no orders – not a single one – she won't dare to proceed. A classic case of supply, but no demand. Your pictures will be locked in a vault and stay there, year after year, gradually forgotten. And your sole consolation will have to come from children's books.' Plainly distressed by the thought he said absently, 'By the way, let me add my own to Pauline's congratulations.'

Lisa chilled with horror. 'You've tapped my phone?' They must have broken in to the apartment and plundered her privacy, just like the first time, the one that started this whole thing. Appalled and hurt, she rushed to explain, 'I had no intention of damaging you . . . whoever you are.' Tormented, she added, 'I . . . simply believed I could do something to rival Beardsley and so on – those from the past.'

'Then be pleased. We rate you in the top rank. I told you, we greatly admire your work.'

'But you aim to prevent me doing it!'

'By providing an alternative option, wholly unprecedented.' He hesitated, as if reluctant to utter the words. 'We appreciate that to sacrifice your gift would be an enormous personal loss. In exchange, we invite you to be the Director of our next event. With your instinctive sensuality, together with your unique insights, we have no doubt you would make it memorable. Anything you require we can produce. I'll be your contact, your mentor –' he broke off with a smile '– though not, regretfully, your master this time. You would have a small staff and expenses to travel, to establish the location, and a budget to stage the meeting itself. Furthermore, you may also choose to participate but that is your decision alone.'

'All very tempting but . . .'

'An opportunity,' he insisted, 'that cannot be repeated. It's now, or never.'

'I'm only an illustrator.'

'Oh no. You are a supreme erotic artist and that is the most valuable background you could have. And your full potential lies ahead. Sometimes I envisage your majestic prime . . .'

'Me?'

'You.'

Lisa pondered silently, playing for time. 'I'll have to think about it.'

He consulted his Rolex. 'In forty-eight hours I shall return. You reply yes, or no. From that one of two actions will flow automatically.'

'Two days isn't long enough.'

He examined her face curiously. 'You forget, we understand your appetites – and your hunger for perverse adoration. The time is sufficient.' He stood up, about to depart.

'Wait. If you realised my deception, why didn't you throw me out?'

'By that time we were certain you are one of us. And we respect your talents – all of them. Our offer is genuine.' He moved as far as the street door.

'Wait!' Lisa's anguished appeal again delayed him. 'I don't even know your name!'

'If you join us, I'll tell you. If you reject us, you won't ever need it.' He opened the door and paused. 'Accept the inheritance of all that you have within you – and all you have learned.'

The Dogana lay to her right, splitting the waterway into two canals: the Grand, to the heart of the city, and the Giudecca, leading to the docks. As the lagoon narrowed, a white cruise ship passed serenely, its rail lined with passengers taking their first excited views. Gulls circled and swooped, and landed near to Lisa who sat on a smooth mooring bollard at the edge of the sparkling waterway. Grateful for the light breeze ruffling her hair, she occasionally shielded her eyes from the glare of the evening sun.

In contrast to the relaxed scene, she struggled hopelessly to resolve her dilemma. In her hand she clutched the mobile phone, a link to Pauline and through her to Jon but now compromised, insecure. Lisa's urgent wish was to keep her promise and complete the assignment. She owed that to her mistress and also to Jon as her benefactor.

Here, in Venice, she had been privileged to experience a special domain of heightened sensation. Among many other lessons she had acquired one of particular importance. Enjoyment of sex is not primarily to do with bodily pleasure at all, but with a constantly renewed state of anxiety and anticipation: psychology even more than physicality. Those were the elements that gave the spice and made encounters significant. *And all of that I could use.*

In fact, she might never exhaust the range of images she had gained.

Even if she discounted her recent prize, which might deliver an avalanche of commissions and a higher price for the originals, her whole life was there, in England. Her house, Miss Gibbs, Kim, Pauline, Jon. All her history.

If she laboured for weeks or months on the best creations of her career, their publication would be doomed.

Perhaps frustration could be steered into a different type of collaboration. Men toy with women's minds but women feed off masculine lust, so both manipulate in a variety of ways. There could be many kinds of disorientating transitions, slipping and blending.

'Enigma,' Pauline said, 'releases fundamental emotions.' *And she's right.*

The natural route to explore those dream-like advances into fresh possibilities would be intensive visualisation followed by drawing. Not an exposé of what she had witnessed – that would be stopped – but a vision of future affairs.

And who is better prepared?

A troubling guilt pervaded her mood. Jon had been expelled from the organisation, driven out for helping her.

It goes far beyond my drawings. Daniel's open-ended brief gave the chance for her imagination, combined with the mysterious instruments of her senses, to extend to their full capability. Ideas could jump straight off the page into live action.

What should I do? Where do my loyalties lie?

'Less than twelve hours . . .'

Reduced by distance to the size of a toy, the ship veered left into the wide Giudecca Canal. Gulls lifted and settled, and the sun's glare drained to the muted pinks and purples of dusk. Motionless, as if welded to the bollard, Lisa argued back and forth ceaselessly.

231

To be the Director of the next event – was that what she wanted?

He said: 'The point of beauty is to provoke obsessions.'
Talent can do that too.

And he also said: 'Surely you know what you most desire?'
'What is it that I most desire?' To work in isolation, on drawings that suggest or describe sexual intensity? Or, in place of simulation, to be engaged energetically?

Lisa felt something entirely new: a blossoming into the flowering of herself – of her body and all her instincts. They were precepts and guides to a new realm.

The sky lost its colouring and stars emerged in huge arcs, etched on a rich velvet of blue.

In one fluent action Lisa stood and used an underarm throw. The flat trajectory surprised her, and the block did not spin end over end. Reaching its apex, it plummeted to a leaping splash, scarcely audible a dozen yards away. Instantly the 'phone disappeared from sight.

To be published in July 2006

FRESH FLESH
Wendy Swanscombe

Out of the shadows of myth an ancient horror invades lesbian Europe, seeking fresh female flesh with which to fulfil his dark dreams of dominance and empire.

Only a handful of women stand between the monster and his final victory, and as time runs short they must risk all in a desperate game with their own bodies for dice. Dracula rises again, and again, in Wendy Swanscombe's *Fresh Flesh*.

£6.99   ISBN 0 352 34041 X

MANSLAVE
J. D. Jensen

Endowed with the magnificence of a *Golden God,* Shane is saved by his mistress from *The Ceremony of Glorious Transformation.* Yet, torn by so many conflicting emotions; his devotion to her; his fascination for her . . . there is also his love for maidservant Li-Me; and not least his own fearful degradation.

So deceptive is the opulent tranquillity of *The Pavilion of The Divine Orchard Ladies* and how fragile must his pathway be through the turmoil of petty jealousies and cruel perversities. Escape is impossible; survival an ever tenuous state.

Ruled by the devious *Grand Lady*, the Pavilion is a dangerous place for servants and royal concubines alike. Even so, neglected by the ageing emperor, *The Honourable Sisters* resort to alternative but forbidden pleasures. Resented and shunned by his felloe novice-eunuchs, can Shani rise above his unwilling role of a freak plaything to *Their Royal Ladyships*?

£6.99   ISBN 0 352 34040 1

UNDER MY MASTER'S WINGS
Lauren Wissot

Under My Master's Wings is the true story of a French-Canadian master and his American slave girl and how they navigate the fine line separating reality and fantasy, love and lies in Manhattan.

Lauren Wissot is an extraordinary and beautiful young woman. Her book begins at a Times Square strip club where she meets David – a beautiful male dancer – and ends on New Year's day after exploring and documenting their numerous orgies and S&M rituals in midtown Manhattan motels.

The content is very strong and explicit. The insights into Manhattan urban sleaze are raw and vivid.

£6.99   ISBN 0 352 34042 8

If you would like more information about Nexus titles, please visit our website at www.nexus-books.co.uk, or send a large stamped addressed envelope to:

Nexus, Thames Wharf Studios,
Rainville Road, London W6 9HA

- - - - - - ✂ -

Please send me the books I have ticked above.

Name ....

Address ....

....

....

.... Post code ....

Send to: **Virgin Books Cash Sales, Thames Wharf Studios, Rainville Road, London W6 9HA**

US customers: for prices and details of how to order books for delivery by mail, call 888-330-8477.

Please enclose a cheque or postal order, made payable to **Nexus Books Ltd**, to the value of the books you have ordered plus postage and packing costs as follows:

UK and BFPO – £1.00 for the first book, 50p for each subsequent book.

Overseas (including Republic of Ireland) – £2.00 for the first book, £1.00 for each subsequent book.

If you would prefer to pay by VISA, ACCESS/MASTERCARD, AMEX, DINERS CLUB or SWITCH, please write your card number and expiry date here:

....

Please allow up to 28 days for delivery.

Signature ....

Our privacy policy

We will not disclose information you supply us to any other parties. We will not disclose any information which identifies you personally to any person without your express consent.

From time to time we may send out information about Nexus books and special offers. Please tick here if you do *not* wish to receive Nexus information. ☐

- - - - - - ✂ -